## PAWN OF WAR,
## PRIZE OF BATTLE...

The Lady of the Snowmist turned and walked behind the seeming great moss-covered stone that was her chair, and stared intensely at Jarik Blacksword.

"You are important to the War. And that makes you of inestimable importance to me—and to all the world."

Jarik stood, and looked from her. "Lady, there are ever wars in the world. It is the way of us. Wars for this or that land, or principle, food or growing-land. But a war that you said has lasted *centuries*—how can that be? What are the stakes—the cause?"

Snowmist straightened, armor rustling and flashing with her swift movements. *"The stakes, Jarik Blacksword, are all Humankind."*

*Ace Science Fiction Books by Andrew J. Offutt*

KING DRAGON

*War of the Gods on Earth Series*

THE LADY OF THE SNOWMIST
THE IRON LORDS (coming in July)
SHADOWS OUT OF HELL (coming in August)

*The Cormac mac Art Series*

THE MISTS OF DOOM
SIGN OF THE MOONBOW
SWORD OF THE GAEL
THE TOWER OF DEATH
THE UNDYING WIZARD
WHEN DEATH BIRDS FLY

VOLUME THREE OF
*WAR OF THE GODS ON EARTH*

# ANDREW J. OFFUTT

# THE LADY
## OF THE
# SNOWMIST

ACE FANTASY BOOKS
NEW YORK

THE LADY OF THE SNOWMIST

An Ace Fantasy Book / published by arrangement with the author

PRINTING HISTORY
Ace Original / June 1983

ISBN: 0-441-46941-8

Ace Fantasy Books are published by
Charter Communications, Inc.,
200 Madison Avenue, New York, N.Y. 10016
PRINTED IN THE UNITED STATES OF AMERICA

# THE LADY OF THE SNOWMIST

# One

They moved out of the woods onto the beach, mailed and armed men with sunlight aglint on their helmets. Almost at the instant of their emergence from the gloom of the forest, the trees began to rustle in the breeze that rose suddenly. It blew straight out to sea. The hair of the men, wheat and jonquil shading into a tawny hue and no darker, stirred where it appeared below their round pots of helms. Bright light shrank their pupils and they gazed blinking upon the long bright strand that slanted down to the sea.

It waited, their stout wooden ship *Seadancer*. Their leader paused. He had been Kirrensark Long-haft and was now Kirrensark One-arm. Now the big man who had once raided shoreline farmers fled women, and a strange somber yunker commanded more than he. On the service of Her: the Lady of the Snowmist.

After a brief pause he paced down the strand toward the long boat they called ship. Behind him came his men, in mail and leather leggings. They moved in silence, with their captive in their midst.

And behind them, the Guardians of Osyr emerged from the wood. A single feather of red or white stirred above the blue-tressed head of each as she moved apart from her sisters. The Guardians of the god Osyr were women, all women. They and these departing invaders of their manless island had made the trek to the beach without incident; their queen was still held hostage by the men to insure safe

*1*

passage to their ship. Tension hung over them all like a pall of smoke on an overcast day, as it had accompanied them all through the forest from their wark.

That man called Jarik called to them to halt, and Kirrensark turned then to shout the same order, for he was firstman and ship's master. But these were only men. The sinuous bodies of the Guardians did not come to halt until they heard the command called out by their queen, their Osyrrain.

They continued to emerge from the trees, and they stepped apart, and stopped. Thirty-one women with full quivers on hips and taut-strung bows held not idly in the left hand. Scarlet feathers and white trembled above blue-haired heads. In silence and tension they watched the men moving down toward their sea-going Thing called ship: werk.

The thirty-second was the Osyrrain's champion. She had never been defeated at arms since her thirteenth year—until yesterday, when the over-tall one called Jarik had bested her. He with the sword of black. Only just, had he bested her! Her quiver rode her hip and her bow was on her back. She wore sword and dagger. The barely adequate skin of a grey squirrel dangled between her taut thighs, her only clothing. A red feather stood erect above her blue hair and on her breast was the dull gleam of the ruby bonded on its tip. The sullen red stones had been bonded thus, in pain, to the outermost curves of the right breasts of all the Guardians.

She was Jilain, and she had done much thinking while she glided through the forests with her sisters in Osyr. Now she stood frozen, with her sisters. None of them had been defeated by Jarik, had wounded him and been wounded by him. None of them had spent the night with him, as had she and the Osyrrain. The others looked alert and angry and Jilain looked troubled and deep in reflection.

"To the ship," Kirrensark called, and turned and walked. Behind his broad back were thirty-two bows and surely over three hundred striped arrows.

Men moved past the Osyrrain and looked at the tall Jarik by her side. He nodded. The Osyrrain looked at him while the men moved on. Buskins scuffed and crunched on sand. They followed their firstman down to *Seadancer*, and set stocky legs and strong backs into it. They pushed the ship down into the surf. The hazel and chestnut eyes of women looked from them to Jarik and their ruler, who had paced twenty steps down the strand. Twenty paces behind waited thirty-two superb archers with as many superb bows. Forty paces ahead was *Seadancer*.

Her sisters watched Jilain, then, while she paced to a point a little nearer Osyrrain, nearer Jarik. Her hands remained empty. Another man had remained behind. He stood on the other side of the queen. He was Delath *Morbriner*, with white-blond hair fluttering below his helm, and he was old enough to have been Jarik's father, assuming he had seen his son born at his age seventeen, which was more than normal among his people. His pale eyes sought those of Jarik, while their fellows floated *Seadancer* in a lively surf and began clambering aboard. Still the breeze blew from the woods, out to sea. Few doubted that the wind was for them, for who could doubt the power of Her? They had seen it; they saw it on each of Jarik's wrists.

On the strand, the silence held, in tension thick and palpable as that impermanent tension that precedes a violent storm. *Seadancer* was afloat and restless, and all but two were aboard and more than ready to depart Kerosyr; the Isle of Osyr, the dead god.

Jarik bade Delath go with the others, to the ship.

"You do not command, Jarik Blacksword. I go when you go."

The two men looked at each other. They were not friends. Morbrin-fighters both; the *machines-that-fight*; they who fight as the wolf fights. They had had their troubles on this expedition for Her, but now Delath chose to remain with Jarik, in danger. A warrior's respect for courage superseded antipathy.

"I remain to hold the Osyrrain, Delath Berserker. I will join you on the ship."

"With many arrows behind you. I go when you go, Jarik Blacksword."

"Go," Osyrrain said. "We will not seek to stop you now."

Jarik said quietly, "Say that again, Osyrrain. Very loudly."

She looked at him, while Delath looked at her, and she repeated her words. Loudly, for her women. "Go! We will not seek to stop you now!"

"At rest," her commander said, hearing the promise, which among the guardians was *helderen*, which meant sacred, and more. "Let them go as the Osyrrain commands."

Jarik stepped away from the queen, and turned. "We leave you, Guardians," he said, so that all heard. "Remove yourselves back, to the very edge of the trees."

"Do not seek to take her, Jarik!" That from the commander.

He let his gaze meet hers, and he nodded. "She remains, Ershain. I have promised it."

Ershain made a little sound and the Guardians backed, to the very edge of the treeline. The very air seemed heavy, despite the seaward breeze. Jarik was sweating, in leathers and linked mailcoat, and bird-songs were only intrusions. Kirrensark alone had not boarded *Seadancer*. He waited near the ship, as a firstman should. He would be last aboard. All but two of his had boarded, and the tension had not abated a whit.

"Farewell, Osyrrain," Jarik muttered, and looked past her for he expected no reply from this woman who hated him very much. "Delath."

Jarik looked at the ship. His back prickled. Sweat trickled and was fire in the whip-weals the Osyrrain had put on his back.

"When you are ready, Jarik Blacksword."

Jarik glanced at the other man. "I am ready, Delath. Go!"

"When you let go this queen of murderers and go, Jarik Blacksword," Delath said. His gaze was steady, expressionless. "Then goes also Delath the Morbriner."

"Delath . . . we have given our word." As he said those words, Jarik felt Osyrrain tense. "*Kiddensok!*" Jarik called. "Delath!"

Dutifully Kirrensark called to his longtime friend and weapons companion: "Delath! Board ship!"

The pale-eyed, cloud-bearded man looked back at the line of bow-armed women, and at their queen, and at Jarik. And he took his hand from his hilt. Then Delath *backed* down the strand, and Jarik knew that Osyrrain seethed at the insult. Reaching the ship, Delath allowed Shranshule to aid him aboard. He turned at once, still watchful. Showing his distrust. Pale eyes above pale beard, and eyebrows no darker than the sand of the beach, and yet his hair was not white with age.

Jarik took a deep breath. He scanned the beach ahead of him and saw no obstruction or depression to turn the ankle of a running man.

He let go Osyrrain's arm. Then Jarik raced to the waterline, his mailcoat jingling and his back gone all aprickle. Behind him, just as his feet splashed for the first time, he heard the shout. The voice was Osyrrain's, and Jarik went cold.

"SLAY THEM!"

"*Bows*!" Delath yelled instantly. "Up bows for Kirren-sark!"

"No!"

That from Jarik, who had clamped his lips and splashed dodgily through the water while his back crawled. He reached the bulking hull of the ship. For an instant he and Kirrensark looked into each other's eyes. Jarik looked back to see women frowning, eyes rolling. Arrows were being moved slowly and uncertainly from quivers toward taut bowstrings. A promise had been made, and among them no promise was broken; it was not conceivable. Yet she spoke for the god, and she had ordered them to loose their arrows. They moved slowly, uncertainly—

One of Osyr's Guardians moved swiftly. She ran leaping ahead of the others. Almost naked, jiggling as only women jiggle, she raced and her sword was out in her hand. She ran toward the Osyrrain, and all stared.

That Guardian did not slow. As she passed, running, she struck. Racing, bosses flashing on her leather helm, shell necklace and squirrel's tail crotchpiece wildly amove, she struck without slowing. She was the best of the Guardians and with one sweep of her blade she accomplished the impossible. No hair covered the Osyrrain's neck, and the sword was sharp and well swung, backed with the momentum of the Guardian's racing pace. The Osyrrain's head fled her body on a wake of scarlet. It thumped to the sparkling sand, and rolled. The treacherous eyes glared and flashed bright as gemstones.

Every body froze and every eye stared—save those of the Guardian who had slain her queen. She ran on down the strand until she was splashing in water, and came to Jarik's side beneath the ship's fierce hawk's head of a prow. She offered him no harm, but instead she turned back to face her sisters in Osyr.

"The Osyrrain gave an Osyrrain's promise!" she shouted, and her voice hurt Jarik's ears. "And she spoke too for Osyr! These men know not the helderen-promise—and yet they *kept* theirs! Would you allow a promise to be helderen only until the Osyrrain decides on treachery? Would you allow her to rob Osyr of honor, because she had none? Guardians! Choose now an *honorable* ruler!"

Jilain whirled then, and reached up to the ship. As she stretched, Kirrensark regained sense and movement. He seized her thighs and lifted that tall lithe woman. Aye, and she well muscled and he with but one arm. The two hands that reached down were Delath's. Dripping, the Guardian of Osyr turned her naked backside to her people, and to the sun, and scrambled aboard that ship of men.

Whirling at once, she reached down for Jarik of the Black Sword.

A woman aided aboard the agent of the Iron Lords and the unwilling servant of the Lady of the Snowmist, made hers by the silver bracers he wore. At the same time two men drew up their firstman.

Ashore, Jilain's fellows stood staring, shocked into immobility of brain and body with their bows and their arrows in their hands. Would that *this* shipload of men had never come to Kerosyr! Would that the Guardians had not sought to use them to father more Guardians and then to slay them, and their male get, as Guardians had done time out of mind. Would that the incredible Jarik had not come with them! First the dilemma of whether to serve a queen who broke her promise, because she wanted revenge.

Now dilemma continued: break a queen's helderen promise to avenge their queen in death? Their standing feathers quivered and blue hair stirred, for the wind was blowing well and the sail was up and hardly was Kirrensark aboard before his shout bawled out.

"ROW!"

*Seadancer* moved. The wind strove at the sail and men

rowed anyhow, while the weavers wove and gods plotted and strove and their servants endured without understanding.

"I am Ershain, and *I* have made no promise!" a voice yelled, and in its excitement it rose into a screech. "Loose, loose, loose!"

The dilemma was broken. Ershain served Osyr, as did they all. Never had men come ashore on His isle and left it again. Bows were raised to a higher tilt, arrows aimed upward. Strings twanged and left hands returned partway with the bows while right arms cranked to pluck forth second arrows while thirty were still in air.

To the ears of those on *Seadancer* came the ugliest sound known to men of weapons. It had been likened to the hum of swift bees, flying on that distinctly un-beelike course called a bee-line. Angry bees. It had been likened to the high-pitched whining hum of those most ferociously territorial insects, wasps, when their nest was threatened or disturbed. Others had referred to the angry keening hum of enraged hornets, which was enough to send a fine horse bolting. Yet none of those impressions was truly descriptive. There could be no sound quite like the keening whistling rush through the air of slim deadly missiles. No sound so hideous as that of the attack of a swarm of bow-shot arrows.

Up they arced, to fall into the ship in a bee-swarming, wasp-speeding, hornet-attacking, eerily keening whiz of death. One rattled off the round helmet of Tole, whose expression became disconcerted. He staggered. Another improbably struck the copper boss on a man's leather jerkin with a definite ring. The striped shaft caromed away to fall into the water and he knew that he was saved, only by luck. Anonymous attack from the skies; indiscriminate stabbing down of blind staffs—what a way for a man to be downed! What a hideous impersonal way to attack, to wage war!

Several of the keening staffs peppered planking and one drove with a harsh thunk into the mast. None fell into the water; not one of those Kerosyran arrows. The horn-plated bows and the skill of the Guardians were beyond that. One slammed into Jarik's upper arm, so that he emitted a mingled gasp and grunt while he jerked violently. Yet he felt only the impact. The arrow stood there for a moment, part of its head wedged between links of thin wire of the god-metal. Its point was caught in the close-fitting jacket he wore under the coat of chain. Jarik plucked it forth, unblooded. Another man cursed as an arrowhead, in passing, did not quite miss but opened a shallow ridge in his arm. Merely a scratch.

No one was wounded in that first volley, which was ragged and loosed in excitement. Men pulled hard even as the sail snapped and bellied.

Though the ship was farther off by yards, the second volley was not ragged. The same wind that thrust the ship away from the island aided the flight of the pursuing arrows, which the Guardians loosed in concert. Thirty shafts whistled high and fell onto *Seadancer*. This time more than one man cried out. So did Jilain, and she fell back.

"Jilain!" Jarik shouted.

"PULL!" Kirrensark roared, and grunted when an arrow banged off his helmet less than a finger's width from his face.

Men pulled. Oars and backs creaked, along with planking and cordage. The ship leaped ahead and water gurgled past her flanks in white foam. Another angry keening whizzing descended.

"Do Not Look Up!" Delath bawled, for helmets were invulnerable to arrows and faces were not.

This time some shafts plunged into the sea short of the ship's stern, while others impacted *Seadancer* and others rattled away. A man's outcry was of shock and pain combined; a scream and a gurgle all at once. The fourth volley hiss-screamed aloft, and this time only one arrow struck; it thunked into the ship's stern. All the others were wasted in the brine. *Seadancer* was away. Now the breeze moved her too rapidly for men to pull oars. Twice a man's height at her waist, the ship sped asea.

Those men who saw were amazed to observe Jarik pounce to the fallen Jilain and squat there. Already she was rising, blinking. She wore a leathern cap with plackets of bone awled and sewn all around, and on the neck- and earflaps. One flap was broken, now. An arrow had struck with enough force to stagger her. She was uninjured.

Blinking as she gazed into the face of Jarik so near, she saw that it was . . . different. The eyes had changed; the lines of it had changed.

*"Ah, you are all right,"* Oak said, and swung away from her. He seized Strick's arm, inspected it. *"You are all right,"* Oak said. *"It hardly bleeds—and do let it bleed, man!"*

Blinking, frowning, Strick said, "Here Jarik, what—"

*Already turning from him, the mailed wearer of the Black Sword swung back. His eyes were ablaze, ferocious. "Don't call me that, damn you!"*

While Strick stared with his mouth open, *Oak shouldered aside Seramshule to squat beside Handeth the Hounder.*

Jilain, frowning, and others, frowning, watched while Jarik moved his hands over the man, from whose thigh stood an arrow. Yet it was not Jarik. None of them knew. No one of Kirrensark-wark or Kerosyr had seen this strangest of the strange aspects of Jarik. None of these had seen Oak the Healer, who shared Jarik's body. Oak, who *saw* wrongness or debility and the solution or cure, by scrying with a sort of psychic eye that *saw* within. They were seeing him now, and knew it not.

*With one hand on Handeth, without looking up, the man in the dark mailcoat put back a hand. "Give me a clean dagger."*

"Dagger!" Handeth burst out. He tried to lunge up, groaned, and fell back. The arrow stood from his thigh and quivered with his movements.

"You wear a dagger, Jarik," Delath Berserker said.

*"You mange-ridden silly jack,"* Oak snarled, *"I am not Jarik, and don't call me that! My name is Oak. Oak! Jarik kills! Oak heals!"* And, while Kirrensark stayed Delath, who lurched angrily forward reaching for his hilt: *"Handeth. Listen. If the arrow is pulled out you will lose too much blood and perhaps die of it. Its head is caught in the muscle. If it stays in, you will lose this leg to the flesh-rot that stinks. We must break off the shaft and cut out the arrowhead, Handeth, and it will hurt a lot."*

Silence draped itself over *Seadancer.* Into it another wounded man moaned. Men exchanged glances and stared nervously, with Jilain, at him they knew as the strangel Jarik who had come to their wark from nowhere, in time to save Kirrensark from attack by ambush, who almost immediately had attracted the attention of the god who had come down from the mountain above their wark, and taken him up into it with Her: the Lady of the Snowmist.

He returned wearing her seamless bracers of silver-that-was-not-silver but some unscratchable, unremovable god-metal—and he and Kirrensark had led them on this mission. For Her. Now—now . . . *who was he*? Could *he heal*? *Why did he behave so*?

"You—how do you know this?" Handeth the Hounder's voice was plaintive; the voice of a patient who liked none of his alternatives.

Blue eyes gone hard as perisine gemstones stared into his. "*Do not mistake me for Jarik, Handeth. I know.*"

"Jarik—" a man began, and Kirrensark took his hand from Delath's chest to wave it for silence. He did not twitch his gaze from Jarik—or Oak.

"Use . . . use my dagger," the Hounder said, and he fell back.

"*Two men hold his arms. Two hold his legs. At knee and ankle, now.* Move!" *Oak had Handeth's dagger as he spoke, and was holding it up, squinting at it while he turned it in the sunlight. Sharp metal flashed.* "*Kiddensok—is there ale left?*"

"Uh . . . yes . . ."

"*Ale!*" *And Oak broke off the arrow, making Handeth grit and grind his teeth and gleam suddenly with sweat. Then Oak cut.*

As it turned out, more than four men were required to hold Handeth the Hounder. There was much blood. No one mentioned a stuck pig. All stared tensely and in silence, save those who turned away, unable to look. Eventually Oak showed the unconscious man the arrowhead. It dripped. When Oak poured ale over the bloody thigh, Handeth jerked even though he was unconscious.

"*Bind this up.*"

Oak moved to another wounded man. This was he who had cried out, and could not prevent his own moaning though he strove to keep his mouth tight.

"*Oh*," Oak said low and fervent, "*shit*." And he went to work.

*Seadancer* fled over the water. Oak worked. As Jarik was the consummate compelled fighter, Oak was the compulsively dedicated worker-at-healing. Men exchanged glances and said little. Understanding even less, Jilain moved close and aided Oak, all in silence. She looked frequently into his face, into his eyes. And she did as he bade and said nothing when he railed at her. None could be more impatient than this man! Somehow Jarik had become a healer. Somehow he *knew*. With the role, he took on the eternal arrogance of the healer.

Jilain accepted, adapted more swiftly than could any of the men, and made herself his assistant. The tradition of the nurse-servant was born, there on the sea when the gods dwelt upon the earth.

The sea formed a shallow bowl so that the horizon was at a higher level on every side than line of sight. Eventually Kerosyr vanished and there was only water and sky. A great shallow round depression, sea-girt, with *Seadancer* at its center. The ship strode confidently over it in foam that seemed crystal and snow.

Most of his companions stared at Jarik, who avowed— with such vicious anger and militancy—that he was not Jarik, but someone with the name of a tree. The word was already old, in their language; the word was "Oak." His name—Jarik's name—might mean "sea-gift" or "beach-found," depending on interpretation and pronunciation. He was after all not of Lokusta whence plied the hawk-prowed ships that had slain his parents . . . except that they were not his parents.

The roll and sway of the ship hardly bothered Oak. Neither did the sun, or the sky blushing its way toward sunset. He thought only of his patients. Men obeyed his injunctions to rig shade over them.

Many men slept that night, once the sun-chariot had been overtaken and gone to rest. Oak did not sleep. Jilain knew that Jarik had not slept on the previous night save for that little time before she had to wake him. He had been busy arranging the succor and escape of all these men. She knew he must be weary. She was determined to remain awake with him. She who had challenged him, and fought him with sharp blades, and cut him and been cut by him, and nearly bested him until she was bested by him after long combat, and who now joined the weave and pattern of her life with his. So the weavers wove their yarn of life. That he was a healer, that he *knew*, was manifest. She adapted cleverly—or womanly—and called him Oak. And she fell asleep.

Oak did not sleep and he did not touch her. He tended Handeth. He tended poor Shranshule Beartooth, who had an arrow in the arm that did much damage, and he tended Hanish, who protested at having the Kerosyran arrowhead cut out of his chest. Seramshule came quietly over to stand over Oak and gaze down upon the sleeping Jilain. She was sprawled naked or may as well have been, wearing what Guardians wore. The squirrel tail adorned as much as it covered. Oak looked up at him.

*"Take those thoughts and those bright hot eyes over there and go to sleep."*

Seramshule blinked, and after a few seconds he swallowed, and after a few seconds more he went elsewhere. Somehow one obeyed Oak when one might have challenged Jarik. Oak worked on, and *Seadancer* slipped on through the sea, over the nighted sea. Kirrensark fell asleep. Oak hovered, and brooded, and worked. *Seadancer* fled before the unnaturally constant breeze.

# TWO

*Yesterday this day's madness did prepare:*
*Tomorrow's silence, triumph, or despair.*
*Drink! For you know not whence you came, or why.*

—*Omar Khayyam*

On the morrow men awoke to find that a nearly naked woman slept among them, and they felt lust. They saw also that Oak had not slept. Or Jarik, for the two were one. It was not possible; it *was*. Already his eyes were rimmed with the hue of slate. All the night he had tended the wounded he made his responsibility, and it was strange to see him so, still wearing the chaincoat he—or rather, Jarik—had of the Iron Lords. Men looked about and saw that there was only *Seadancer* now, alone on the vast plain of the sea. There was no there, the opposite of here; no land within sight.

Some nervousness, though hardly all, was allayed when a silver-grey dove flew in from nowhere. It came gently to light on the shoulder of Jarik-who-was-Oak, and they knew that the bird was from Her.

"I am busy," Oak said to the bird. "Go to Kiddensok. I am busy."

All had noted that Oak pronounced Kirrensark's name as Jarik did, giving the letter *r* even less pronunciation than they. (How could one man be two; how could two men occupy one body? His head was not so big. How could it con-

13

tain two brains?) No one failed to note that after a little while the dove jumped from Jarik-Oak's shoulder and fluttered, lifting. It alit on the armless shoulder of Kirrensark. A Her-sent gull had guided them here. Now some wondered only that this was a dove, not a gull, for men were adjusting of necessity to god-sorcery. The other bird had guided them all the way to the isle, and to the Temple of Osyr. None of these men had seen dove or gull in the village of the Guardians. (Jarik had.) Every man felt a bit of shame about his gullibility and willing lust and his activities in that forest-bound wark; about his *use*. Nothing much was said of it. Men muttered of the sun, and the sea, and Jarik and Oak, and the shamelessly naked woman aboard their ship. Men checked over blades unused on the island. Only Jarik's Black Sword had drawn blood.

The Man Who Was Two Men attended the wounded and he issued commands in a most peremptory manner. Amid so much other strangeness, men of weapons somehow accepted that. He told Hanish that he would be hale. He told Handeth that he thought he would be fine, so long as he remained absolutely still and "thought good thoughts" about his future. Handeth blinked at that; could this weird healer know that he had been despairing in his mind?

"It is Jarik," Delath at last said. He was talking as much for his own understanding as to the others, rubbing and rubbing his hand over his leather leggings that had once been that yellowish-tan which was the color of doeskin. They were far darker, now. "It is Jarik," he said again. "And it is not Jarik. It is Oak. I call him Oak." He glowered about, he who went *morbrin*, berserk, and was better at fighting with sharp blades than any two or five others. His eyes were the color of an inch of rainwater in a silver pan. "Call him Oak."

The chainmailed figure squatting beside Shranshule turned and stared at Delath. His slate-rimmed eyes were terribly bright. They seemed to burn, like the eyes of a man with a fever.

"Who are you?"

Delath stared, for a long while, into almost glassily staring eyes. Jarik's eyes?

"You know me, Oak, healer. My name is Delath, Barranath's son of Kirrensark-wark."

"Ah yes. Del-ath. Another superb killer. Yet no friend of Jarik's. Well—friend of mine, Del-ath. I may need you. This man is bad off. I fear for his arm."

"Fear?"

"Yes. Fear." The blue eyes stared. They seemed cold, yet burning. Flame and ice. "And do you do the same, man of weapons; *fear*! For his arm is in danger. If it has to come off, you will be needed."

"How can it be that Hanish took an arrow in the body and Shranshule was struck only in the arm, and it is he who is in such danger?"

Oak raised his eyebrows. He seemed to consider. "I have decided to answer you," he said, and such words surprised everyone. "The arrow that took Hanish in the chest struck at a slant because he was moving at the time. Now strike your own chest with your fist, Del-ath. We are padded there—and the plate of bone is very hard. It is designed to protect the lungs and the heart, and it does well. Human armor, you see. You must have . . . experienced some trouble some time, in trying to strike into an enemy's chest." Oak's eyes seemed to commence burning at that thought of Delath's experience and expertise, and he paused for a few moments. "The arrow sent into Shranshule struck his arm directly. It tore through skin and muscle and nerves and imbedded itself in the bone. The *bone*, and it was hard to draw and cut out. Hanish's chest was hit, and hurt, by an arrow that was almost glancing. Shranshule's arm was wrecked."

Coon turned away toward the rail. He was pale, for he was young and he had not seen such wounds, or heard such talk. Combat was supposed to be glorious, with glorious camaraderie after, and everybody being men together. Coon, who had been called that so long and so often that some did not know his proper name, had been thrilled to come on this expedition. Now he wished he were at home. Where was the beauty in fearful men and burning sun, in endless sea and moans, and the talking of slicing off a man's arm to save his life?

Jilain squeezed more water from her cloth, onto Shranshule's forehead.

"Must—you talk . . . about me . . . so?" Shranshule demanded, and Oak turned to look down upon him. Only

Delath and Jilain saw the drawing of his face and the compassion in his eyes.

"You are a brave tough bear, aren't you, Shranshule Beartooth! You were misnamed, man. They should have called you after the whole bear."

"Uh," Shranshule said, wincing. "Well, if you—going to have to—take off my . . . arm, do it and get it—uh!—done with. May be it won't hurt so . . . so much then. Just . . . uh! *Blight* but it hurts!—just don't *talk* about it. I have a weak stomach."

Someone chuckled and clamped his own mouth; Oak stared down at the fallen man, and shook his head. "You do not have a weak anything, Shranshule Bear, save perhaps a head!"

"How," Delath began, and paused. "How can you know these things about his body, and about our bodies, J—Oak?"

For a long while Oak stared at the morbriner, while *Seadancer* skidded over the water under a luminous postdawn sky. "No one has ever asked me, that, Del-ath." And he was silent again for a time. His eyes were not pleasant, this healer with patience only for the injured. "I cannot tell you. I . . . know. I *see*. I am Oak. It is what Oak does. I . . . come, when Jarik—when someone Jarik cares about is sore hurt, or Jarik thinks so. I *know*. I just know how. Men of your ilk slay and wound. I heal, and mop up your spilt blood. My kind is needed."

"Aye," Kirrensark murmured. "More than mine."

After a nerve-fraying silence, Delath asked, "And my kind?"

Oak stared at him. "No one will ever know, Del-ath. Your kind, Jarik's kind—the poor bloody damned killer!—will always prevail. My kind must exist because your kind does. I must exist because you do. I must labor because you will not stop your bloody labor: Our kind—humans, I mean, Del-ath—is not sane. Be ready, though. Shranshule is in trouble, and I may need you." He looked at another man, his greasy old belt pulled through the loop in front and dangling down almost obscenely. "Shranshule needs some ale, now."

Delath gazed reflectively on Oak, and his water-grey eyes rolled so that he was looking at his old friend

Kirrensark. The firstman seemed now only an aged man with one arm and many many memories. A god commanded them. A gull had led them and now a dove shipped with them. A very young man had directed their expedition for the god on the earth, and accomplished its mission. He had the White Rod of Osyr, taken from the very hand of the statue. And now a very young and eerie healer ruled the ship and Kirrensark did as he bade. Now there was a naked woman aboard—aboard a hawkship! She served the healer and men could not look at her without swallowing. Kirrensark could but observe. He could but abide, and wait, and be. And think about his accomplishments of the past, perhaps. He had been ruler and hawker and killer, this man Jarik had come to slay and had saved instead, with the Black Sword and his awful competence.

Jilain had long since put aside her bow. Now and again the sun flashed off its plackets of bone, gleamed dully on its campion-hued grip. A man picked it up to examine it, in its great differentness. When he sought to pull its recurved length, he gave the woman a shocked look. *That slim girl* . . . no vertebrae showed on her. Her back must be overlaid by solid muscle! And below that—he swallowed and tried to think about the bow.

"I would bid you remember yourself and eat . . . Oak," Kirrensark said, pausing over the name. He was a big man with a big head.

"I would bid you see that a better canopy is rigged to shade Shranshule," Oak said. He considered, looking at the canopies over the others. Cloaks and whaleskins. "Eat. Yes. It is a good idea, for from food comes energy. Yes. And to drink, as well. I am not used to considering the needs of this body." He looked down at himself. "Is this heavy iron coat necessary?" He looked down at it deprecatingly, his warcoat of linked circles of the god-metal that was mightier than iron as a man was mightier than a boy.

Gane the Dogged looked all around before he chuckled, a bit nervously. "We are all alone on the sea," he said.

Suddenly Jilain of the dark blue hair extended an arm. She pressed Oak's wrist in her long-fingered hand. "Please keep on the chaincoat, Oak."

He looked surprisedly at her. Studied her. "Bargain. You are on a ship full of men. I shall keep this body covered if you will cover yours."

Jilain frowned a little, and looked around. She did not blush; she had no social conditioning that told her to do. "Oh. What—"

"Wear my . . . my good coat of leather bossed w—with bronze," Shranshule said, not easily. He tapped her thigh with the knuckles on the hand of his good arm. The thigh was tighter than his own. "It will . . . please me. And . . . peradventure I shall not—be needing it . . . more."

She stroked his forehead. "That is kind, Shranshule. But it will not fit."

"*Not fit!* Healer—help me up! I must show this tender girl I am no small boy!"

"That 'tender girl,'" Oak said, "very nearly defeated Jarik and his Black Sword, Bear. He bears a wound of her—two, on thigh and forehead. Best you call her *elye*: lady!"

"Jilain will do," Jilain said, ignoring the mutters elicited by Oak's words. This . . . *woman* had nearly bested *Jarik*?! "And what one meant, Shranshule, is that your leather garment is far too big."

The supine Shranshule rolled his cloudy-sky eyes. "I think you have chest enough to fill it," he said, without a gasp.

Sudden laughter swept the ship to whelm the sound of water gurgling past the hull. It was too loud, that laughter, and went on too long, for there was much tension to relieve, on *Seadancer*. Too, not a man aboard but was aware of Jilain's unmanly chest, and of the ruby bonded to its one lobe. The gem flashed every time she moved that arm. All were aware—unless perhaps Oak was unaware or not noticing, but Oak was after all a creature apart.

Shranshule chuckled, and then went pale and groaned, for he was capable of no movement without pain.

"Jilain," Oak said dourly, laying a comforting hand on his patient. "Cover yourself in this bear's bearhide."

"I am not cold," Jilain said.

The arm had to come off. Oak spoke quietly to Kirrensark. Oak's eyes were terribly bright, within their dark-rimmed sockets. *Seadancer* bore wood-working tools, for a ship might need repair or even so much as a new mast or oars. When Oak asked for a saw and the help of several men, Kirrensark paled.

"Ah! It's a terrible thing to do to a man."

"It was done to you. Would you rather be dead?"

"Alive," Kirrensark said softly, "though there are times when I have my doubts."

"That is Shranshule's choice. I do it or he dies. I may have waited too long already, in too much hope. Stupid, stupid!"

Kirrensark put his hand on the shoulder of the tall, powerfully built warrior become healer. "You have done more than anyone could have done, Oak. You need sleep, badly. Do not blame yourse—"

"Don't patronize me!" Oak hissed with an intensity filled with malice. "I will sleep when this is done. When I sleep, I sleep long and long, while *he* owns this body and misuses it. Just unpack that blighted saw!"

When Oak was preparing (complaining about the tools he must use), Delath suggested one clean blow with an ax. Or the Black Sword, perhaps. Oak glowered and his eyes were like knives that pierced.

"Don't be stupid, slayer! The shock of such a blow would kill a man in Shranshule's condition! It must be sawn off. Right now Jilain is trying to fill his gut and brain with ale so he will feel less."

Delath was flushed and almost quivering. "You . . . try me, Healer."

"Slay me then, slayer. I will not fight you. I have work to do." And he stared suddenly into Delath's eyes. Just as straightforwardly and in a quiet tone he said, "I need your help, though."

Delath gave it, and it was done. Shranshule passed out almost at once, clinging to the squirrel's tail Jilain had "traded" him for his big leathern mailcoat. A third of *Seadancer's* complement lurched to the rail, to be sick, and Coon could not understand why he was not among them. Blood soon covered the whalehide sheet on which Shranshule lay. Of a sudden blood spurted high. Oak grunted a command, sharply. Delath swallowed and hesitated, staring at the scarlet fountain. Jilain clamped her hands on Shranshule as Oak had directed. The freshet of blood lowered, ceased to spurt. The fire Oak had com-

manded stank. Shranshule lay still, in his faint, while his
arm was removed. The stench of the smoking iron on flesh
was worse than the stink of the fire in which the iron had
been readied, and even in his unconsciousness Shranshule
lurched and sweated a barrel.

Oak gave it over an hour. He staggered when he had finished, and with an angry glare at Jilain *ordered* them to get
him out of the mailcoat. Out of it and the padded
underjacket, he stood panting in a sodden tunic—and he
shivered. This time a man gave him a severe look, and
swung a cloak about him. Oak went to the foremost part of
the stern and stared ahead. He hardly squinted. Behind
him steam hissed and rose, for the fire must be killed, not
merely dumped overboard; sparks might return to the ship
and smoulder for hours before killing them all in a floating
pyre.

Shranshule lay one-armed, cauterized, bandaged,
shaded. The sun was bright. The dove remained aboard
while the continuing strong breeze blew *Seadancer* in a direction experienced men swore was homeward; toward
Lokusta. As if any could be sure; but they swore nevertheless. It beat rowing.

A hand came onto Oak's shoulder. He did not turn. The
shoulder was cloaked, wet-tunicked, and no longer mailed.

"One does not understand, Oak."

"One does not! *Two* do not understand! Jarik and Oak
do not understand, woman! Three then, with you. Hmp!
And many more do not understand Oak and Jarik. Get
some sleep." He had not glanced at her. It was hard, being
Jarik; it was hard dealing with this other personality that
shared his body and hated him so.

"One would try to understand, Oak."

"So would I. You should nap. We are not through. I
think I waited too long with Shranshule." Oak stared
ahead.

"One does not know what—"

"I know that *one* doesn't know, woman! No one knows.
Only me. I—"

"One has a name. Why do you continue calling her
'woman'?"

Interrupted, he stiffened in affront. Yet he *decided* to
answer: "Have you noticed how I call most of the others
'man' when I address one?"

"Well, yes . . ."

"Leave off then, and try not to be a bigot. I have no different rules for females. Now I think I waited too long to remove Shranshule's arm, and that was stupid. I put it off because of unworthy emotion—only a butcher would want to take a man's arm off. The wound was high though, near the shoulder, and the poison came swiftly into the blood. I fear it may already have entered the body. Stupid, stupid."

She moved her fingers on his shoulder. They were unexpectedly strong fingers. Under them was a tension-stiff shoulder. "No. Not stupid. Oak is . . . great."

He snorted. "Oak does not even exist. Oak is a chimæra. Jarik's nightmare, that rotten slayer! Jarik's sickness. I was born eight years old, do you know that? How many people are born eight years old, and able to bandage wounds—even the wounds of a man minutes from death! That was my first act. I was born at eight, into the body of another, and he was still in it. I was born of insanity and my first act was one of insanity. I bandaged one Orrik, a dead man. . . . our father."

"One understands none of this, Oak—"

"*One* understands precious little of anything, woman, but there is no sense bragging about it. Go and sleep."

"How," Jilain said, "can a healer, one so concerned wit' the well-being of others, be such an arrogant, nasty creature?"

Oak stiffened under her hand, and did not turn. "Listen, you—"

"Why do you not look at this one when you are about to rail at her, healer?"

Oak rounded on her and his eyes were full of blue fire. "Damn you! You are the only decent person aboard, woman! Why must you pester me? Why must you be . . . emotionally caught up with us?"

She challenged: "Us?"

"Us! Jarik and me! We are hardly alike, that poor twisted unhappy killer and I! You asked a question. Well, it is hard for us, Jarik and me, to look straight at the one we speak to. It is not your place or business to make mention of it, plague you! As to what you call 'arrogance'—it is not stupid or wrong to admit one's superiority. What is wrong is for those who are manifestly superior to deny it. It is stupid *not* to admit one's superiority. You are stupid, and you don't admit it, and so you are stupid, deliberately. Bovine. A perfect assistant."

The queen's champion of Kerosyr stared into his eyes. "One will not bother to insult you in return as you would like, healer. Have you more poison to spew? Spew it, then. This one is strong."

Oak stared. "Strong indeed," he murmured at last, quietly, and he looked as if he was about to touch her.

He did not. He whirled from her to stare asea again. "Invidious woman! How *dare* you? How dare anyone be so strong as to be *able* to remain equable when another wants trouble, and goads you. Have you no need for release? Where is your ego? You have right to one, Jilain Kerosyris! Listen. Attend me. Listen. Hear Oak, for Jarik hasn't sense or nerve enough to speak his thoughts, his true thoughts. If that bloody machine-that-kills has thoughts! He is not sure enough of himself to speak them. Listen. You . . . attend me, now." He was spewing words, fountaining a stream of words while he sought the ones he wanted to say to her. "Listen! You are . . . you are superior, Jilain. 'Spew then,' you said. Ah your shoulders are strong, Jilain, both physically and in the mind. You are strong, woman. You are . . . you are our strength. Jarik's and Oak's, who need it. Stay, Jilain. Jarik . . . Jarik is strong with weapons and weak of mind. No, no, that is not what I mean. There is no word. He is weak of . . . of mental construction. Ah, that's stupid!"

He struck *Seadancer*'s rail in frustration, and *Seadancer* fled on, eastward and northward. Off to steerboard a big fish leaped, armored in sleek blued silver. It returned in curveting joy to the water amid a dancing explosion of crystal droplets. Otherwise, despite the wind that drove *Seadancer*, the water was placid, glassy. The sea seemed bored.

"Jarik . . . Jarik has a mind, he thinks, and it is not weak . . . it . . . it has a disease in it," Oak said, groping, staring at nothing. "Yes. A sort of disease in it. I am strong with this talent, and weak as well. Jarik . . . covers. I cover. You do not cover, Jilain Kerosyris. You can be our strength. We need—O we need, Jarik and I! Can you bear that weight, isolated unworldly islander who knows nothing really and is about to enter the world—born even older than I was? Listen. Attend. We are two, that bloody barbarian killer and I. Jarik and I. We are two. You are a third, and perhaps that—perhaps you can make us, make us one—three as one!"

Again he struck the rail. "Bah! What a ridiculous concept! There are no words, not enough words. Three people, two bodies, one unit. Ridiculous. Jilain . . . Jilain, plague take you, *go and rest*. We . . . we . . . I . . . we think highly of you, Jilain. You are . . . to me, for me, with me while I have labored over these men, you have been . . . you have been . . . what I mean is, I—you are . . . pox and plague! I may need you more, woman! Do you go and sleep now!"

Her hand came onto him again. "One understands, Oak."

"Stop that! You cannot understand! You are no god on the earth!"

"One knows affection. One has had lovers. Some will be sorry, Oak, that this one has left Kerosyr. Lishain will weep for this one's leaving, for this one's not being there with her by nickt. And this one will weep for her, sometimes in the dark of nickt. Do you know that? This one knows what you say, and cannot say, Oak." She moved her hand from his shoulder to touch his cheek, though he did not look at her. "*You* need rest and sleep, Oak, and Jarik does. This one will sleep when you do."

Oak stared asea. "Stupid," Oak muttered, and Jilain, in Shranshule's brass-bossed mailcoat of supple old brown leather stained dark unto black, left him. "*So honorable*," Oak muttered in a low-voiced sneer, while men looked at Jilain, for her legs were long and beautifully curved with muscle under tight skin. On her forehead she bore the mark of Jarik's sword. On his forehead, he bore the mark of her—or/and Oak did.

Oak was right. He had waited too long. The poison in the blood had gone from Shranshule's arm into his body where nothing could be done about it. He was in pain, and it would be worse. Fever burned in him. He sweated and shivered, muttered and babbled. Already he was starting to experience that which was not; the wakeful nightmares of sepsis.

"Kill me!" he got out coherently, with effort and in a hideous voice. None thought he was delirious then: "Show mercy and kill me!"

"I cannot," Oak muttered. He rose to shout it in anguish: "I cannot! I cannot kill . . . Jarik? Jarik, killer, you are needed."

But a man lay yet unhealed, and Jarik did not return to control of that fine body and maimed mind. So long as he was needed as healer, Oak ruled the body and the brain. And Kirrensark stared without comprehension. Once he had heard a man beg for the mercy of death. He had been unable to grant it. He had heard Jarik agree; that stranger who had come from nowhere to save the life of Kirrensark, without knowing who he was. He had heard Jarik agree. He had watched Jarik grant that man the mercy of death; a man who had waylaid and fallen upon Kirrensark, with two others.

Now Kirrensark looked on Jarik—no matter that he called himself Oak and was most visibly obviously manifestly a healer—and heard him say that he could not kill. Kirrensark closed his eyes. His head hurt and he felt old. His arm tingled, where there was no arm. Nothing to rub or scratch.

Oak went to Delath.

Oak spoke quietly. Delath refused, and refused, and agreed. He knelt and muttered rite-words. He stripped himself bare, unwinding even his breechclout, and he prayed more. Then Delath, in mercy, slew Shranshule who was in agony with blood poisoning. The stroke was swift and far more merciful than the long death in pain he faced; far more merciful than poison.

Oak stood and watched. Staring, glaring. His eyes glistened. Delath met his eyes.

"I did not enjoy that."

Oak gazed steadily at this homely, not ugly man with the nigh colorless eyes. Then he nodded his respect and thanks to Delath, and turned away to stare at nothing. Jilain watched him, and perhaps she understood.

Eventually he moved. He went about seeing to his patients. All would be hale in a bit of time. That one who would not heal had received the ultimate healing, from the hands of Delath. The healer had done his work and

*Seadancer* was at peace—physically. *Seadancer* flew over the waves and windspray sparkled in air. Oak fell down and could not be aroused. They arranged him so that he lay in comfort. And Jilain, too, slept. After a long while, after some darted looks and remarks from others, Delath went and sat beside Jilain, and he looked at the others. He looked mean. No one went near either of them.

She awoke hours later, but the Man Who Was Two Men did not wake.

When he awoke, just under two days and nights had passed.

# Three

*My spirit wrestles in anguish*
  *With fancies that will not depart;*
*A ghost who borrowed my semblance*
  *Has hid in the depth of my heart.*

*—Hjalmar Hjorth Boyeson*

He awoke in the stern of a ship plowing the sea almost silently. Almost in silence; there was the creak of
rope and of wood, the sound of moving water; the murmur
of two or three conversations. He opened his eyes and
looked up into anxiously staring hazel ones, set in a face
framed by blue hair. How could he have thought those the
eyes of a dog? And the mark of his sword's point marred
her forehead: ∧.

"What color is your hair?"

Those were his first words in so very long; she twitched.
"Oak?"

"Ah." A frown briefly cluttered his forehead, which was
also sword-marked. "So Oak has come, has he? Did he
heal everyone who was hurt?" He turned his head and only
then discovered that it was pillowed on her thighs. Good
thighs; they were womanly round and manly firm with the
strength and tone of them. The crown of his head pressed
against her lower belly, which hardly existed. Thus he felt
her long, long sigh. Thought came to him of what else lay
beneath his head, at the base of that firm belly, and he

thrust that from his mind. He also thought it best to tell her:

"I am Jarik."

"This one is glad, Jarik. You—"

"Will you never call yourself 'I', Jilain?"

"You have asked three questions."

He heard his belly growl, and felt it. He fancied that his navel and backbone had become unwilling lovers. Surely they were in conjunction. How long had Oak remained, this time? Jarik had no memory of the sensation of leaving his body that was too familiar to him, or of those . . . whatever the visions were. Harbingers of the future? *How long since I have eaten*? (At another level was the thought, *Is Oak gaining strength, that he was here and I felt and knew nothing*? But that was not to be considered. It could lead to terror.) His bladder was as full as his stomach was empty. He decided to ignore his body's demands for both ingestion and elimination, and he chose which question to repeat.

"Men were wounded, I know. Did Oak heal everyone?"

"You do not remember, Jarik?"

"I remember that an arrow hit you and you fell and I went to you. I remember nothing more. But you are not hurt."

"No, not at all. It has been four days, Jarik, although you slept for nearly twa of them. You remember none of it?"

"None of it. When Oak comes, I am not here. I know nothing. I asked—"

She told him what Oak had done, in her accent in which o's were extended and softened, and such as "fight" and "thought" were "fikt" and "thokt," and in which "One, two, three" became *Woon, Twa, Thray*. As memory came back to him he asked again about her. She assured him that she had not been hurt. All were hale on *Seadancer*, Jilain told him, save Shranshule. He told her that he did not even know Shranshule. She asked about that; how it was that he had "sailed and sistered" with men he did not know. He was astonished to discover that she knew everyone among the Guardians, which was everyone on the Isle of Osyr: one wark they called *wairk*.

The men of *Seadancer* discovered that he had at last wakened, and questions were asked.

Jarik sat up, felt dizzy, and fell backward—to be caught

by Jilain, who was lithely strong though her arms showed little musculature. He wanted to urinate, and he wanted food and drink—and he wanted more to remain with Jilain. Sitting, he gave the men of Kirrensark-wark, of *Seadancer*-werk, a shamefully brief explanation of what he knew of Oak, which was little. That of course was no explanation at all and satisfied no one. It was all he knew, he told them. When someone close to Jarik, beloved of Jarik, was hurt or seemed to be, Jarik lost all sense of himself, and Oak came. It was as though he was unconscious, he said (not troubling to introduce the subject of his visions and his experiences outside his body), except that Oak commanded this body and brain. He answered a few other questions and then tightened his lips and told them he would answer no more. That made no one happy and was manifestly unfair to men both confused and curious—and a bit frightened of the Man Who Was Two Men.

Unfair! The accusing word was like a knife thrust at him. Jarik would not stand up for them, but he sat very straight. His eyes came alive so that some thought that perhaps Oak had returned. Jarik was the warrior and slayer and Oak certainly was not; yet they feared Oak more than Jarik.

"*Fair!*" he snapped. "None of it is fair! All is unfair! I had no wish to come here with you on this ship. I have no wish to be servant to *your* god Snowmist—who is not soft as snow or mist, but shiny as silver and ice and just as hard. Lady Silver-and-Ice!" He thrust out his arms at them. "It is not *fair* that I wear these bracers that make me slave to Her. *Slave*, to your Lady Silver-ice! It was unfair that I had to descend alone and go alone to the temple of Osyr the Dead God, for that White Rod *She* desires! It is not fair that I was beaten. Beaten! Beaten with a whip, by the Guardians while you lot disported yourselves with them! Fair! You are alive because I saved you! And you say 'unfair'!"

And then he remembered, and Jarik grew a foot and years: "I am alive because Jilain cut me loose of Guardian ropes," he said, admitting his reliance on another. "Scavengers! Go away. Oil your metal against sea-spray. Oil your leather against salt which hardens and cracks it. Pick your noses and wash your armpits with salt water. Jump into the sea." He waved his arms, ranting at them. "Stand on your empty heads. I want to talk with Jilain Kerosyris, and that is

what I am going to do. It will be the first time in many days
that I have done what *I* want to do!"

And he lay back, with his head on her strong round
thighs.

"Ignore them," he muttered low. "If any remain staring,
pretend they are not there. They are not my people."

She looked down at him, her hair falling in separating
strands of azure and sapphire and cerulean and perisine.
"Who are your people, Jarik?"

He closed his eyes.

At last she said, "The Man Who Is Two Men."

His eyes came open. He looked at her, upside down.
"Yes."

"Well, Jarik of the Black Sword, now you are the One
Who Is Three, for this one is part of you."

*A part of you is a tree, and a part of you is a woman, and
two of you lie on an island, close to union.*

He remembered those words, thought-words of his
Guide, those times when he left his body to journey where
the Guide took him. Now he understood. A part of him
was Oak, and oak was the name of a tree. Jilain was the
woman, whom he had met—at crossed swords!—on an
island. Was this their union? They had left the isle. Was
this union? Was this being whole, Three Who Were
One?

Now Jarik understood, without understanding. It was
impossible. If it was so, was it fair to Jilain? Was it fair to
him?

He heard a flutter, and saw the dove. The dove of Her.
Impossible. He stared at the sky with eyes the color of the
sky.

*Impossible is only a word. Fairness is an invention of hu-
mans, and we humans do not make the rules. There are gods
on the earth, and there is strife among them. The weavers
weave, and the weavers are blind.*

He listened to her again, in his mind: *Well, Jairik of the
Black Soord, naoo you are the Woon Who Is T'ray, foor
this woon is pairt of you.*

He said, "What will you do? You belong to Kerosyr, on
Osyr. To the Guardians, manless women. You know nothing but the island . . . and nothing there resembles the
world of—of reality. The world, the broad world, the real

world, off Kerosyr; it is . . . different. And most cruel, Jilain Kerosyris. You will be a—an innocent child."

Her brows rose, and she looked at him with pride and some hauteur. "One wears the red feather," Jilain said sternly, "meaning that one has lain wit' a man. And one is the best—the second best warrior ever to end bow or draw soord on Osyr's island! Innocent babe, indeed! Why do you say such a silly thing to this one?"

"I cannot explain. I didn't mean to insult. It is this: you will find things unfamiliar to you. Many things and most things, beginning with the *people*, who are most different of all. You will find cruelty, and malicious people, and terror, and mistrust and sadness, sadness."

"Have you then had so terrible a life?"

It was a normal enough query; how could she know she posed it to one whose totally honest answer was so different, and ugly?

Quietly, sadly, he said, "Yes."

She gazed down on him, and said nothing. His stomach rumbled while she felt herself tighten, not with hunger, at his single word. She stroked his cheek. Her fingers moved up onto his forehead. It was a good forehead, under the tangle of shoulder-length wheaten hair.

"A good forehead," she said in a low voice. "This one regrets that she put this cut here."

He squeezed the hand on his face. "No. It's only a little cut."

"It will leave a scar."

"Only a little scar. I gave you one. Carefully, deliberately, I cut your forehead—maliciously. We will each bear a little scar of the other, all our lives."

He remembered how he had put it there. *I will fight no woman*, he had arrogantly said, and maliciously added, *much less a girl*! And she, the queen's champion of Kerosyr, had said, *Refuse to fikht this one and you will die, for she—he—who would not fikht an armed woman once the battle-lust leaves him would not slit the throat of an* unarmed *one—boy*! At the time he had been holding the Osyrrain, their ruler, and Jilain had been right. And so they had fought, she and he.

She was skilled, as well as being the fastest foe he had ever faced. She evaded strokes and slashes he could not have moved fast enough to avoid. She forced him to give it all his skill, else he be slain. This woman! He had had to chop up her shield to get at her. She had struck his forearm hard enough to leave a bruise he had no doubt still showed there. He gave her such a bruise by kicking her lower calf hard enough to knock her down—almost. And while he congratulated himself on that: *You'll limp tomorrow, bitch!*—she had nearly killed him. He did not quite avoid her point, which carved this backward L between his wheat-hued eyebrows that put blood on his face. He had kicked her again—in the leg, again to save himself, in desperation—and Oh but there was strength in those dancer's legs of hers with the unusually well developed calves! And he chopped her shield to flinders—while she gave him a shallow little cut on the thigh he never even realized had caught him. It bled and she nearly got him again and he kicked her ankle. Then he launched the most terrible chop with the Black Sword, and the shieldless woman's iron blade could not withstand it. It was sheared through. He remembered her shocked expression and tone: *You . . . bested this one!* And he, with blood trickling between his brows and down his leg, bade her stand. And she did! She stood to receive the death blow, and stood unblinkingly while he extended his point toward her eyes. With care he pricked her above and between her thick black brows, and she made no sound and did not move. He turned the sword, just a little. Blood trickled from the wedge he had incised so deliberately.

*Then I turned to advise the Osyrrain that I had defeated her champion—and only that rotten queen's eyes told me that Jilain never gives up and doesn't apply rules to combat—she nearly got me in the back with her dagger, and I had to defeat her* again, *with bare hands!*

Thus he thought now, days later aboard *Seadancer*, and again he thought, *What a warrior! What a woman!*

The ship cruised, not rapidly now, before a gentle breeze. At the prow, foam was bleached beneath a sky of iridescent blue. The dove of Snowmist left again, to fly before them and enable Kirrensark to make a slight course correction. There was no place to go on the long boat called ship. Privacy was hardly available. A man stood with his tunic's hem in his hand and his leggings partly unlaced, raising the level of the sea. He and the others gave Jarik and Jilain what privacy they could, without liking it. What a pity that such an arrogant bullcat was also so disgustingly competent—and had indeed saved them all!

For a time Jilain and Jarik said nothing, while they touched, and the weavers wove with yarn that entangled two lives.

"As to the cruelty of your world," she began after a long while, and he blinked and lifted his brows questioningly. "Oh. Were you asleep?"

"No. Thinking. Enjoying. *Being.* I hunger, I thirst, I have to empty my bladder. And I had rather be here with my head on your legs."

"One will wait while you do these things. One's legs will be here."

"With my bruises on them."

"Yes. They do not hurt."

"I will wait," he decided, or rather did not decide, for being motionless was better than moving, than deciding. Above all men Jarik knew that small changes, small moves, could bring enormous changes. The weavers had woven his life's skein with much red, and black.

She lifted her eyes, and after a few moments she made a tiny gesture. Response was swift. The youth came to bend over Jarik. Jarik saw his stained buskins, and above them leather leggings once tawny and now walnut-hued and here and there splotched darker still. At mid-thigh they vanished up under his tunic, faded from brown to hazelnut, with loose sleeves to the middle of his work-thick forearms. His belt was a hand's length longer than the lean youth was around and, pulled through its brass ring and doubled back and looped over and drawn through the loop, dangled. The belt was broad and thick. It bore three bosses of bronze and a copper-riveted tip. The attire was about the same as that of the others, and so was the hair that straggled down unbound; the youth of seventeen wore no helmet now, and there was yellow and orange in his straight stringy hair. He was lean, strong of jaw and chin, straight of nose, with an almost invisible beard that was hardly worthy of being distinguished with that name. There was an odd darkness around both his eyes—in the sockets, not in the eyes—that had led to his nickname. Over the years—and as he grew strong and tall—"Coon-face" had been shortened. Perhaps he worshiped Jarik. Doubtless he worshiped Jilain.

"Ah, Coon," Jarik said. "I'm glad to see you unharmed!"

Coon blinked, for such words were not like Jarik; not like what he thought Jarik was like, that is, and expected of him.

"Coon," Jilain said softly, and Jarik thought that she had got her voice from a dove along with her prowess from a swift youngling bear. "Jarik thirsts. But he and this one wish to remain here alone as any can be on this ship. Will you help, please?"

Coon stared at her, spellbound. His eyes asked what he might do.

"Will you fetch quietly some ale for Jarik?"

The youth stared a little longer before nodding, jerkily. "Oh. Aye! And for you?"

"No. Only for Jarik."

"And Oak," Coon said in a tone of reverence.

Jarik's face lost its pleasant expression, but Coon did not notice. He went away as if on holy mission.

"He's addled over you," Jarik said.

"What?"

"Coon is infatuated with you."

"Oh. And wit' you."

"Oak. It's always Oak they love and want. Once I was taken in at a little wark of fishermen because Oak had saved one of their trappers. They were sore disappointed, because they had only Jarik." He remembered the great half-circle of stone or pitted metal in that village of Harnstarl—Blackiron—and the strange sword all of black that had stood from it. He remembered that day of horror when he had yanked forth that blade and put it to awful use. The Black Sword of the Iron Lords. Those gods lived within the mountain that rose above Harnstarl as Snowmist lived on Cloudpeak above Kirrensark-wark, and Jarik had . . . visited with them. He was their agent, who wore their armor finer than iron and their Black Sword finer than anything. His mission was to slay their rival god, kith but not kin, the Lady of the Snowmist.

She heard what he said, and she knew a little more of him.

"You do not drink ale?" he asked.

"Guardians make beer, though we drink water, mostly. Drank," she amended. "That is, they. . . . One will have to learn to say 'they' of the Guardians, while 'we' are . . . something else. Anyhow, this one too has to drown a spider."

After a couple of moments he decided that was Guardian for the act that all peoples euphemized: draining the bladder. "Oh! I will move, then—"

Her hand pressed him back down on her thigh. It was sweaty there, under the tangle of his blond hair. He smiled, then frowned. "Has that been difficult? On the ship, with men only?"

"Oh, it is fascinating! What does one know of men? One stared and stared, until one discovered that they do not like one to look. It was rude, but one did not know. Yes, it has been difficult. On Kerosyr we say 'One must drown a spider,' and do so. Some look and some do not; it does not matter. Some prefer privacy. For—that other, we say 'One must go alone' and it is very private. One held her water as long as she could, until Oak noticed the fidgeting and asked what the matter was. Demanded to know what the matter was! Oh, but he does demand! A king, Oak is. Though he would make no good one, the impatient arrogant cat! He demanded to know, and one told him the cause of her fidgeting. First he told this one how silly and stupid she was. Then he called Kirrensark and told—*told*—him that he must always see that this one has privacy. Kirrensark understood at once. He had not thokht of it. So—one has privacy, when one has need."

Jarik was chuckling. "One does!" he said, and his voice rose loud.

"Hush, Jairik Blacksword! So . . . one eats and drinks but little, for it is troublesome, the going alone on this ship, and the men are [a word unknown to Jarik]."

"What? The men are what?" The language had been theirs in common, he knew. Over the years and scores of years, differences had grown between the speech of her people and those of Lokusta, as it had been the Lokustans' speech and that of Akkharia, whence Jarik had come when he was Orrikson Jarik. Phrases changed; pronunciations changed and euphemisms and expressions were born; words and phrases were born.

She felt some anger in him against the men who were whatever-she-said. She assured him that her word meant "uncomfortable." He relaxed. Then he said it after her.

"Uncomfortable! Aye!" And Jarik laughed aloud at that. Many heads turned his way, for the somber wearer of the Black Sword and the enslaving Bands of Snowmist was not known for smiling, much less laughing. Laughing aloud while lying on his back, he choked himself on laughter, and sat up with a jerk. A terribly serious expression flowed over his face, and his grunt was a moan. Giving Jilain an apologetic look, Jarik hurried to the rail.

Men wondered why he laughed as he urinated—going alone.

Much later he was able to sit beside her again. He saw her bruised legs.

"Hello. I tried to kill you."

She looked at him most seriously indeed, as though trying to memorize every pore of his face; what showed above the reddish-blond beard Oak had not bothered to scrape off.

"Yes. One tried to kill you," Jilain said, almost in a whisper.

"You bear my sword's mark on your forehead. You will have a little scar there. Like this." He showed her a finger held in a crook, knuckle up; an inverted V.

"You will bear this one's sword-scar on your forehead, too," she told him, almost in a whisper.

Jarik nodded. "Well," he said low. "Now I would fight *for* you, Jilain."

Again that intense, studying look. "Yes. This one would fikht for you, Jarik Blacksword."

He squeezed the hand that touched his cheek. "In a way, you killed for me."

"No." She shook her head with a rustle of blue hair. "That was justice. She made promise, and broke it. That cannot be, from the Osyrrain above all others. She was not honorable with regard to you earlier, either, whick you know bothered this one even then. One slew her for Osyr. It was justice." She looked down. "One does not feel heroic, however. And expiation will have to be made."

The word she used was unfamiliar, but Jarik said it over

in his head and recognized it as the word for "expiation." He repeated it as a question.

She nodded. "It will come. Payments have to be made for our acts."

He knew he was hearing a Kerosyran belief, and he knew that he would remember that phrase all his life, and not fondly. Of a sudden he squeezed her arm, which was bare below the short sleeve of Shranshule's leather coat.

"Hail, warrior. I am your brother, warrior."

The form was unfamiliar to her, but she heard the sound of a rite; of something *helderen*. She said, "Hail, warrior. This one and you are sisters." Her voice was only just audible.

Jarik smiled, though he felt a tickle that was almost a sting behind his eyes. He did not like it. He looked at her, and looked away. "You began to tell me something. You began long ago: 'About the world's cruelty—'"

"Yes. One remembers, and one would say it still. You spoke so strongly of the cruelty of your world, whick made you no happy wom—ah! Man, man, this one means. A man would not like to be called woman?"

"A man would not, Jilain. Would a woman like to be called man?"

She considered. She shrugged. "It does not matter. This one knows what she is, and words will not change that. What do words matter?"

He heard. He would remember that, too. She had proven herself. She had no need of words. He wondered when he would feel the same to be true of himself—he who had bested her in blade combat and by hand, and doubted whether any other man aboard could do so.

"Well," she said, "consider. You know most of it, Jarik Blacksword. What could be more cruel than Kerosyr? Women who live without men—and on the occasion this one changed feathers, she knew the difference! This one *liked* it, Jarik, the coupling with a man."

Yes. He remembered. So she had said. "Some do," he said, "I am told." He did not smile, nor did he look at her. It was hard for him to believe that she had offered, she!— more, she had asked him to, and he had said her no.

It was not easy, being Jarik.

"It is forbidden to say so, among the Guardians! Did you know that?"

"To say that, uh, one enjoys coupling with a man?"

"Yes. *Enjoyed*, for there is only the once. One conceives or one does not. Men are dishonest, we are taukht, and dishonorable, and unnecessary. Except once! All a woman needs is herself and another woman, we are taukht. One captures men, and uses them. One changes one's feather with them, changes it to red in order to beget, and continue the Guardianship of the God. That is all. It is only for reproducing, the coupling with men. Is that cruel, Jarik?"

"I suppose, uh, if one, uh, disagrees," he said weakly. Realizing that "to change feather" with them was a euphemism for "lie with" or, as they and some men said, "use," Jarik thought that yes, it was worse than cruel. *It is sick*, he thought, but he said no more and did not look at her, he who was not well. It was hard to be judgmental, when one knew that one was not well.

Besides, he was taught another way. One did not talk or think about women . . . doing that. For once, Jarik tried not to be shocked, to be more than the man his upbringing and his society had made him. It was hardly easy. A bigot of Kerosyr would condemn him more than he would her.

"What more cruel," she said quietly, looking away from him, "than to welcome those hapless men who come to Kerosyr, and treat them well, so well—and then slay them? While those whose feathers they change must live forever on that single memory? Oh it is true that some Guardians did not enjoy it and did not want it again, that coupling with a man. And some merely said that they did not." She was quiet for a space. Then, "And what more cruel than to slay all the issue that are male? Oh it is not that Guardians do not love Guardians, and exchange nikht-pleasures! It is not that such is not enjoyable. But . . . that is not . . . the same." Her eyes went away for a moment, far away. "For Jilain," she added, and gave her head a jerk that whirred short-cropped blue hair about her head. "What could be more cruel than the fate of the Pythoness, who from birt' is trained for that post—and from the age of ten sees naukht but the temple, which she never leaves . . . and is slain in honor of Osyr and in sacrifice to him when she is twoscore years of age?"

That last Jarik had not known. He had liberated the Pythoness, after she had tried to kill him, and she had been happy—for the few hours before one called Clarjain had

murdered her. That had enraged him, and his real trouble
had begun when he sent Clarjain's soul racing after that of
the Pythoness. He believed what Jilain said. He noted that
she made no mention of the bonding of gemstone to flesh,
which must be accomplished in pain. Yes, she was right.
Still, Jarik remembered his own life, and he clamped his
teeth.

"Much exists off Kerosyr that is . . . more cruel, Jilain."

"This one shall survive. This one is Guardian, warrior.
The best but one! Second only to you, Jarik Blacksword.
And one would wager that one is better wit' the bow than
you, best warrior!"

"I have not seen you use that old bow of Kerosyr," he
said, in deliberate challenge, although his skill with a bow
was little better than with the loom or the flute.

"You will see this one use it," she said, sitting straight.
"Others would have been dead or wounded on this ship,
had Jilain been among those on the beach when this ship
departed Kerosyr's shores. Jilain is the best."

"And as modest as Jarik," Jarik said. 'I believe you,
Jilain. But warrior *women* do not exist."

"This one exists, Jarik. Jilain exists."

"Uh—what I mean is, no one employs warrior *women*,
Jilain Kerosyris."

"Employ?"

"I am. . ." His voice dropped even lower. "I am employed by the Iron Lords, gods on the earth. I serve them. I
am also employed by the Lady of the Snowmist, but that is
unwillingly. For Her I had to come to your island, for the
White Wand of your god."

She cocked her head like a bird double-checking before
trusting itself to one swift peck at the grain. "And you tell
this one that no one uses warriors who are women?"

He nodded.

After she had said nothing for a long while, he heaved
and turned to face her. She was staring at him in shock, in
disbelief.

Then she laughed, assuming that he jested.

# Four

*The fate of man lies with the gods;*
*His life's fabric is by their leave.*
*Let no human misdoubt the odds!*
*The gods decide; the weavers weave.*

*The infant pules, and mayhap grows old—*
*Its life's fabric is by gods' leave.*
*Changes come, mind and body enfold*
*The fabric that the weavers weave.*

*Each hap marks the mind with a scar,*
*All lead to what he will achieve.*
*Mayhap each aids; doubtless some mar.*
*Events befall, while weavers weave.*

Racing, the ship slobbered in a way of a racing horse champing its bit, and that foam shaded from frothy white to crystal bubbles to grey to a washed-out green like that of dying plants. All about, sunlight trembled on the waters undisturbed by *Seadancer*'s dipping prow. The sky was almost eerie in its unwavering luminosity. More eerie was the unnatural breeze that never paused or changed direction, but blew them steadily to the north and east. All aboard the ship were aware of it but no one spoke of it. They were not in the hands of gods, but of one god. Her dove accompanied them still, and from time to time soared forth on brief sallies that signaled small course corrections to Kirrensark and his steersman.

39

. Then an orange stain spread across the sky, and deepened into rose with gold only at the western edge. Slowly, one by one, the stars appeared in pearl and white, blue and pink and watery green.

Jilain and Jarik talked quietly in darkness. She talked of Kerosyr and he of the warks of Lokusta in which he had lived. They compared customs and knowledge, suppositions and expectations, and he talked about the land he presumed to be that of his birth.

The Lokustans called it Akkharia, he told her. His people had not. He had lived in Oceanside, a farming community above a chalky cliff overlooking the sea. They were farmers, not seafarers. He was called Chair-ik there; it was their pronunciation, as some also said Jairik and some iYairik, or something like. He was different from those people of Oceanside, even from those he called parents, in the color of his hair and of his eyes. And in other ways; he was of a restless nature that hardly existed in that community. Akkharia, he told her, was an island—so the Lokustans said—not far from Kerosyr, though it was a considerably larger island.

Somewhere far inland they knew, or presumed, a king lived. He was "their" king, presumably. None had ever seen him. Somewhere nearer dwelt the lord of the barony of which Oceanside, Tomash-ten, was a part. The name of the barony was Oaktree. Jarik could not remember its lord's name, and was not sure he had ever heard it. A few had seen the baron. Orrik of Oceanside had liked to tell the tale, glowingly, with pride and some wonder, of How The Baron Came to Tomash-ten And Only Two Sevenights After His Accession. The boy Jarik was had tired of the story. "King" and "Baron"—those were only words. Oceanside was the world, and it was dull and not big enough.

Jarik told Jilain of his sister Torsy. Though the difference in their ages was less than nine months, it had not occurred to him then that she was not his sister. He was Orrikson Jarik then, and had not known that Orrik was not his father, nor his wife Jarik's mother.

Tomash-ten was dull and placid and Same, deadly boringly Same. All that people did was always done the same way, and that was The Way. Every bit of it changed;

the world changed, one day when Jarik was not quite eight.

First had come the two hawks that did not flap their wings and that shone and glinted in the sunlight. They came from the sea or seemed to, but Jarik saw that they swung wide to approach the community from inland, that the awed, staring, pointing farmers of Oceanside would not know they had come from the sea. Then Jarik had not understood; now he felt that those great gleaming birds were spying out the land.

("Birds?" Jilain asked.

("Yes. Birds. As birds, a gull and a dove of Her, have led us to your land and are leading us home. They use birds, the gods on the earth.")

Then came the ship, though at the time Jarik did not know what a ship was. He had seen only fishing boats—two. At its prow was the fierce head of a hawk and off it came helmeted, mailed men who slew and slew everyone in placid, calm, peaceful, complacent, nearly weaponless Oceanside. And Jarik saw it all or nearly, for he and his sister were shirking, watching in secret from a clump of bushes at woods' edge.

Jarik saw his stepmother Thanamee sworded through the belly. That belly was gross with him Jarik knew would be a brother. The old women had said it would be a brother to him, too. He had looked forward to having a brother; looked very much forward to it. Orrik and Thanamee had already decided on what they would name the child: Oak. That man from the hawk-prowed ship, that hawk-man or Hawker, had slain two then, all in a stroke. Another had slain Orrik. Jarik would never have a brother, now.

Jarik and Torsy were not killed. Everyone else was. Everyone else, and there was fire as well, roiling greasy black smoke rolling and puffing up from what had been Tomashten. Why?

Not quite eight, Jarik saw Torsy faint. He jumped up to run out there and kill all those bad men, and then a blackness saved him. A blackness came before his eyes, and over his brain like a cloak, a pall. While black smoke rolled and puffed skyward, Jarik fell down unconscious. When he awoke, he was kneeling beside Orrik and Torsy was screaming his name. Orrik was dead. Yet he was bandaged. A badly frightened Torsy told Jarik that *he* had bandaged his supposed father . . . but he had been mean and snarly to her, and called himself Oak.

("While I was senseless, Oak was born and tried to save Orrik. While I was senseless, I . . . traveled, saw visions. I saw Her that day, Jilain. I had never heard of the Lady of the Snowmist! But that day, while I lay senseless, I *saw* Her. Years and years passed before I saw Her again— *really* saw Her, that second time. I saw the Black Sword that day, too, though it was far across the sea in Blackiron, and I did not see it in fact, with my eyes I mean, for nine years. I remember that in that . . . that dream, I called myself Jarik son of Orrik of Oceanside in the barony of Oaktree of the Kingdom, and I remember saying that I was 'Jarik, son of Orrik, true son—no, servant of the Lord Baron and the Lords of Fog Themselves' and that I was taking vengeance for my half-brother, Oak!"

(Jilain said, "You said, in your dream you said—*half*-brother? Then you did know."

(Jarik reflected. "Yes, I suppose I did—and yet I did not. Somehow I knew it, but did not know I knew it. Do you think we all have two minds, Jilain?"

"No—that is, one has never thokht about that at all. Now one thinks that you have two minds, Jarik. You see? Oak was there then—and Oak knew that you were not Orrik's son."

("That doesn't make sense," Jarik said. "Since none of the rest of it does, it may be right."

("Whose son are you then, Jarik?"

("I—do not know. Ask . . . ask Oak, if ever you see him again."

(At that weirdness he felt her shudder, and he bit his lip, and then went on with his story. It was as if he was compelled to tell her of that young Jarik, of Oak and his borning. And of that first . . . dream?)

"The one I was going to kill, in vengeance for Oak, sneered and said, I remember, 'You don't have a half-brother or a brother either, Baron of Oaktree!'—and I killed him. Yes, he called me that. Baron of Oaktree. He told me I had no father or mother on this earth, and all the while I was . . . I was chopping him up. In my dream, Jilain, at age—not quite eight. It was then that he died, and I saw *Her*. *She* was there. She spoke, too."

He sat, remembering, until Jilain asked him what She had said.

In a strange new voice, Jarik half-sat, half sprawled on *Seadancer*, and repeated the words he had heard in that vision—that first of his several visions—so many years ago. "*'You are come to slay me, Jarik, poor mystery man idiot Jarik without parents. Come to slay me with your reward already in your hand and dripping blood. You cannot slay me, Jarik, poor adopted abandoned exiled brainless peopleless Jarik. Not me. You cannot be suffered even to live! You are less than an ant beneath the world-stamping feet of the gods on the earth, Jarik the ever-Different!*'" Those were her words to me in that dream, Jilain, so many years ago—and in my hand I held the Black Sword I have of Blackiron, and the Iron Lords. But then, I had never heard of Blackiron, or the Black Sword, or the Iron Lords—or even Lady Snowmist!"

He ground out her name with an ugly voice and an audible twisting of his mouth, and Jilain Kerosyris knew that he was no friend or respecter of that god he said he served unwillingly, the Lady of the Snowmist.

"Did you speak to her? Then, in that vision?" Jilain sat close. She felt chilly, and only part of her chill came from the air over the night-darkened sea.

"I awoke then. Beside Orrik, with Torsy yelling and blood on my hands. Because I had bandaged his wounds, you see. Or rather Oak had. It was a good job of bandaging, too. I could not do that well, now. But . . . now . . . Jil—Jilain . . . let me tell you what She said to me less than one month ago. So many years later! This time I was really there, in her keep above Kirrensark-wark, and She was really there, where She had taken me. She was no vision. She said, 'Poor Jarik! You are but a rusty hoe in the hands of a stout farmer. A tool. Had you—'" Jarik paused, because he was not ready just yet to tell Jilain what his mission was, for the Iron Lords; that his mission as their agent was to kill Karahshisar, the Lady of the Snowmist. He did not want to tell Jilain that he had tried, and failed, and endured awful punishment, and awakened with these terrible bracers on his arms. They made him hers, for if he strove against Her or even tried to disobey Her, the pain and terrible cold in his wrists was instantaneous, and moved rapidly up his arms into his body. Nor had the bracers, the Bands of Snowmist She called them, any seam. Nor could they be cut. Only She could remove them, and so he had to fetch the White Rod and now he must carry it back to Her, a fearful controlled slave. Perhaps of all the things that had befallen him, all that he had endured, this was worst. Because he was so in need, so in need to belong and to be in control, the precise opposite of that of which slaves are made. His resistance of authority was as if systemic. Gladly had he believed the Iron Lord, and joined with the Iron Lords, and become their liege man, for they showed him how he could Be someone; truly important. Gladly had he taken their superb armor coat and kept the beyond-superb new sword he had himself appropriated. Gladly had he let them transport him—somehow—across the impassable mountain to the farmlands at the base of her keep on Cloudpeak. Right gladly had he greeted Her when She came down, all misty until She coalesced into a vision of silver and grey and white, snow and mist, and more than gladly had he agreed to be *transported* by Her into her keep. There he had tried to carry out his mission.

And She had mocked him, and enslaved him. Sneered at him and enslaved him. Defeated him and enslaved him. Forced him to set forth on this mission for Her—in company with him Jarik had for so many years hated above all men in the world. For it was Kirrensark who had led the men who annihilated Oceanside, and Jarik's life.

He was her slave, and perhaps that fact was the very worst of all that he had endured in all his life.

Jilain said, "Jarik?"

Her hand was on his arm. He left out the sentence Snowmist had spoken: *Had you succeeded in killing me, you'd not have lived out this day!* That he elided, and told her the rest of what Snowmist had said, for it was incredible that She had said those words, after so many years. "'The Iron Lords could not suffer you to live. Nor are you the sort of tool they would merely hang up in a place of honor on the shed wall. You would be less than an ant beneath their world-stamping feet!'"

Jilain trembled. "The same words."

"The same words," Jarik said.

"What . . . oh Jarik, this is . . . one's mind will not accept any of this!"

He challenged directly: "Do you believe me?"

Small-voiced, she said, "Yes. One believes you, Jarik. Oh, Jarik." And she pressed close, with her hands on him.

Jarik would not return the pressure, or put his hands on her or his arm around her. He had his reasons, which he thought were very good ones. Horrible ones. He did not want Jilain Kerosyris to die.

After a time she said, "What . . . what else did She say, this god who lives and talks?"

He remembered that she knew nothing of that, either. Her god was dead. All there was of Osyr was that statue in the temple on Kerosyr. A temple that was older than old; far older than the Guardians, Jarik was sure. The statue was fine work, in some black stone. The White Rod had stood out in stark contrast, held in one hand of the statue. That hand was made so as to hold the White Rod, which was a separate object, made of something like white horn. The dead god of Kerosyr no longer had that short staff. Jarik had it. Rolled in oiled sharkskin, it was stored away under the prow with the weapons of men who might be tempted to use them, in such close—and truly, boring—proximity.

"I will tell you another time," Jarik said. "Not now. Let me tell you of Oak."

Jarik and Torsy were not killed, that day of Oak's birth in Akkharia. Everyone else was. Since then, Oak had returned three times—four, now.

Once, when Torsy and Jarik were departing their second home, a Lokustan wark where he had been Strodeson Jarik. (He had been exiled when he had slain the firstman's son—purely in unwilling defense of self and goaded by sneers and insults against Torsy.) Two men came on Torsy while Jarik was foraging, and they attacked her. They were men of weapons, and experienced. Jarik was seventeen or eighteen, with a fair mailcoat and an ordinary sword. He killed both those men, in minutes.

When he bent over Torsy and saw blood on her, Oak came. As it turned out, Torsy needed little help and no treatment. Oak, who had feared internal wounds, *saw* none.

Another time was next day. Torsy and Jarik found an injured man in the woods they were passing through. Torsy squatted beside him and got some of his blood on her. Jarik thought it was hers, and Oak came. Oak repaired that hunter, badly injured in his own trap. Oak did everything right, knew everything. He and Torsy were gratefully taken into their third home, that man's village of fisherfolk. That was Harnstarl: Blackiron.

They abode there for some time, years, but Jarik was Jarik, not the healer they wanted.

One day Torsy went into the woods with a girl Jarik might have loved. They were about the normal business of beating the squirrels to fallen nuts. The three raiders found them; mailed weapon men from the sea, and they raped and murdered the young women. Thus Jarik found them, and Oak could do nothing. It was then that Jarik returned to that little wark, a grim and quivering figure none dared challenge, for his face was awful. He took the Black Sword from its strange mounting in the wark. He returned with it the way he had come, with never a word to anyone. Over a day later he caught that trio of men off a hawk-head ship, and they were as half a man against the maniacal animal who came ravening among them with his awful weapon, the Black Sword.

While he was at that ugly business, the other men off that same ship attacked the village of Blackiron. Jarik had not known: the Black Sword was the wark's link to the Iron Lords and should have called them down from their mountain keep in such a time of danger. Jarik had the weapon. He learned only later that he had been responsible for the Iron Lords' failure to come. Yet with it, a ravening morbrin *thing* that day, he attacked the attackers. Slaying and slaying, he turned away the attack and thought that he was a hero. Then he saw one of his friends struck down and, the attackers beaten off and in flight and a friend wounded, Jarik collapsed. Oak came.

Thus Jarik told Jilain a bit of himself and of Oak, and they learned much of each other, Jilain and Jarik. Each wanted to know all there was to know about the other; each wanted to share information. He held back only a little, though there were things he did not get around to telling her.

"So much horror in a sleepy fishers' wark called Blackiron," she murmured. "How long ago was that day, that awful day?"

"A month," Jarik said (though what he said was "a cycle of the moon ago").

"*Oh.*" She had thought it a matter of years. She was shocked that it had been so short a time in the past.

Jilain pressed to him and wondered how it was that a person could endure and withstand and survive so much as he had all in a month, for his time on her island of women had been far from pleasant. He had had no respite, none!

Jilain had never heard of war. Jilain had never seen combat among more people than two at once. The Guardians had no enemies. They had no god that walked and talked and did deeds.

He did not respond to the pressing against his leather-coated body of hers, although he was not stiff. The bossed coat she wore was far from comfortable to a woman accustomed to nothing save weapons belt and quiver, a feather in her hair and—only at times—the tail of a squirrel depending before her loins. She would not complain however; she had heard his travails, and would not mention trivial discomforts.

Surrounded by the sound of snores and of the sea, they fell asleep with their hands touching, only touching. And the weavers were weaving, weaving.

# Five

*"The Lady of the Snowmist is pure evil, Jarik: reddest, ineffable evil. She is dedicated to ridding this world of men as we know them, to be replaced by . . . something else."*
—The Iron Lords

*"Poor Jarik! You are but a rusty hoe in the hands of a stout farmer! A tool, Jarik. The Iron Lords could not suffer you to live . . . less than an ant beneath their world-stamping feet!"*
—The Lady of the Snowmist

*"It is impossible that contrary attributes should belong at the same time to the same subject."*
—Aristotle

In the morning she rose at once under a pink-and-gold sky, and with her left hand she stroked her right shoulder.

"Thank you, spirit," she said softly. After that strange little rite she began to stretch the way a cat might stretch, in long, lithe, sinuous, slow movements. And she stood on tiptoe, seeming to reach for the sky with both up-straining hands. Men saw, and watched, and felt their throats go dry.

Jarik rose from his hard bed, and she watched how he gathered his coat of chain. It was only a dark small wad of jingly links now. She saw how carefully he slid his hands through the sleeves, all the way through, so as not to tear them on metal links. Then, ducking his head, he lifted the one-piece warcoat of many links over his head and straight-

**48**

ened slowly. Clinking, glinting dark, it slithered down over his padded undercoat, which was of dark old leather, and most unhandsome.

Over the chaincoat he strapped his belt and thonged it, so that his dagger swung at his right hip and the sheathed Black Sword hung all down his left leg. Its plain hilt was wrapped with a supple strip of red leather that was thin and long and long. In this wise the hilt was disguised, for no sword was so plain and somber.

Unhelmeted and his wheaten hair stirring in the salty sea-breeze, tangy in the dawn-light, he turned to her.

"One would ask about your stroking your shoulder and giving thanks to a . . . spirit?" he said.

She did not smile at his use of her word "one" in place of the pronoun; she had not noticed the difference. She did look at him all wide-eyed. "Why, one but thanked and stroked the spirit of sleep."

Jarik nodded. "Y . . . es," he said slowly, not making fun and trying not to appear stupid. "I do not know the rite. What spirit?"

"Why—everybody knows of the sleep-spirit!" That slipped forth, and for an instant she stared into the cerulean brilliance of his eyes and saw the flash of anger or irritation there. "Uh—your people do not?"

"I have no people," he said, a bit tight of lip. "Those of Lokusta and Akkharia do not, no. So there is a spirit of sleep. And why do you thank him of a morning?"

She explained with care, not wanting to seem superior or impatient or to make him feel lessened. She did not care to see that flash of the eyes again. "It is hard to believe that everyone does not know it. Every night we die. We lie down, and all consciousness leaves us. Body and brain are as if dead—they die. But the god sends to each of us a spirit of sleep. It lives here on our shoulder, watchful lest we lose consciousness or pass into sleep. When we do, it breathes for us. That way we awake. One is appreciative of such service! So, each day one thanks the sleep-spirit for doing the work of breathing for us while we slept and could not do for ourselves. Your peop—you and those you have lived among do not thank the spirit, then. Well, one supposes that it does not matter. The spirit would continue to breat'e for us each nikht, for that is its function."

"But—we *do* breathe when we sleep! Everyone does!"

"Since the sleep spirit is there to do that for us," Jilain told him with natural patience, "yes, of course. Everyone seems to breat'e for herself while she sleeps. One can even see the chests of sleepers amove." She shrugged, satisfied that her point was obvious, and proven.

"But I mean we—"

Jarik broke off. He realized that there was no way he could prove to her that there was no sleep spirit. There was no way she could prove to him that such helpful and conveniently invisible creatures did exist. It occurred to him that the point did not matter, then. She believed what she believed, and he what he believed. In both cases, what they believed was mostly what they had been taught. Such things were not worth discussing, other than as curiosities, for comparison and understanding of another. Otherwise . . . it did not matter.

Thus Jilain affected Jarik as she did in other ways, for from her he was learning and was to learn more even than tolerance and respect for logic—and even illogic, when it did not matter.

"I see," he said at last. "I think I had better go alone."

She smiled at that use of her phrase. "This one too."

*Seadancer* split the sea with sure-footed instinct and grace, under a bright sun crowding a sky the color of Jarik's eyes. He asked Jilain about her bow, and she waxed enthusiastic. She fetched it at once. Men watched her as they always watched her. Jarik and, strangely, Delath watched them. She returned to him with bright eyes and the bow. She was proud of it, loved it, and was manifestly anxious to tell him of it. Others listened.

No one else aboard had seen such a bow so constructed and so curved. Lokustans were not archers. The bow was for hunting and occasionally for ambush. It was made of a suitable strip of wood, suitably cured, and a slim strip of gut. Arrows were employed only in very major combats, and the dwellers in the warks of Lokusta had little science of archery or of bow-making.

Jilain displayed hers with pride. It was a sleekly reflexed composite work of art and skill, several inches shorter than she and a foot shorter than Jarik. Its core, backed and strengthened by well-chosen sinews, was bellied with good horn the color of cream mottled with black and bearing a resemblance to marble.

Jilain let him know that the underlying wood was used only after having been seasoned for six or seven winters! This would have seemed ridiculous to Jarik, to whom patience was an alien trait. Yet he had seen these superlative bows in action. It occurred to him that since a woman obviously could not be a warrior, Jilain would have no problem; she would be a maker of fine, fine bows, and much in demand. This he thought while she showed how the bow's ears and handle had been stiffened with plaques of bone; bone that had been chosen with care, cured, polished, lacquered, and polished again.

Jarik was shaking his head. "No one could have such patience. How much time to *make* such a bow?"

Jilain ran her fingers over it, caressing. She was a superb hunter, not truly seasoned as a warrior though a marvelous one, and it was obvious that the bow was her dear friend as a man's short-hafted war-ax was to him—and the sword, for those few who had them, for their making too was a high skill and art. Smooth fingertips ran lovingly over smooth shining bone.

"After the curing," she said, "eight days. Thirteen for Jilacla here, because two others were discarded unfinished." Her smile was one almost of embarrassment. "One is very particular."

"Jilacla," he repeated after her. "You name your bows, then. What does it mean?"

She shrugged. "You know that. 'Jilain's friend.' It is! One spent thray moonths adjusting this beautiful friend to our—to Guardians' standards, and to her own."

"Three months!"

The voice came bland and dry: "I assume that Guardians' swords are not named, as they are not made on Kerosyr."

Jilain looked up at Delath. "True. You are rikht. The soords of the Guardians came from men who have landed on Kerosyr."

"And died. And is such attention lavished on the arrows of Kerosyr?"

"Hardly," she said, "but Guardians do take care in their making, Delat'."

"Good, then," he said, and his voice continued dry and

bland. "We have twoscore and three Guardian arrows
aboard. A few have blood on them, true, and some J—Oak
ruined, cutting them out of good men; but they should be
serviceable."

Jarik rose in a jerk. His whole stance was such that had
he been a dog his ears would have been back and his hac-
kles abristle. Beside him Jilain too arose, and her hand
clamped his wrist.

"Good, Delat'," she said, gazing coolly into his eyes.
"Peradventure this one can find use for them, against
game, or our common enemies. You forget though that
this one knew about those arrows; one struck her helmet
guard hard enough to knock her down. But for the helm,
one would be beyond Oak's skills, in death. Certainly that
arrow was meant for this one, who joined you against her
own."

Delath stared into her face for long moments. "Joined
. . . me?"

Jarik said, "Delath . . ." and Jilain interrupted the tone
of menace:

"Joined with you men, yes. With Jarik. And Oak. Are
you their enemy, Delat'? Do you wish to be this one's enemy, Delat'? Why?"

Both men were astonished and close to being appalled.
Delath had given challenge, and Jarik had risen to meet it.
Had Jilain said nothing they would have exchanged words
unto the drawing of sharp metal. Yet she had spoken. Her
open face, her tone, and the words were akin to the hurling
of water on fighting dogs. Confrontations and challenges
were one thing; direct statements and this sort of challenge, a simple agreement and simple straightforward
questions, were quite another. Men did not know how to
cope with such. It was not their way. Delath looked from
Jilain to Jarik, and Delath turned and moved elsewhere on
that ship that provided so little space for putting distance
between people at odds.

"He is determined to be my enemy," Jarik said, staring
after the other man.

"It would not be sensible to fikht another only because
she wants to," Jilain said. "He, one means. This business
of sailing asea is difficult. Tempers are short and women—
*men*, men men—are bored. A combat mikht well grow into
a melee."

Jarik stared at her for a long while. "Hail, warrior," he murmured. "I am your brother."

"And this one your sister, Jarik Blacksword. Oh—is it acceptable that this one be your sister rather than brother?"

He smiled. "Yes!"

They talked for hours then, and both of them learned, while being surprised by much they heard each of the other. *Seadancer* slipped lightly over the wave-chopped water, hardly dancing. From time to time the dove of Her flew out before them, a guide to aid the correction of course. Once Kirrensark and the helmsman had acted, the bird returned to hover and alight. Jilain and Jarik talked, and others looked often at them. They admired much the bareness of Jilain's legs, so pronounced below the short skirt of Shranshule's armor coat. It had covered him to a point just short of mid-thigh, and was only a little longer on her. Still, men of Lokusta were not accustomed to the sight of any portion of bared female leg, in public. At least the mailcoat spared them the distracting sight of the rest of her, and the flash of ruby tipping her breast, bonded there to flash there forever, a nurtureless gemstone nipple.

Above them, the dove fluttered and flew out again. Jilain and Jarik, strangers on this ship and two parts of three becoming one, did not notice. They were intensely busy with and unto themselves.

Flapping, finding wind currents, the dove flew ahead. Kirrensark gestured and grunted a few words; he at the helm was already making his adjustments to his steering oar, which he tied anew. Beads of windspray danced all asparkle on the air.

First there was a dot, and then the big bird appeared. It was blue-black and larger than a dove. First one man saw it, then another, and their shouts attracted the gaze of every eye skyward.

The bird *shone*. It gleamed in the sunlit air as though metallically. Even as high as it flew, a racing black missile, its large size was evident. It soared as the gull had soared, that led them to Kerosyr. It did not flap its refulgent wings of jet. Like an arrow arced high into the sky, the metal-shining bird soared, and seemed to glide, and gleamed in a bright flash as it changed course in the splitting of an instant. It swooped above the dove of Her, and it dived, dived.

Those on *Seadancer* watched it fall, like a hurled stone. They cried out. To no avail. High in the sky well ahead of the ship, the large blue-black bird struck the smaller, silver-grey one.

White feathers flew and fluttered like the spinners from maple trees once they tired of summer. The dove flapped, flopped. It seemed to slide sidewise, flapping in a way that could be seen was desperate. And it dropped, with a last flutter. It fell like a dropped stone, not a thrown one, and hit the water with a small splash.

The sea swallowed it and became a ripply mirror once more.

Kirrensark's voice broke the silence of shock then, sharply: "String bows!"

Jilain lurched away from Jarik while men snatched at bows and flexed them to hook the other end of their gut-strings.

Glinting, flashing as if deliberately in triumph, the blue-black bird of prey flew in bright sunlight. Directly over the ship it dared course. Strings twanged nasally and arrows leaped skyward, singing. Only one struck that fell bird; a spirally striped shaft raced up true. With a ringing sound, it caromed off its airborne target. Yet before it had fallen to the sea an identical arrow struck the bird; a shaft launched from that same bow that was named Jilacla.

This one, too, incredibly rebounded from the body of the black hawk, again with the unexpected clanging sound that was *eerie*.

The bird banked, wheeled, sped away—in the same direction in which the dove had been leading them. Unflapping.

"The Iron Lords," Jarik Blacksword murmured while he stared at a bird that had taken no note of two arrow impacts. "That was an iron bird." And he added, "Of destruction."

# Six

*We have forgot what we have been,*
*And what we are we little know.*

—*Thomas W. Parsons*

The sun was white bordered with jonquil and gold, in a clear sky the color of an infant's eyes. *Seadancer* plowed on across the water with no need of oars or the dove that had led her. Still, she no longer scudded so swiftly, nor did the spirits of those aboard her. The breeze that had so long been a constant fact of life had less power, and even faltered now and again. It was impossible for the wark-men not to make a mental connection of this with the destroyed bird that had represented Her. Amber-wearing men were nervous, even morose. Their voices were subdued. The symbol of the god on the earth—*their* god, their protector—had led them, and had been destroyed in an instant! There had been no resistance, no fight; hawk attacked and slew dove without carrying it off to eat it. Were other gods so powerful? Could the dove have represented Her in a way beyond being her agent and her guide for these her people?

Again they were aware of intimations of mortality—but for a god?

Jarik of the Black Sword was silent and wrapped in a thoughtful dolor like a cloak of charred coal. He was surly as well, and men quickly learned to leave him be. So did the one woman among them, with less willingness and far more concern for him. The others had little concern for his mental state and well-being, which he felt—without total accuracy—to have been the tale of his life.

Jarik Blacksword was wondering at the power of the Iron Lords, and of the Lady of the Snowmist. Her colors were beauty and theirs were somber. Her bird was beauty and softness and theirs was power and predation. The dove was easy prey for the hawk.

Others murmured and muttered, casting fearful glances aloft even while they tried not to look fearful, tried to talk themselves out of being fearful. All were a part of the pretense and none challenged another.

There came no more dove or gull and there came no more the hawk. There came no further incident of any sort. Far from land, the men of Kirrensark-wark thought of home and their families. They talked in low voices. They glanced from time to time at the somber man who wore the bracers of Her; the Bands of Snowmist. In addition to binding him to Her, were those seamless silvery bracers not also supposed to warn him of impending danger?

Yes.

Then why had they failed? Was not that fell hawk a clear enough source of danger?

Yes—but not directly to Jarik, Jarik told them, and turned away.

They wondered in their minds and aloud, but Jarik would not talk.

Jarik did not dare. He was agent of the Iron Lords, but he was among loyal people of the Lady of the Snowmist; people who lived at the very base of her mountain. It appeared that his patrons wielded more power than theirs, but asea, all alone among them, he dared not speak of it. There was a simple answer to the question of what befell a man when he was far from shore on a small ship among men given cause to hate and fear him. Jarik was brash; he was not stupid. The others wondered, opined, surmised; he tried not to do. He made his way to the stern and, standing well away from the steersman, stared asea along the rippling bubble-dotted line of *Seadancer's* wake. He thought on the Iron Lords. Behind his staring eyes he saw the Iron Lords, and he heard their voices. He remembered how those voices rang metallic and hollow, rang dully from within daunting iron masks that were part of iron helms. Black, all black.

They were not iron, he had learned. No. They were god-metal, which was stronger than iron. Jarik knew. He wore a chaincoat of the black god-metal, and the Black Sword was stronger even than it. Sword and armor were of and from the Iron Lords. Yet his Black Sword was not so powerful as theirs, which appeared identical. One of them had extended his sword, and Jarik had seen that it was pointed at a man, an attacker of the wark called Blackiron. That Hawker stood fully eight paces away. And when the sword was pointed at him he burst into flame, and died where he stood. Utterly consumed he was, in clothing and in flesh and hair and bone.

"*I am the lord of Dread*," one Iron Lord said.

"*I am the lord of Destruction*," another said, for they were all identical, all three.

"*I am the lord of Annihilation*," the third said that day in Blackiron, and he too extended his sword. He twitched it as he did, and this time not one but two of those hawkship attackers of Blackiron burst afire and died in roaring flame of white and yellow, so that nothing remained of them.

They took up the wounded of Blackiron then, and vanished with them. Before dark they returned those people—healed. Only the dead could not be healed. And the Lords of Iron brought it forth that the ravening avenging maniac with *their* Black Sword, had sent three attackers to the realm of the Dark Brother—and laid low no less than six others, some of whom were also certainly slain. (It did not matter, for those terrible swords that spat fire burned all the remaining attackers, wounded and dead alike. Jarik's sword would not do that. It clove. Oh, it clove!)

When first they came, they saw him as Oak the Healer, and heard him deny Jarik. When they returned, they called him that, but Oak was gone and he was Jarik. So he told them. "*Ah*," an Iron Lord said in an aside to the others, "*once there are none to tend, he reverts to his main personality, then.*" The helms of his brother gods nodded, but only they understood what had been said. And they took him up to their keep within the mountain, though he was not anxious to go; to disappear in Blackiron and reappear inside a mountaintop. There Jarik had visited and talked long with those gods on the earth. He remembered how at first he had asked them which they were, so that he might know them apart, though they looked identical.

"*I am the lord of Annihilation*," one said, from a yellow chair, and "*I am the lord of Destruction*," another said, from the chair-for-two that was among other things Jarik had never seen before. Naturally then Jarik had looked expectantly at the third of those gods, but he did not speak. Annihilation advised him: "*One learns not to utter the profoundly obvious*," and Jarik remembered. "*And not to ask the profoundly obvious*," Destruction said, and Jarik remembered that lesson, too. He was not all that fond of talking anyhow. (Not until recently. Not until Jilain.)

That third god had not spoken for long and long; it was profoundly obvious that he was the Lord of Dread, and was not silence an ally of dread? (Later it was Dread who suggested that Jarik, foundling, had been abandoned originally because he was a male child. He had only suggested that, not stated it. Now Jarik understood, and knew that even gods did not know everything; for Dread thought perhaps Jarik had been born on Kerosyr.)

Learning that Jarik had been adopted into an inland wark of Lokusta, they asked if those people there had spoken of *Elye Isparanana*. And Jarik had said Aye to them, for *Elye* was "highly respected woman; Lady" and *isp* was "snow" and *arnan* meant "mist," as *'arnan* or *harnan* meant "fog." Jarik told the Iron Lords what little he knew of Her: the Lady of the Snowmist. He told them how now and again, across years, Milady Snowmist came down and took up a youth, and returned him only a day or two later—and after that the Chosen was not only very popular with maidens of the wark, but enjoyed perfect health, all the days of his life.

"*We cannot tell you what she does with those youths, Jarik*," the Lord of Destruction told him; "*we dare not tell you, mortal lad. For what she does with them is horrible, revolting. A monstrous thing.*" And then he told Jarik that She was dedicated to absolute evil, to ridding the world of mortal humans to replace them with . . . something else. She must have sent those killers to Blackiron, he opined, in direct challenge to the Iron Lords, whose chosen wark it was.

"*Evil*," Dread muttered of Her then, in his deep voice of dread.

Jarik remembered other things they had said to him. One thing he was told was that the fire-hurling was an ability of the Iron Lords, not of the swords. "*Gods may not slay gods*," Annihilation said. "*It is a law of the universe. Too, long and long ago the Lady of the Snowmist wove a powerful spell, and it keeps us here, confined. As she herself is confined to her territory, her domain. We cannot leave here to extend our protection to others as we wish, for she prevents us. The power of the gods wanes in proportion to the distance from their own territory.*" It was hardly unknown, he told Jarik, that often gods must ask the aid of mortal men.

(Though that was unknown to Jarik, he nodded sagely and listened.)

"*She will know the identity of your parents, Jarik*," he was told. "*We are convinced that it was at her bidding that you were left to die, as an infant. . . . For reasons known to herself, Jarik; doubtless it would somehow further her plans. Perhaps she foresaw that it would be you who would come in time to end her reign of evil. Not for vengeance; for all of humankind, for men as you know men.*" And they told him too that She knew much of both past and present, and of the time to come, as well.

Jarik learned the true names of the four gods, then, and they were similar. Were they kin? No, Annihilation told him; Karahshisar, Milady Snowmist, was of their *kith*, not kin. "*She is of our people*," Dread said then, and Jarik listened attentively, for Lord Dread did not speak the profoundly obvious—or often. "*Was*," that god corrected himself. "*Now, as you have seen, she is our enemy. The enemy of your fellow men, of all humans. Like you, Jarik, we are exiles; homeless, kinless on this—in this place. Because of her.*"

Jarik absorbed that, and spoke, using the respectful pronoun: "She is of your kith, and imprisons yourselves. She is god of my people and bade them leave me to die. Then she is not sister or kith of yourselves, Lords, and she is no god of mine. She is our enemy."

He heard himself say that word *our*. Surely they smiled within their helmet-masks, helm-masks of harsh dark godiron. For they wanted Jarik to act for them against their enemy Karahshisar who was Snowmist, and now he had renounced Her and spoken words that allied him with these gods. A glow of excitement sent heat flushing all through him. *I*, Jarik had thought. I! Jarik! I am important! I belong at last! Ally and agent of the *Iron Lords*!

Now, only a month later and seemingly longer, he stood tall at the rearward rail of *Seadancer* and stared asea. Stared at nothing, while he remembered and tried to sort out the confusion and darkness in his mind. He reflected more, dwelling on that interview and their words to him. For he had had great need then to be important and to belong—and even more now, when he wore the bracers that made him a slave to their enemy.

*To my enemy*, he thought, and his face was grim and taut.

More important than he knew or could know, he stood alone and tried not to suffer.

Behind him, Strave Hot-eye approached Jilain, carrying his bow that was as long as he and all of wood. His cognomen was meaningless, now, and had been nearly so when he had got it. It had been loaded on him in his youth, when supposedly he had been less able to keep his eyes off the maidens of Kirrensark-wark than any other hot-eyed youth. He was the best archer among the men aboard *Seadancer*, but none called him Strave Archer or Strave Bowman.

"*Elye*," he said; "Lady; will you talk with me of bows?"

Jilain jerked sharply at his voice. She was sitting with her knees up and her hands around them, while she stared at Jarik's back.

"Oh! Y-yes. Of course. Call this one her name; it is Jilain."

"Strave," he told her.

"Oh yes," she said, as if she remembered, though she had not.

"We cannot compare bows or skill, Jilain. This is all we use, and it was your two arrows that hit that bird of sorcery. Mine missed. Would that I had thefted away a bow of your people when we departed!"

Her smile was fleeting. "Bows can be made, Strave. One can show you how to make such a bow as this. You—"

"I heard you telling Jarik of it. I listened because I am interested, La—Jilain. Perhaps we can begin, and try. But it will be hard to wait seven years!"

She nodded. "One can see that," she said, although her people were not afflicted with the impatience of these men. "Still, if one is to do it, there must be a beginning. After the sevent' year, wood for bows is always curing, so that one need not think of waiting any more."

"Well—what I wanted to ask you about was the way you hold arrow to bow." His eyes came alight with the enthusiasm of a boy, which he was not. "You seem to cross your hand, somehow?—to hold the shaft even less than I do, and without a bracer. It was too fast and I too was shooting, so that I did not see. Will you show me that—your technique?"

"Oh of course, Strave." *Surely they do not use the child's pinch?* "One had not noticed . . . would you first show one how you draw and loose?"

He showed her. Her thick dark brows rose as she saw him lay the shaft along the left of the bow. Though he did not use the pinch—actually holding the arrow's nock-end—she had never seen or thought of the grip he used instead. Naturally; she had learned what all Guardians learned while Strave had learned the way of his father, of Lokusta. He caged his nocked arrow with the index finger hooked around the string above it; and below the next finger's last knuckle and the mere tip of the next finger. Thus he drew in demonstration, while Jilain stared.

"One would see you release," she said, as he began to relax the tension in arm and string.

Strave looked around. "Ah—Kirrensark? We need practice, me and Jilain."

"One of you does," someone called, and a few men laughed; a very few, for most were too morose.

"I hope we have enough arrows aboard for . . . *practice*," Kirrensark said, with the frown of a stern father bidding willful children to have care.

"Oh, we have plenty," a man called. "Delath was at pains to tell Jilain so." And he ducked a backhand swing from Delath, who saw no humor in the remark but would not look at the speaker.

"We find that we hold and pull and release differently," Jilain told the firstman. "We would compare, whick cannot be done without actually loosing a shaft or two."

"Fr'm what I saw she don' need no practice!"

"Don't aim at the mast," Tole called. "It's seen enough hard knocks, that mast has."

"Ah, blight all this blather," Strave muttered.

He pulled slowly so that she could watch, tilting up his bow so as to send the arrow harmlessly aloft and into the sea ahead of them. He did, and Jilain heard both the twang of the gutstrip and the sharp little snapping sound. She only glanced at his arrow as it streaked away, although she squinted a little, measuring.

"That slap one heard . . . the string striking that leather cuff you wear?"

Strave nodded. "Right. The—"

"And did one not see the arrow flex leftward?"

"Yes, of course. An archer adjusts for that, when he's good. We both know an archer is not made in a day, or a year either. The string follows it—snaps to the left, I mean. So I merely wear a bracer a little different from these ax-wavers." Strave wore a sword. A good archer had perhaps traded fresh game for someone's swordmaking skill.

Jilain was nodding. "Ye-ess . . . one does see. Very different. Well, here is what this one does, and those of Kerosyr."

"Well," someone said, "do you want to trade or don't you?"

"Just wait a little. Let's watch these two. I like to watch her."

Men, grateful for any diversion so long as it was not another sorcerous attack, summoned more interest than they might have done under other circumstances. Being ashore, for instance, with something to do. And women.

Strave did see that slight twist of the hand he had thought he noticed earlier: she hooked her right thumb over the string from the left. Two fingers came around to hook over her thumbnail, which was pared. Her thumb was below the arrow as she drew that strange and handsome Kerosyran bow. She looked asea as she started to pull. Then she stopped and relaxed.

"Your arrow—it floats point down!"

Everyone looked. Those who could not see the bobbing feathers so far away did not admit it. Strave saw.

"An arrow always floats so."

She shook her blue-haired head. "Guardian arrows do not."

"Oh. Your points are all bone?"

She frowned, tilting her head to one side, uncomprehending. "Not all; Guardians sometimes use stone. The sun-winking fleckstone."

"Our points are of iron, Jilain."

"Iron!"

"We brought only armor-piercing arrows with us." His mouth twitched in the hint of a smile. "Although we didn't need them!"

"And so it floats point downward! Yes, one . . . *armor piercing*," she repeated, as his meaning became clear. "Oh. Then . . . then you have arrows designed for. . ."

Jilain broke off, and swallowed. These non-Kerosyrans used arrowheads designed for use on human beings! The Guardians of Osyr had no such arrows. Yet she could not comment or show disapproval; these men well knew that the Guardians of Osyr killed. To anyone's knowledge, Jarik was among the first men ever to visit Kerosyr and leave alive.

Again she began drawing her string, while Strave squinted at her thumb and fingers. "Wind," she murmured. "Arc . . . distance—oh, we are amove . . . hmm . . ."

She pulled, elevated her bow a trifle, and loosed. Strave wanted to examine her thumb at once. He found a heavy callus, but no mark of a snapping string. Obviously the arrow tended to flex rightward, with her technique, and there was nothing on the right to be struck by the string! He saw at once that this also sent the shaft whizzing on its humming way with no hint or possibility of being sent awry. His eyes narrowed, Strave was even then conceiving a thumb-protector, a tiny bracer or ring of leather, surely . . .

Then men were calling out, pointing ahead. He looked, to see her arrow floating horizontally—almost exactly beside the bobbing fleche of his submerged shaft. Strave looked at her with increased respect, and so did the other men.

He and she sat down to discuss bows, and grips, and arrows, and the loosing of them. And bracers, and calluses.

When she handed him her bow another surprise accompanied it; that bone-shining, serpentinely curving composite was far from easily pulled. Jilain earned more respect.

Jilain shrugged. "Your thumb is stronger than your fingers, is it not?"

"Ah." Strave smiled, nodding, and they bent their heads close in conversation. Two archers, conferring. The one telling the other how he might improve his grip, his pull, his accuracy. That one was a woman and one a man was of no import.

And in the stern, alone, Jarik was mentally reviewing the most thrilling occasion of his life.

To reach the wark at the base of Snowmist's aerie on Cloudpeak, he must cross Dragonmount. That long, jaggedly towering range, he told the Iron Lords, was impassable. They made no reply, to his embarrassment: they would not speak the obvious. Obviously no mountain was impassable, when the sea was so close—or when one was allied with the Lords of Iron!

He remembered his words, as he sought to keep any plaintive taint from his voice: "And how can it be accomplished?—the death of a god?"

The Black Sword that was now his, along with an armor coat as gift from the Iron Lords, would slay even Her, a god, he was told, "—*and those she raises to menace and do death on you. Though you must have as much care as ever . . . warrior.*" Thus the Iron Lords, and Jarik hesitantly suggested that the Black Sword might slay even them, then. Oh no, he was told:

"*Think you we would place the means to slay us, us, into the dirt-grubbing hands of those stupid villagers below? Or into the hands of a man-of-weapons, warrior, such as you?*"

He heard what these gods truly thought of mortal humans . . . but more loudly in his brain he heard himself called *akatir* for the first time: weapon-man or warrior. Jarik's heart surged and within him his ego struggled to swell and be recognized. He paid no attention to their contempt for his kind: mortal men; he was ready to kill for the Iron Lords.

Jarik, who learned to distinguish them by voice and realized that Dread was both eldest of the three and *old,*

learned then what became of those youths the Iron Lords
occasionally took from Blackiron. They chose the best
among the young males—and he did not return. Now Jarik
learned why: that youth became an Iron Lord! He was assured that they *were* immortal; oh yes. The body aged and
had to be replaced, the Iron Lords told him, but each *entered a new body* before the time of the mind's deteriora-
tion. It occurred to him that that was most probably not
true. Likelier the Iron Lords seized the minds of those
whose bodies they would occupy. For if they could do the
one, he reasoned in the very teeth of the unreasonable,
why not the other?

Perhaps accidentally, perhaps unwisely, Destruction
confirmed that intelligent surmise: "*All our memories flow
into a youth of the village. Thus we live on, Jarik. We are the
Iron Lords, gods on the earth; we live forever. I was born
Eskeshehir; I remain Eskeshehir.*" For that was his real
name. Jarik replied that he did not care to be an Iron Lord,
and they promised him that he would not be. They promised him much else, once he had killed Her who was their
kith but not their kin. Their fellow god.

And the weavers wove while the gods moved and manip-
ulated, and Jarik was god-transported to the other side of
Dragonmount the impassable. Perhaps Lord Dread had
been sorry to send him away so: "*We send away him with
the best potential of all in Blackiron,*" that aged god had
said, who must be ready for his new body.

That the Lord of Dread might still covet his form Jarik
did not consider.

Thus, saving the life of a man he did not know was
Kirrensark on whom he had so long sought vengeance,
Jarik came to Kirrensark-wark. He came not as Orrikson
Jarik, or as Strodeson Jarik, but as Jarik of the Black
Sword. He rejected Kirrensark's daughter Iklatne that
same night. Next day he rejected Kirrensark's offer of
her—and then She came. A few hours later, in her keep to
which She had taken him, he tried to kill Her. And he had
failed. And She had told him that They had lied; that the
Iron Lords lied, lied, and were evil, evil. And Jarik did not
know what god spoke truth—or if any of them did.

Now Jarik sighed, and clutched *Seadancer*'s rail with
sun-bronzed fingers until the knuckles went white. He had

lived in misery and now despite Jilain he remained in misery. Who was right and who was wrong? Who lied and who did not, or did both; Iron Lords and Snowmist? What was good and what was evil? Who was he, and Why? How was he to know?

When was he to be someone?

*Soon*, he thought grimly, staring back at *Seadancer*'s grey-white wake.

He had accomplished her damnable mission, and pox and plague on Her! He had promised Her nothing, and he would never forget what She had done to him. To him the Iron Lords had done nothing; for him they had done more than somewhat, while promising more. And with them he had made a bargain. To them he had made a promise.

The ship was carrying him toward Lokusta, and Kirrensark-wark, and Her. Jarik knew what he must do. He had promised.

"Jarik?"

The voice came from behind him. It intruded so that he stiffened with a small jerk. He did not turn.

"Will you eat, Jarik?"

Jarik turned. The youth who had approached him saw no menace in his face, but agony and a fixity of resolve and purpose. He could almost feel it. He stepped back a pace from the force of Jarik's eyes.

Then Jarik smiled. "Yes, Coon. Let us eat a bite or three, Coon!"

And he who longed so, needed so, stepped forward and put an arm across Coon's shoulders and thereby made Coon someone; made Coon important. For to no other of Kirrensark-wark had Jarik Blacksword been comradely.

# Seven

*If an external thing gives you pain, it is not this thing that causes you pain, but your own judgment of it.*

—Marcus Aurelius

The sun became a fat egg that broke over the horizon and Jilain came to Jarik where he sat alone. She sat nearby. Around them, men were lounging, disposing themselves for sleep. The new air of tension, however, still lay on the ship. This night, Kirrensark had decreed, three would remain awake and watchful, not two or only one. And no man said him nay. The sky deepened and darkened and after a while there were stars sparkling like spots of snow, and rubies, and emeralds, and the amber beloved of most Lokustans.

After a long while Jilain Kerosyris moved to sit quite close to Jarik of the Black Sword. She put a hand on him, on his thigh near the knee.

"Jarik? You think the hawk came from the Iron Lords?"

"Yes."

"You know these living gods? You have seen them?"

"Yes."

"You have heard them speak?"

"Yes. They have spoken to me."

"And you to them? I mean—do gods . . . converse?"

"Yes. I have conversed with the Iron Lords. Gods also have names."

Perhaps he had been too long in silence. Perhaps he merely wanted to keep her near. Perhaps he had need to talk. He did not know, though he was not interested in conversation with anyone else. He was aware of her hand on his thigh. He felt it, through the leathern leggings he wore next his skin, save above where he wore a wrap-folded breechclout in the way of the fishers of Blackiron. He wore it snug.

As for Jilain, she was interested—and also she wanted him to talk. The subject did not matter. This had not been a pleasant afternoon, with him wrapped in some dark cloak of memories.

"Tell me the names of the Iron Lords?"

"They bear names to frighten children with. They are the Lords of Dread, and of Destruction, and of Annihilation."

"Ugh." The tiniest tremor ran through her, but the night air asea was chilly. "What terrible names for anyone to bear!"

"They are not anyone," he said; "they are gods. I have seen them, and what they can do. They do have other names, though. Would you hear those?"

"Are they less fearful?"

Jarik smiled a very small smile. "Yes, but they are harder to say! The Lord of Dread is named Seyulshehir. Say-ool-she-here. The Lord of Destruction is named Eskeshehir. Esky-she-here. And the true name of the Lord of Annihilation is Nershehir. Those are their names. They told me that they do not have meaning, but are names, merely names."

"They are so much names! Still . . . so are Kirrensark and Seramshule, one supposes. But one should not care to have to call anyone by those names! Still, they are not so . . . fearsome as the others."

"That, I think, is why they wear those other names. They are fearsome in appearance as well." She was rubbing and rubbing his leg, though the nap on the leggings was long since worn down. A bit nervously he said, "They told me the true name of the Lady of the Snowmist, too. Her name is Karahshisar."

"That is . . . very strange," she said in a distracted voice as if her mind was elsewhere. "Yet it is a prettier sound, this one thinks. Is She pretty, the Lady of the Snowmist?"

"No. I mean I don't know. I doubt it. She wears a mask. They all four wear masks, Jilain. I thought all gods wore masks, until I saw Osyr, on your isle. That was only a statue, of course. And Osyr is dead, of course."

She did not argue the point; Guardians did not consider Osyr a dead god. "Jarik? Do you remember how after one cut you loose and handed you your dagger, that nikht in our—the Guardians' wark—and you looked long at this one? You said you wished that one's name were not Jilain, but *Jilye*; *Jilish*."

Heat rose in him, and he felt uncomfortable. "I remember."

"And later one asked about that, and you said that in your land the names of all women end in that *-ye* sound, and that the term of fondness is to change it to an *-ish* sound. Your family called you 'Jarish'?"

"Yes," Jarik said, less comfortable by considerable. "I remember, warrior." Deliberately he reminded her that they were warriors together.

She was silent for a time, rubbing and stroking, while she summoned words. "One told you that one had enjoyed one's experience wit' a man, but that one had not conceived of it. You would not do that wit' this one, for you said you would take no chance of leaving a son on Kerosyr to be . . . to be . . . killed." Her voice had dropped very low.

Jarik said nothing. He remembered, and he was aware of her nearness and her hand on him, and he heard her words. He wished he were somewhere else, or that she was, or that he had continued talking of the gods.

Suddenly she leaned closer still. Quietly and most privily, she asked him a question.

He answered, "Never."

She jerked as if struck. "But—we are no longer on Kerosyr! This one shall never return there. If—if we did, and a son of yours came of it, one would cherish it and love it!"

Jarik said, "Never."

She looked down, and despite the moonlight she did not see the ship's planking between her outstretched legs. After a time of silence she said—to the planking—"But . . .

this one likes it! One remembers! One loved it! It is good, the thing a man and woman do together."

For the third time, tight of jaw and grim-faced, he said, "Never."

"And you bear this one no ill will? Why, then, not?"

"And you who loved it; you bore no child of it, Jilain Red-feather?"

Sadly: "No." Her hand slid from him.

"I am sorry," Jarik said, "since you are. Yet I am glad, too. I know at least that you have borne no son to be murdered because he was a son, and no daughter someday to murder a man because he is a man. I am sorry, as you are. But . . . no, Jilain, warrior; sister. Never."

"You will never call this one Jilish?"

"I did not say that," Jarik said, feeling sincere in his desire to be stricken instantly with some awful pox, that he would not have to continue to talk with her. He had spoken with deliberate cruelty, seeking to offend her into silence, into stalking away from him. It would not lessen his misery, but it would end this immediate discomfort.

"You do not want this one?"

Even in darkness, Jarik did not look at her beside him. His voice was dull, exanimate.

"Listen, Jilain, warrior. Listen. Once I had a stepmother," Orrikson Jarik, later Strodeson Jarik, said. "She loved me, I think. I did love her. I did. And a stepfather too; we, I know, loved each other. They are dead, bloodily slain, and with iron birds present. Hawks. Then there was Torsy, my sister who was not my sister. We were long companions. We endured much together and we did love each other. Torsy was slain bloodily. There was also Stijye, in the wark of Ishparshule where I was reared by another set of foster-parents. Stijye and I exchanged youthful kisses and fondlings and vows in the night—ah! That seems a hundred years ago! One called Stath also wanted her. He challenged me and I slew Stath, bloodily, who was son to Ishparshule and he fell down dead in blood. For that I was exiled, and Stijye saw me as naught save killer and an outlaw she hated. In Blackiron, that fishers' wark I told you of, there was a girl I was fond of. I was trying to belong, oh to *belong* and to be, and thought perhaps she would be my woman. Alye; Alye her name. She was bloodily pierced, raped, and slain in blood. Do you hear? Now too I have lain with the Pythoness of Kerosyr, though I left her sealed. And she was slain, bloodily."

He did not mention the Osyrrain. Her he had stroked much of the night, torturing her with pleasure without love. And next day she was slain, bloodily. By Jilain. The killer did not matter, though, in Jarik's mind.

"A pattern, you see," he went on in the same chilling, dull voice, while he did not look at her. "Even as of a quilt done all in scarlet. Scarlet is the color of the pattern the weavers weave for Jarik, Jilain. Or the pattern that Jarik himself weaves all unwillingly for those he loves! I bring death to all I love, you see; all who love me. I will never lie with you as a man and a woman, Jilain of Kerosyr. I will never love you nor allow you to love me, who is Jarik the *Accursed*!"

And he thought: *Jarik the Miserable.*

The silence of night-dark was shockingly disturbed then; the voice was Kirrensark's.

"Then what, idiot, is to become of her? Good with weapons or no, matchless with bow or no, in the real world—our land—she is merely a waif! A lovely bauble for the playing with, and for the using of."

Jarik went stiff, but Jilain felt him relax a bit. She lay staring into darkness. She could not imagine herself being "played with" any more than she had ever thought of herself as "lovely." *These men*, she mused, *surely have somewhat to learn of Jilain*!

Jarik surprisingly did not take umbrage at the interruption and the firstman's harsh words. He shook his head. "Perhaps . . . perhaps I will ask the Lady of the Snowmist. It may be that She will help her who so helped us."

"Aye," Kirrensark rumbled, and he dared voice the dread possibility: "If She was not Herself that grey and white dove. . . ."

Another day began with Shralla whipping her horses so that her yellow-white chariot set out on its daily journey across the ridgepole of the sky. The men of *Seadancer* awoke, and added to the water in the sea. Their movements were not energetic, and they were irritable. Clouded although the sky was bright, the ship seemed to have

shrunk. Not touching had become important. Stout men of
weapons did not look forward to another day of dullness
and un-occurrence.

The world was small: Mottled brown ship, salt-sprinkled
green sea; blue heaven, ruled by the golden chariot of
Shralla, pursuing her lover across the sky.

No calm slowed them, although the breeze of Her was
diminished, weaker. No gale arose . . . not even a way-
ward wind to play capricious or vicious games with the ship
of men so tiny on the great ocean. No storm delayed them
or sent them skidding and heeling helter-skelter off course.
They knew the direction of Lokusta. Last night had been as
clear as the stormless day, and several who had sailed before vowed that the stars confirmed their course. See, there
was the Stag and there, over there was the Life Ruby rolled
from the pouch of the Gem Lady, ruler of the night. Now at
this time of year, when the Stag was just so, and with a
thumb a man could span from the eastward antler to the tip
of the Slayer's spear, then certainly . . . and so on.

This day Kirrensark had wakened before dawn to watch
the sun rise in chill beauty that warmed and warmed while
he marked the positions of several bright stars until they
faded in Shralla's light. Aye, uncertain as such reckoning
was, he felt confident that they were on course for Lokusta
and Kirrensark-wark.

Food held up well though it was dull, and they had
fetched plenty of water from Kerosyr. Without the dove,
and with boredom like a sheath over their hearts, they
fared on homeward. Every man—every person—of Kirrensark-wark wore a piece of amber as amulet on cord
around his neck, and some of those amulets had been
traded as many as five times, on this voyage. It was something to do.

Jilain asked Jarik about the Bands of Snowmist, and he
told her that they bound him to Her, giving him unbearable
icy pain if he sought to go against Her or her wishes. No,
they would not come off. In addition, they warned of impending danger by going chill—bearably chill. They were
both badness and boon then, she said, and he gave her a
look and went silent. Already she had noted those smooth,
scratchless and unscratchable armlets that so snugly encased his forearms to the wrist-bones. She had seen that

they were without sign of seam or closure. Magic. God-magic.

Jilain talked with Strave then, with Coon close by. Strave answered her questions about Milady Snowmist, and told her about those who were Chosen. Coon listened as raptly as she.

Later in the day Kirrensark spoke to her, quietly. "Among our people no woman's legs are seen save by family. Those she loves and who love her. These men keep staring, but I will not ask you to wrap yourself with something unsightly, Jilain."

*Good*, she thought; one *would not do it anyhow*. "Women of Lokusta wear leggings, as the men do? Leather?"

He shook his head with a little smile. "No—well, in winter they do, but under their skirts. Women wear skirts, all over Lokusta."

"What is a skirt?"

He glanced sharply at her at that; he saw that she was serious. It was strangely difficult for him to explain, and he saw that she thought the concept was silly. It would hamper one's movements, she pointed out. And above the skirts? Did women wear nothing above? The same necklaces these men did, perhaps?

No, and that was even more difficult for Kirrensark to explain. He assured her that she could borrow something of his daughter's . . . though his Iklatne was shorter.

"Iklatne? Your daukhter . . . does Jarik call her Iklatnish?"

He shook his head and did not smile. No matter that Jarik had made himself hateful to Kirrensark and was not much likable besides. He had saved Kirrensark's life; he was favored by Her; he was of the right age and obviously of Lokustan birth; he was the best man with weapons the One-arm had ever seen. Would that Jarik did call his daughter Iklatnish! Would that he thus became Kirrensark's son, in a way. They had produced four sons, Kirrensark and his wife Lirushye. One had died at birth. Now the others were gone to the Dark Brother, too. The youngest had died seven years ago. Jarik had admired his dagger, which had hung on the wall of Kirrensark-house ever since the youth's death. But Jarik would not accept it as a gift. He would accept nothing of Kirrensark, who had so long ago led the raiders that extirpated the Akkharian farmers' community where Jarik had lived.

Jilain did not notice Kirrensark's brown study, despite her unusual sensitivity. She was looking sideward at Jarik while trying not to appear to be doing so. A smile was playing tag with the corners of her mouth. She was glad he did not call this Iklatne person by the fondness-name.

*Jarish*, she thought.

"One cannot imagine being content," she said after a time, "in one of these 'skirts' of the women of Kirrensairk-wairk. Still, if sikht of a woman's legs is distracting to the men of Kirrensairk-wairk, one would not wish to be a source of such distraction. One has no experience with this dwelling of two sexes together! Perhaps leggings mikht be found to fit this one?" She looked about the ship. "His would be too short . . . his too big in the waist, and his! Coon's, perhaps. Mikht Coon have an extra pair of warrior's leggings, Kirrensairk, that one mikht appear proper with her legs concealed?"

"I doubt it," Kirrensark said uncomfortably.

"Well, once *Seadancer* reaches land, one will provide her own leggings, then. Surely game and the hunting of it cannot be so different, in your land."

Kirrensark sighed. No, he thought. He would not tell her that women did not hunt; men did! No. He decided abruptly that he needed to have converse with the man back at the steering-oar. That was a dull chore on this voyage, so the firstman saw to it that those aboard took short turns.

The sun was westering when a man called "Land!"

Immediately he showed how foolish he felt. It was not land he saw.

"Ship!" another man said, and "ship," another said, and Coon went up the mast faster than a hungry woodpecker.

"Aye!" he called down. "Ship, ship! A ship!" Then, "Hawkship!"

The men on the hawk-prowed ship named *Seadancer* looked at one another. Some were surprised at Kirrensark's command, but they did as he bade, donning armor and helms and readying bowstrings while Delath went to unlock the swords and axes stored under the steering platform in the little compartment there. Jarik forced his way forward, with clinks from his dark mail of the god-metal.

"That ship fares from the direction of our goal," he said, staring at a striped sail too far distant for its colors to be discerned. He could have blotted it from sight with an upraised thumb. Both thumbs were busy; absently he was seeing to the secureness of his belt through its buckling loop. Jarik would not suffer the Black Sword to be taken from him and stored away; Kirrensark avoided arguments with Jarik.

"So it does," Kirrensark said. "And it comes for us."

"A ship come looking for us?" A hopeful voice.

"We must be close to land, then." Another.

"We are well asea," Seramshule said with a seaman's wisdom. "How likely that another ship find us, on this largest plain in all the world?"

"How likely that the wind remain unstintingly behind us?" someone asked rhetorically.

"Coon come down!" Kirrensark said. "Tole go up, for you have more experience aloft."

The other hawkship grew and grew and the sail seemed orange-red. It grew more, until it was discernibly orange striped with crimson. They did not need Tole's eyes to know that atop its mast something glinted in the afternoon sunlight. A metal mast-head, must be. The two craft drew closer together, and closer, and the plain of the sea seemed less vast.

Coon knew that this was adventure, and he knew excitement. And he knew fear. He had been handed his short-hafted ax. He held it tightly.

"That ship," Jarik said too thoughtfully, "comes almost directly on our course-path."

"Yes." Kirrensark's voice was tight, muted. "And its sail bellies no less than ours."

It was then that gooseflesh crawled aboard *Seadancer*, and crawled over the arms and back of more than one man. Two ships asea and, unlikely, on seeming intersecting courses. Each moved in the direction opposite the other's direction of movement even while each moved toward the other. Both sailed before wind. And each sail billowed, full of air; bellied out toward the other ship.

"Not . . . possible," a man murmured.

"Sorcery," Grath Redshank said, softly.

"Why is this so?" That from Jilain, never before asea or so much as on a ship.

"The wind blows us straight toward that other ship," Jarik told her. "And the wind blows that ship straight toward us. That is not possible. It is sorcery. God-power." Without knowing, he was rubbing the fingertips of his right hand over the seamless cylinder of silver that sheathed his left wrist. "And atop that one's mast . . ."

They stared, feeling the eeriness of it. They saw oars rise along that other vessel; saw their blades drop into the water on either side.

"Kiddensok!" Jarik snapped, and more than one staring man jumped.

They saw the sails reefed on the approaching ship. Sheets down; oars out. And Jarik knew what it was that glinted atop the oncoming mast.

"That craft is not here by chance. It is powered by sorcery or gods. And it is not from Her. The Lady of the Snowmist did not send that ship, Kiddensok!"

"String bows!" Kirrensark snapped, without looking away from the approaching vessel. "Ready oars. Seramshule, Grath—stand by the sail."

"Jarik—?"

Jarik squeezed her shoulder without thinking about it. With his hand there on the dark leather, he turned to shout. "Does any man recognize any man on that ship?"

Amid replies of "No!" Tole called, "No, but I recognize that fell *bird* atop her mast!"

Spray flew high from the others' oars. "They mean to attack," Delath muttered. "Kirrensark?"

"Weapons ready," Kirrensark said, "but hold steady."

"They mean to attack us," Jarik said, while Jilain looked from him to the approaching craft and back to him. "Those are no friends. One has more control of oars than sail and wind, and men row to the attack. The iron hawk is with them, that killed the dove of Her."

"Iron?"

"Arrows out," Kirrensark said. "Nock. Wait now, wait. Wait. . . . The distance is too great."

"Not for long," Delath said, and it was almost a snarl.

"The Iron Lords," Jarik muttered to Jilain—and to

Jarik—"or *someone*, has sent that bird-guided ship full of men to attack us. Consider what we have seen. Doesn't it appear that the bird flew ahead to find us as well as slay *our* guiding bird, then returned to guide those men to us? We are not to reach Lokusta."

Kirrensark glanced at him. "That is not possible, Jarik Blacksword."

"You are right, Kiddensok. The gull that led us to Kerosyr is also impossible. And the breeze that stayed behind us all the way—going and returning. With perfect weather day and night. The dove that was with us is not possible, either. Neither is it possible that a hawk flew out here, out to sea, and slew that dove, with no attempt to carry it off to eat. That big black hawk itself is impossible, when two of Jilain's arrows glanced off it!"

"Stop," Runner murmured. "Oh stop talking so!"

Weapons belts were strapped on. Daggers and swords were loosened in their sheaths; the heads of axes were uncovered so that their evil iron curves were free and glinting.

"Suppose it's that White Rod they want," Delath said.

Jarik did not look down at it, or touch it, the wrapped staff of Osyr he had fastened to his belt. Milady Snowmist had sent these others only to convey and to escort Jarik. Jarik She had sent for the staff from the hand of the dead god's statue. None of them knew why She wanted it. Obviously it was important to Her. And to others?

Jarik said, "What else?"

# Eight

*I belong to battle as the heron to the reeds*
*till I give my body back.*

—*Marge Piercy*

The other vessel loomed larger still. Its naked mast seemed trying to pierce the sky, stark without its sail. Now faces could be seen. And the broad, sun-glinting wing-spread at the top of the mast. Bows, too, could be seen. They were strung.

Jilain asked, "What will happen?" and Kirrensark explained.

Volleys of arrows would be exchanged. A ramming would take place or a grappling if possible, if the others did not veer off. Boarding, amid loud yells. The chopping of flesh and bone with ax and sword. Blood splashed and running underfoot with nowhere to go. Dead men. One crew would lose and one would win, while both lost men. He spoke in a dull voice these terrible things, as if he said it all from rote.

Jilain had never heard such. She had never seen such. Now she looked thoughtfully the length of this long broad boat, at the man in the stern, sitting to the right of the steering-oar. Was he the most important man aboard, now?

—Yes.

Jilain looked back at the other ship, and around at the

naked blades of axes and the grim faces of their bearers. She saw pale, bone-tight knuckles clutching those hafts of tools never meant for use on wood. And Jilain snatched up her bow.

"Give space, for this one and Jilacla."

"Here," Kirrensark said. "We're not in bow range yet!"

"You do not have Jilacla, either," Jarik said, suddenly wondering if it was possible. "Give her space."

"Look there—she's drawing the string clear back past her ear! Strave? You ever see the like? Seramshule?"

"Weird way to hold a string too, I say. That's the strangest—huh! Barrenshule? Didn't you try to pull that bow?"

"A trick—"

"Shut up." That from Strave Hot-eye, who received some mean looks.

Jilain opened her right hand and brought it slowly down from her ear. Her striped arrow had whished up, and up. It arced. It plunged in a long graceful trajectory . . . and it drove into the other vessel's steering-oar no more than two finger-breadths from the steersman's hand. Since every man on *Seadancer* was staring at that, they did not see her release her second shaft, so swiftly following the first. They did however see it appear in the body of the other ship's steersman.

The man half rose, throwing up his hands. His big oar lurched and struck him. His ship lurched too, as he fell back and the long stern-set oar had its head as a plunging wild stallion.

While men cheered on *Seadancer* and loudly slapped their thighs, pandemonium seized the other ship. Its noise came across the water, in many voices and conflicting cries and instructions. Pandemonium held that unguided vessel—

And released it. Another man took the steering-oar. Up came his ship's beaked prow amid a heroic flash of white spray.

Within a minute he was slain by a spirally striped arrow.

"Lady be merciful!" Barrenshule swore softly, and Strave was grinning as if he were somehow responsible for the prowess of Jilain and her Jilacla.

Now an insect cloud seemed to buzz up above the attacker ship. Arrows came keening at *Seadancer* while shields were erected for the protection of a third steersman. Only one of that covey of shafts reached *Seadancer*, and it was wavering when it thudded weakly into her side, just above the waterline.

"Huh!" Stirl Elk-runner sneered. "I could do more damage to this ship with a good kick!"

Some of Kirrensark's men shot, too, but it was too soon. No matter how strong of pull and strongly pulled, Lokustan bows would not bridge the distance with anything approaching accuracy. One man emulated Jilain's "trick" of turning his hand, *so*, and pulling past his eye, *so*, and his bow broke.

"They will be sore fearful over there by now," Jarik muttered. "They will think it's sorcery that drives these stripe-wearing staves into their steersm—"

Jarik broke off. A chill wind blew up his back. He remembered! He had *seen* this. He had *experienced* this, and all before ever he sailed with Kirrensark. Before he had seen or thought aught of Guardians or anyone named Jilain of Osyr's Isle. That night in the keep of the Lady of the Snowmist, when She had tormented him with several real-seeming visions that were not real—that night he had experienced just this scene, this attack! Now he was doubly sure that some at least of his visions showed him the time to come, and there was no happiness in the thought. He remembered. . . .

The sea lapping and gurgling along the sides of the ship he was on. The strange tall short-haired woman aboard among men, clad in armor. Young and comely she was, a warrior woman with a quiver of arrows at her hip. And down on them, blue-black and shining, on moveless wings, came swooping the iron hawk. Using her strange doubly curved bow (quadruply curved bow!), the woman sent an arrow at the attacking bird. Jarik was sure he saw/had seen a spark as the shaft glanced away with a clanking sound. This he had *seen* nigh a month ago, though Jilain's hair now was hardly so long as he had *seen* it then—and *even then in the vision she had a new-scabbed cut on her forehead*! Jarik remembered that awful vision. Down came the iron hawk, for him. . . .

He had awakened in sweat, in Snowmist's keep, sure

that he was dead; for the bird had dived down and horribly, painfully, bloodily slain him!

Now he went cold and fearful, Jarik of the Black Sword.

*Seadancer*'s arrows had fallen short and the attackers, in need of any sort of jubilation, shouted taunts and jeers.

Jilain stood alone, though Kirrensark was close by. And Jarik, who stared at her. Delath was storming and snarling, trying to silence the crew. Jilain was carefully checking and re-checking windage; examining an arrow with eye and fingers and fussily plucking a bit of feather at its nock-end; gauging distance and plotting arc with strange sightings along arm and fingers and thumb; plucking her Jilacla as though the bow were a musical instrument.

"Jilain! Lady!" Strave Hot-eye was rushing to her. "Wait! No arrows are better than an archer's own—but you want these armor-piercers!"

She turned, looked at him, nodded. A frown moved over her face, though, as she took one of the shafts he proffered.

"The lengt' is about the same; that is easy for one to compensate for. But—this arrow will be end-heavier than one's own, won't it? Hmm."

"Yes," Strave said, bobbing his head. "Yes, but the problem is, if you make good your shot *your* arrow may still be wasted, and what's the good of that?"

She decided, and took his arrow, nocked it, closed her eyes while moving her arms just a little, bobbing the bow, getting the feel of it with this new, heavier-tipped arrow, raising it a trifle, opening her eyes. Jarik watched her and did not know he was biting his lip. Nor was he alone.

"This one for the wooden head on the front end, then," she said, and Jarik saw her take a deep breath, and hold, this woman who did not even know what to call the foremost end of a ship.

"Wait!" Strave called.

She heeded that interruption. He had seen the wave coming. *Seadancer* dipped, rose, glided, and Jilain drew and released.

Much noise from the other ship—not coming so fast now, as all stared at the ship they had considered prey—as Strave's arrow arced and dropped and barely impacted the vessel's bow. Behind her men groaned.

"Ha!" Jilain called. "Two such arrows, Strave. The

same, just the same now, archer!"

"Yes, archer! Right!" he said, grinning, selecting from his quiver.

"Why don't Strave do something?"

Strave half-turned to face that man. "I am. I am handing arrows to a better archer." And he did.

Again she checked and gauged, for the distance had changed, and the ships were pushing ripples at each other while their separate winds were beginning to come into conflict. Again she filled her lungs with breath she would hold. *Seadancer* dipped, began to rise, and Jilain gasped "Perfect!" and she sped off two arrows ere they were atop that little swell. Only Strave saw the slight change in elevation of her bow between the two swift shots, and he too was holding his breath.

Each arrow keened high and screamed down amid shouts and wild waving of arms on the other ship—and then a hush closed over that craft. A third helmsman had been slain by lofted arrows, while crouching *behind* his bulwark of shields!

While his men cheered and danced, Kirrensark bellowed his command: "A volley! A volley! Loose, loose, loose!"

The big black hawk flashed blue as it launched itself from the enemy mast-top. It drove at *Seadancer* like a hurled spear. Jarik felt panic grabbing at him in cold, clawed hands: *It's going to kill me. This is the vision, repeated—it's going to kill me*! Somehow his hand was frozen at his side; just at the hilt of the Black Sword. And frozen was the term, for a chill commenced to emanate from his bracers.

The bird swooped, half-wheeled, dived—not at Jarik.

Unerringly it singled out and drove down at its ship's worst enemy. Jarik could not move. Jilain could, and did. She did not waste an arrow on this unNatural creature or *thing*, but snatched up the shield she had set aside as useless. Not now. Swiftly she dropped bow and drew sword. Her stroke missed and she was already ducking when she swung it. The bird struck the upper edge of her buckler with a *bamm* sound, seemed to bounce upward, and was away. Unflapping.

The sound of the impact of the bird had been no less than that of an ax on her buckler.

Men had seen that shield give before the bird's impact,

but Jilain straightened and sword and shield were combatively up. Amid the clamor of both ships' crews, the hawk swooped and banked to come driving back, all with incredible speed. Even so, it was Kirrensark who moved to effect. It was his big three-quarter moon of an ax head that intersected the creature's dive at Jilain. A terrible clang accompanied the impact. The great bird was knocked off flight—and swooped up and away with no sign of injury. It glinted indigo and jet in the sky, and neither screamed nor flapped its wings.

Kirrensark stood glaring in astonishment at a badly dented ax head.

"At their ship," Delath had presence of mind to shout, "Volley!"

With another bluish metallic flash in the sunlight the bird wheeled in air. Again it came driving down. The spread of those extended, moveless wings was equal to the length of Jilain's sword, which this time struck it before it reached her. Another of those impossibly screeching, unnerving-because-impossible clangs rang loud—and Jilain's swordblade snapped. The broken off section shot past the bird and off into the water. Already her buckler was whipping up. The bird struck it with a great *whump*. Wood popped and cracked. Splinters flew. The shield was slammed back against its bearer. The bird's claws had pierced the shield's thrice-toughened wood, and it clung. Men stared in horror, seeing the woman's legs, calves bulging in strain, buckle under the weight of the awful bird of sorcery.

Jilain fell back. Still she was silent; had anyone been aware of eeriness other than this outré attack, he'd have noted the strangeness of this woman in combat and in stress. Never had she uttered a sound.

Jarik did, now. A mad yell tore from him and he interfered as if a volcano had detonated within him. Out came his sword to sweep away and back while he charged. Runner was in his path, and Runner was bowled aside and over as though he had been a mere boy rather than two hundred pounds of ugly blond warrior in forty pounds of helmet and warcoat and weapons belt, bearing a four-pound ax and a shield weighing thirteen more. He went back over a bench with a crash, a snarl, and several curses.

Jarik, with a maniacal cry and a great sideward stroke, slashed. His rushing blade seemed a black stripe drawn in the air.

The Black Sword of the Iron Lords struck the bright-shining black hawk—of the Iron Lords?—and sliced through it. No blood splashed. No entrails flew. The huge bird went flying over ship's rail in two halves. Each plunged with a sizable splash into the water and, of iron or god-metal, sank in an instant.

All had taken note that its wings had never flapped. Nor had any sound come from that ferocious curved beak. All had seen that no blood spurted from it. Now every man saw that there was nothing at all on Jarik's unshining black blade. Nor was it notched or even marked, though Kirrensark's good war-ax of iron was badly notched. Goreless and bloodless, that unnatural demon-bird died.

The sword's wielder lurched down beside Jilain. She was bleeding, and conscious though muzzy. Even as Jarik's brain blurred with the hovering of Oak's reaching for the surface of a shared mind, he saw that only the wound he had put on her forehead had been knocked open, and that by her shield. It bled anew, in a trickle only. On her cheek, from bracer or shield, showed a scratch within a bruise. Her hazel eyes found focus and glowed up at him. Jarik hardly knew what he did. She had just slain three and been singled out for that god-demon's attack because of it, and was injured and groggy. And she was a woman who noted the attention and anxious concern of the man she had chosen.

"This one is all rikht, Jarish," she told him, and showed him a pallid smile. It was the first time she had said his name that way.

"Lie still," he said, and though he was Jarik he snarled the words as a command, as Oak would have done. He let go the Black Sword, leaving it against his bent leg. Both his hands rose to draw a thong from behind his neck. At its end swung a warmly glowing chunk of amber, cut into a thumb-sized ward symbol. He placed the cord over her head so that the weight of the honey-colored stone fell onto the warcoat she wore with a little rap of amber on leather.

She smiled, but she had to force it; never had Jilain seen such mad eyes. Those eyes were not soft blue perisine

gemstones now, or flecks of sky, but two chips of cobalt
that were at once hotly glaring and yet of ice. Flaming ice-
bergs; frozen volcanoes of blue fire.

Straightening, he hurled himself to the rail. Only she had
seen that fearsome glassy glare, those staring mad eyes.

Like a madman he stood tall, presented a fine target
while he waved the Black Sword high. Seemingly begging
for archers to try their skill. Challenging the other craft as
an entity. Begging its crew to come and die. And suddenly
by his side was a man twenty years older but no less mania-
cally inimical. White-blond hair floated out beneath his
round iron helm in which a dent and scratches showed like
badges of experience. Then Kirrensark too was there, roaring, shaking his notched ax and his beard, with nothing pitiful or ludricous about that big girthy man's lack of one arm.

Only Kirrensark knew what he was doing.

From behind them and aftward, four arrows left
*Seadancer* together. Never could anyone be sure which
man's was the bow that sent the other ship's straw-bearded
master toppling backward with an arrow sunken deep in his
corselet of stout boiled leather.

"Belches!" Jarik bellowed in a mighty voice. "Excres-
cences on a frog's back! The BIRD directed you, on behalf of
the Iron Lords! Without it, you are without them—and
without them you are LITTLE men and dead men! For this is
a sword of the Iron Lords, you gusts of gas from a fat old-
ster's belly! What else could have SLAINNN that foul bird
that was no bird?"

Beside him, pale-eyed, fire-eyed, Delath too had gone
morbrin. "Come," he roared, "and DIE!"

"Oh Sweet Lady, to see this! Both are gone morbrin.
Neither knows what he says or does!"

The attacking ship sheared away as if gusted by those
mad voices. Not so much as a single arrow streaked at those
maniacs, who stood tall and within range. Mad-eyed and
foaming for the letting of blood, Jarik and Delath demanded that they pursue and slay, slay, slay, sink the other
ship, wash it in blood, chop men and ship into scarlet
kindling. . . .

They were restrained and calmed by men wary of their
blades, for they were in an insane fever for battle and
blood. In that emprise the two morbriners wreaked far

more damage than the attackers, in bruises and abrasions on the shipmates who at last restrained them. They lay panting, snarling, held down.

"They attacked *me*," Jarik morbriner said once, panting. "The Iron Lords sent attack on *me*!"

Oh so slowly those glaring eyes of blue and of grey lost the ugly glitter of the morbriner. A few feet away Jilain was hale and fine, and none had heard her bright-eyed murmur:

"O Osyr! How one loves it! How is it that Your daukhter Jilain never knew she was born for battle and danger?" And her right wrist pressed hard against her breast while she clamped in her hand the chunk of ancient amber that hung from a leathern cord around her neck.

Then Jarik and Delath were recovered from that fit of madness that came now and again on some few men, and it was Jilain who was hero of *Seadancer*.

The day waned and ended in the peace of a sunset that was orange and the color of roses splashed with gold. Combat-companions slept well with a feeling of accomplishment. And had any sought to touch the woman among them, surely ten would have attacked him.

Next day Jarik and Jilain stood for long, each with hands on the other's shoulders, and looked each into the other's eyes. The men of *Seadancer*, of Kirrensark-wark, saw that about his neck and on Jarik's chest hung a necklace of shells. Nor had those shells been touched by any man.

That cool day Strave Hot-eye had a thought, and smiled, and tugged off his leggings to display dirty breechclout and hairy, knotted legs. Ceremoniously he folded away his leggings. He said nothing, but soon Tole's leggings were off and piled on Strave's, and Coon's, and those of Stirl and Runner, and Jilain was no longer alone bare-legged on *Seadancer*.

A crosswind gave them trouble, and they spent hours battling it. That was good, for it was something to do. Kirrensark worked at smoothing out his damaged ax, and shot glances at Jarik. Once they were sure they had bested the contrary wind, those men of his wark saw land. Aye, and this time it was land; it was land they knew.

Standing well out, the men of *Seadancer* ruddered up the

coast to familiar landmarks. Marks of land; land they knew; a land that rose to sneer down at the sea but admitted it here and there by way of deeply slashed inlets. Most willingly they answered the questions of one aboard who had never been to sea. She was a fellow warrior. They did not today call her Jilain, or even Jilain Kerosyris. Jilain Demonslayer, they called that hero of *Seadancer*. Nor did Strave Hot-eye mind or say a word when she erred and called him "sister archer." For both of them knew what they were, and words would not change that. Besides, he knew she intended only to compliment him, battle companion.

And *Seadancer* came to Kirrensark Long-haft's wark on the high shores of Lokusta, where the sea crashed and roared with the voices of a hundred wolves; and they made landing amid a great welcoming.

There followed a feasting and much license, for women were glad to see their men home and the men twice as glad and in need besides. Willingly maidens bestowed that which they had saved and protected. The presence of Jilain aboard, and her untouchable, had only increased the desire and need of those seafaring men. Produce of this night's sowing would be seen nine months hence, and welcome, for there was battle to come, and battle again.

They were not aware of it, and would not have given it thought had they known: a wind age, a sword age, a wolf age had come upon the earth.

In that celebration Jilain took part, in a loose tunic of blue the color of her hair and the hair of Kirrensark's fat wife Lirushye, whose tunic it was, dyed with the same water-steeped leaves that provided the color of the hair and brows of every woman of Kirrensark-wark. Thus they did not see Jilain's hair as unusual, for they thought she dyed it as they did theirs. Only her black brows they thought strange—but that year a new fashion was born in Kirrensark-wark, and blue eyebrows vanished.

The leggings Jilain wore, fawn-hide and hardly stained, were old but little worn. They had belonged to a firstman's dead son named Kirrensarkson Kirrenar. They fit, nearly, though it was not easy for that archer-warrior to sit. Leather, Kirrensark assured her grinning, would stretch. And he added, "Blight the fact!"

She was warrior and hero and combat-companion, but she did not participate in the license. None dared touch her save Jarik and Kirrensark—who touched her in the way of a father. And Jarik of the Black Sword lay neither with Iklatne daughter of Lirushye and Kirrensark, nor with Jilain called Demonslayer of Kerosyr, though both wanted him sorely. Indeed, he was careful to avoid such possibility by taking pains to become thoroughly, disgustingly drunk.

# Nine

*"A white-bearded man with an unlined face and eyes like water in a stone basin sworded open Thanamee's swollen belly so that he took two lives at once."*

—*from* The Iron Lords

Kirrensark's cousin Ahl was ambitious, and not content with his own holdings. He had kept his bargain with the Lady of the Snowmist because he dared not do otherwise: Ahl had kept to his own lesser domain and made no attempt on Kirrensark-wark in the absence of its firstman. He had also kept a spy high in those bad eastward hills. That man set off for Ahl-wark the moment *Seadancer* put in to shore and the gladsome clamor rose in the wark of Kirrensark. Now the firstman was home, and the bargain was at an end, terminated by its own terms. Just after dawn of the morning of *Seadancer*'s return, Ahl made attack, with nearly all the men of Ahl-wark.

Kirrensark's people were worse than unprepared. Men were swollen of tongue and head from ale and sex, and many were hardly rested from lengthy engaging in the latter. In seconds all three sentries and the two women with them were dead in their blood. Thus it was roosters and dogs that gave the alarm, and a shrieking woman who had gone to privy. She died too, and it was horror and injustice that wounded Handeth became a widower on his first day home.

Jarik, though his head was thick and exerting inward pressure on its caging skull, was up. No miracle was involved. Some of the gallon or two of beer he had downed wanted out. His mighty bellowing shout was soon joined by others.

"Attack! To arms! Attack! We're attacked!"

Soon men were bustling forth, with or without armor, but at least helmeted, armed, and bearing shields of wood bossed with bronze or iron.

Still, it was impossible that in their state they could successfully defend and prevail, even against men whose leader had foolishly marched them nearly all the night. What was needed in Kirrensark-wark was a miracle. Or great heroes.

The attackers gave up all stealth when their prey came boiling forth to meet them. They came running and bounding in among the very buildings of the wark, men in leathern armor flashing with bosses of iron or bronze, and a bare few in chain- or scalecoats. The hair streaming from under their helmets and behind ranged from white to tawny and no darker, and the noise they made was horrendous clamor.

Always there must be a fastest runner and thus a first. The first among those of Ahl-wark fell to an arrow that was striped in a spiral wise. One man tripped over him while others pounded past and over. Five bounding paces the second man took in his strapped buskins and brightly glinting coat of scales sewn laboriously onto leather, and an identical arrow dropped aslant into his forehead, and burst within. The others ran on to the attack. Axes whooshed up and down and sharpened iron blades banged and clanged on bucklers and on iron and leather with fearful noise. A bit of bronze boss flew from a sundered coat of leather, and the first defender fell without a cry. And another. And another, while two more attackers fell to arrows from the bow of her whom Kirrensark had last night heartily announced, again and again, as his warrior daughter-son. Her name was not Iklatne. In Kirrensark-wark, Jilain had found immediate employment of her skills.

The roaring shout was hideous and bull-like as Delath burst from his home. In his hands an ax; on him neither armor nor shield. His pale eyes glared like sunlit ice and his pale, pale beard writhed with his snarls and roars. Whether he saw any man that day, as a man, was never known. Yet he slew or maimed more than a half-score of Ahl-wark, and received only two cuts the while. There was no dealing with a man without sense enough to know fear and have care for himself. He was *morbrin*; the machine-that-fights, and the machine was for killing. Bucklers were cracked and sundered under his flailing ax and men spun away in horror and pain with shield-arms wrenched or broken, and they were the lucky ones. Once Coon saw the mad Delath's ax rip open the two thighs of one man and continue that same stroke into the side of another to bowl him over with a huge wound gaping in him, and all in one sweep of Delath's arms. Coon had seen it. Coon told of it for years thereafter.

Darkness came on eyes grey and blue that day and ruddy lips turned the color of eyes. Sharpened iron shattered shields and flesh and bone while Kirrensark-wark became a chaotic jumble of hacking axes and swords whose clangor filled the air to the skies and hurt the ears. Like a madman plunging blindly, in the grip of his battle-rage that was a demon within him, Delath plied his dripping ax that split shields and skin and skulls. All about him others hewed and shielded in more normal ways. Combatants slipped in gore and wallowed among the dead to rise dripping and hideous even when unscathed. Battle cries and the clamor of dread chopping reverberated from the surrounding slopes and the wark ran red with blood.

Some few women of Kirrensark-wark fought, but she who was newcomer among them was no less warrior than any other warrior, save only the two who fought morbrin.

Five stout men were later found with her painted arrows in them, and she was seen to slay two others at least. Her skill was great and her swiftness hardly believable. Loose on her was the short-sleeved mailcoat of dead Shranshule, while her leather leggings had belonged to a dead son of the firstman Kirrensark. The horn plaques on her Kerosyran helmet of leather gleamed brighter than iron. Her first sword came from a slain man of Kirrensark-wark that day, and it broke, and her second came from a wounded man of Ahl-wark. Like a great spring released, she bounded with it into combat, fighting with strangers, alongside strangers, against strangers.

A lean grey sword came seeking Kirrensark's life and he smashed the hand that wielded it to leave that man unslain while his whistling ax clove a buckler to lodge in a shoulder. Tole's point sprang out between a man's shoulder blades so that Tole had to set a foot against a standing corpse to free his sword for the dealing of more woundy blows. The sword had served Tole's father and it served Tole. After that day there was little left to sharpen. But by then swords lay about for the taking.

Delath raged through the attackers like a mad bull goring wolves, so that men fled his coming, else he would certainly have slain more. His ax was a blur that dealt maiming wounds and death. It hummed in the air, that ax, and its wake was marked by scarlet droplets. The very air about him seemed to form a shield. Men feared him and fell back. Some even turned and ran, to face and hew at normal opponents.

Delath was not nigh when Ahl's son Barakat Cloudlocks sore wounded Kirrensark—and lost first hand and then intestines to a leather-mailed woman in a strange helmet.

This Ahl did not see, for he was busy backing from a ravening maniac in a coat of dark, dark chain. This one moved with the dynamic speed of a wolf both famished and angered, and his blue eyes no less glittery than those paler ones of Delath. This was the second morbriner unleashed that day to halve the male population of Ahl-wark. His sword was black and nothing stopped it. It came upon Ahl in a whistling storm of fury and the unnatural sword sheared through his wrist as though it had been mere birdflesh. The hand flew, a ghastly bronzed spider trailing scarlet.

As he had afore, Jarik forgot all save strength and horrible skill. His brain was of no use to him and he did not use it. In the grip of the kill-machine rage that day he and the Black Sword clove shields and arms, swordblades and hands, bowels and legs, helmets and skulls. Once four men surged at him in a great wave of lifted shields and whistling axes and swordblades. When one was dead and another dying and a third staring at a thigh and knee that would never again support him, the fourth blanched and backed and then fled.

The glitter of bright scarlet ran freely, like oil from his

weapon's strange blade while Jarik forged on. Even as he fought to wrench it free of an attacker cleft from navel to thigh, Jarik's left arm straightened in a rush. As if weightless his shield shot out at the warrior coming at him from the side. It slammed into that man's buckler with staggering force. Jarik's left foot kicked him neatly up under the skirt of his mailcoat of scales and the wight fell puking. He was lucky; had he not fallen he must surely have died to the morbrin-fighter. That dance of Jarik Blacksword, while he fought simultaneously with both hands and one foot, was not ludicrous.

Men slipped in blood; men stumbled over fallen men. Here and there a helmet or ax lay forlornly. Several feet from any corpse, an ax lay with its haft still clutched by the hand that had wielded it.

Ahl had become Ahl One-hand in this attack on his one-armed cousin, and he became prisoner and hostage while his wark's survivors fled. Behind lay more friends and kinsmen than fled, and only a few were able to groan. Even the sky had gone gloomy.

To save Kurensark-wark was needed a miracle or heroes; what saved it was a miracle of heroes.

Delath fell down gasping and panting. He was wet and running with sweat and the blood of others. He was hauled to his feet by a younger man whose hair was like wheat in summer and whose sword was black. They stood panting and gasping, with the blood of others all over them and in Delath's ash-blond beard. Neither was able to talk. They stood and dripped, striving for breath while their eyes glared ferociously about in quest of more foemen to be slain. Sweat ran from them and darkened their clothing. Their arms and legs quivered and their chests heaved.

To them came that warrior that was a woman, with a sword dripping in her hand. There the three stood, with arms about one another. They made a fine picture of comrades in triumph; truth was all were so weary and breathless that they were holding one another up. Others among the successful defenders waded in gore while stepping across shields and corpses. They knew what they owed these three. Half those who had fallen had fallen to Jilain and Jarik and Delath, for they were warriors three and maniacs two. They were treated with awe and respect that must soon become high camaraderie. After the glare faded from those two morbriners' eyes. . . .

As, staggering, they shifted to take Jilain between them, Jarik leaned out to look across her. "Delath! Hail, warrior. I am your brother, warrior."

Very solemnly Delath looked across Jilain to Jarik to say, "Hail, warrior. I am your brother, warrior."

"This one is your sister, warriors!" Jilain said between them, and they laughed in delight and companionship—and soon broke off, for they had need of their breath.

"Ah, Delath," a man enthused, who had only three teeth visible even when he smiled. "You've not been so magnificent since that day the insanity come on us all asea, and we raided them farmers over on Akkharia's shore!"

Jarik stared at the chesty, gutty man, whose name was Treth Alemaker. When Jarik turned his face slowly to Delath, Delath was looking soberly at him. Still they held each onto an opposite shoulder of Jilain, their sweat-slick arms crossed on her back. Jarik looked again to Treth Alemaker.

"What great battle is that which I missed, brewer?" he asked heartily, pushing the heartiness; ingenuous as only one so fair and so young could be—and so accustomed to dissembling.

Delath also tried to be casual. "No war tales now, Treth!"

"Oh, we was all Possessed that time," Alemaker said, delighted at Jarik's prompting. "Almost a score of years gone, it was. Over the water we went, ahawkin', and we come to this cliff of land like a white wall standing up outen the sea. We clumb it—"

Jarik was certain now that the man spoke of Tomashten, his Oceanside, where he had been Orrikson Jarik and happy until That Day. The day *It Happened*, as he had thought of it for over a decade. The day the man Jarik then thought was named Kiddensok or Kiddensahk led his "Possessed" men there, to kill and kill and rape and kill and burn. To end Jarik's life, and begin it.

"We didn't even know what we was doing until we'd come back home here. Oh, Milady Snowmist come down off the mountain *that* day, and She give us a tongue-lashing we none of us has ever forgot!"

And Jarik thought: *Snowmist disapproved, then. She did not order it.*

"Treth . . ." Delath began.

"Jarik—you're hurting this one's shoulder . . ."

"Ah, and you was the one, Delath! Look at you now; you three's saved the wark this day! But *that* day—! You was just plain gone mad, Delath. I remember how once you even slit open that young woman all fat with child! We all—"

Delath let go Jilain's shoulder. Slid his arm from under Jarik's. Strode forward. He knocked Treth Alemaker down and kept walking, threading a path among corpses and weeping women and past shields and helms and axes and wounded men. He walked to where Kirrensark's women hovered over the firstman.

Strangely blank-eyed, Jarik stared after him. Then he turned away to walk in the opposite direction, as if aimless. Away from the wark.

*slit open that young woman all fat with child*

Aye, Jarik thought. Aye. And her name was Thanamee Orrikswife, and the child would have been called Oak. Was no white-haired man I saw murder them both at once, Thanamee and Oak! Was one with hair of such blondness that it seems white and is, in summer. And he killed her, with the morbrin rage on him. Killed Oak within her, who would have been brother to Orrikson Jarik. Delath did that!

*I am your brother, warrior.*

"Jarik?"

He did not turn at the sound of Jilain's voice. All these years he had lived for revenge. Existed for, fed on the thought of vengeance. At last, only a month ago with the help of gods, he had found him who led the attack. He found a one-armed man, now wounded anew—whose life Jarik had saved. *Then* he had learned his name: Kirrensark/Kiddensok. Kirrensark would not tell Jarik the name of the man who had killed the child-swollen woman in Akkharia. And now he had found the monster himself. He had found him who slew Jarik's stepmother and the brother that would have been. Because of the careless mouth of Treth, seeking kinship with hero-warriors, Jarik had found the killer. And he was Jarik's fellow hero and now combat-companion and war-brother, whose life he had saved. Oh ye gods, why are things this way? Oh ye weavers, what twisty skeins ye weave!

*I am your brother, warrior.*

Hero of Kirrensark-wark, Jarik Blacksword! Savior of the wark of murderers, the murderers of his family and life; Jarik Blacksword! And he could not have his vengeance, for he could not slay either of those men. That was what he had dreamed of and lived for! Jarik paced, and the savor of this day's triumph had become the taste of dirt in the mouth of Jarik Blacksword.

# Ten

*Evil is not a foreign body which some clever surgeon of morals can neatly excise; it is a part of ourselves which we have to learn to live with. Grief is not a poison we can vomit out of the system; it is an ingredient in human experience which we have to assimilate. We can accept all this, and still be in love with life, which we cannot really be if we merely repudiate the darker side of it.*

—Robert Donington,
writing of Siegfried

Jarik walked away from the bodies and moans and wails, away from the odor of bowels and bladders voided at the instant of death. He was wrapped in himself as in a dark, dark cloak and yet he was cold, cold. He did not fall down or stumble, nor did Oak come. Nor did Jarik depart his body to see future or past while trying to escape the present. He was Jarik; Strodeson Jarik and before that Orrikson Jarik and before that . . . Someone's son Jarik. He was Jarik, alone though Jilain stood staring after him with empathy and pity and yes, longing in her eyes. In his eyes was pain. And he walked, for it was all he could do, and in a way Jarik coped.

In a way, Jarik always coped. His mind writhed and twisted and warped, but he coped and endured. He continued to function, and to try.

He was a young man whose looks, whose physique and

prowess others envied. He was a hero. Surely he did not deserve this lot that was his, the constant night-sent misery. He walked, without looking back. It was in him, toying with him and tugging at him, to keep walking. Away from this wark. Away from Delath and Kirrensark. Away from Jilain. Away from Her. Away. Into the sea, perhaps. With him in sword and mail, the sea should soon solve all his agonies. Away. Into the mountains, perhaps, in quest of a bear stronger than he.

It was his life he wanted to walk away from. Jarik wanted to walk away from Jarik.

He could not. He did not. He walked for a very long time, and then he turned. Jarik returned to the wark to receive glances both confused and anxious from Jilain. Too, he returned to discover that he had missed the great happening. *She* had come; Her.

Powder and some strange adhering coating She had sprinkled on the stumps of the four maimed but living men, including Ahl. Him She had taken time to tell, in her clear silver voice, that he was without honor and lucky to escape with his life. Kirrensark she had lifted up with little effort, while his blood dripped down.

"I shall soon return," She had said, and She had . . . vanished.

Jarik did not even ask about that. Yes, he believed. He had seen gods and talked with gods. Four, in all. He knew that gods vanished, in their traveling; he had vanished with them. Now Kirrensark had. Jarik believed without difficulty that She, in her silver armor and helm-mask, had picked up Kirrensark, even big Kirrensark. And Jarik believed that She had indeed disappeared, all in an instant. He had seen it afore.

He was, however, unconditionally sorry to have missed Her this time. The bracers flashed on his wrists. His blade seemed to itch and quiver at his hip. It was clean, and black. Blood ran from the Black Sword the way oil ran off ice.

"Jarik?"

It was Jilain. Her voice and tone had gone all girlish. He looked at her, and felt a boy. He wanted to embrace her, to hold her and be held by her. All about them others were doing things about blood and bodies, dead and alive. All about them people wept and moaned, or kept touching or hugging as if to be sure they were alive and unharmed. Jilain looked as if she wanted to hug and be held by him. Jarik wished she would, so that he could do that without having to do it; without having to initiate it. He wanted to hold and be held. Few needed it more. Suppose though that he was wrong about her, and she did not? Suppose he did or tried, and she stiffened or pushed him away or both? Why was such a mighty warrior so cursed; why was he so unsure of himself?

He looked at her. It was at once good and terrible, that his eyes could see across the ten hundred hundred miles between them.

She came two paces toward him. She stopped. She stared into the cerulean brilliance of his eyes.

"Oak's eyes are so different," Jilain said. "Oh one knows that Oak is you and you are Oak. But *his* eyes . . . they are somehow opaque and reflective, like the sea. One sees . . . one sees *you* in your eyes, Jarik."

He thought that she had said that before. Had she? Was it a memory or a false memory? Was he now having trouble distinguishing between his real memories and those of his visions? (Or were they real? Suppose . . . suppose that all this, all his life, was just a vision, and that only the visions were real?) He was sure that she had once called him "Jarish."

She said, "It was Delat', then." It was not quite a question. "Kirrensark led them, and Delat' killed your mother. The one you called mother. And that Oak that would have been."

He nodded. His face bore the expression of a lich, one of those legendary but unseen walking dead.

"Oh Jarik."

He was not able to do anything other than nod again, and look miserable.

"Oh Jarik."

Her voice was smaller. She looked as if she wanted to hold him and be held. Once again Jarik was reminded that it was hard, being Jarik. It had not occurred to him that it was hard, too, being Jilain.

He made no move. Across twelve feet, they stood and longed.

His arm had begun to sting. He explored and found a cut, and crusted blood, surrounded by a bruise. Jilain insisted that it must be tended. Thus he was touched by her, at least. He was glad for his little wound.

She came.

This time many saw Her coming. The strange pearl-white mist that wafted liquidly down the mountain called Cloudpeak and across the plain, like the thinnest of foggy milk flowing to the wark. It moved toward Jarik of the Black Sword, that eerie mist of liquefied pearls. It came to pause twelve paces from him, the distance he and Jilain had stood apart while being so far. There it swirled milkily until it coalesced and rose up, and in it She appeared.

Long before he had seen Her, Jarik thought that he had seen Her, in that vision the day *It Happened*. He had been eight, then. And She had come to him thus the day after he had arrived here in Kirrensark-wark, just over a month ago.

All in refulgent silver and white and soft grey She was, in her form-clinging armor that was like fabric or the skin of some serpent created of sorcery. Excellent of female form She was, a vision beautiful and nigh blinding in the bright sun of day. On each of her wrists, over the silver-grey armor, a silver bracer flashed. They were identical to those bracers that encased his forearms. The hilt of her sheathed sword, too, was silver, and its pommel was a strange gemstone that was colorless and nearly transparent, and yet faceted so that her slightest movment set it all alight and aglint with many hues.

This was the god on the earth.

She stood before Jarik and gazed upon Jarik. So he must assume, although nothing of eye or flesh showed on Her. Her helm was a low dome that seemed to sprout white wings. To it was attached her mask. All her face was covered by frosty, sparkly silver as if it were coated in snow frosted by a freezing rain. High-arched brows were part of the mask, but there were no eye-slits. He knew full well that She saw just the same. Also a part of the mask was a mouth that was shaped to seeming softness, rather than the ugly slits in the blue-black helm-masks of the Iron Lords. Those metal-wrought mouths were like wounds.

With Her, She brought Kirrensark One-arm who had been Kirrensark Long-haft.

He was hale and smiling. He and his wife Lirushye and then his daughter Iklatne hugged and wept and hugged, for he was cured and healed. A miracle, of the God on the Earth. Eyes worshiped Her, then and there among them. A living god who worked miracles among her people although not quite among them, and religion was aborning on the earth. The god had worked a miracle and all knew it. She had no face, but no one minded.

While Lirushye clung to him, Kirrensark threw up his arm; the stump of the other She had not replaced. "The god would talk with Jarik Blacksword," he called. "Leave them."

People faded reluctantly away, without looking away. She paced toward Jarik. Three and four and five steps, with the fluid sinuousness of a cat—or a serpent in flashing scales. Or one of the Guardians, he mused, and Jarik wondered.

"Jarik."

He looked at Her. He stood stiffly, and looked at an eyeless mask. He nodded. It was his name; it was all the acknowledgment he would give Her.

"The hero Jarik," the Lady of the Snowmist said.

"The god who works miracles," Jarik said. "Milady of the Snowmist." He paused only briefly before continuing in a clear, loud voice.

"I came here from a place called Harnstarl. Across the mountains yonder—the impassable Dragonmount. Harnstarl is under the protection of the Iron Lords who are gods on the earth. In Harnstarl is a sword, a god-Sword of the god-metal. When Harnstarl is threatened, the Iron Lords know of it by that Sword of magic, and they come to aid their people. The gods themselves. Thus those other gods afford protection to those who look to them as gods and protectors. Today in Kirrensark-wark many were hurt and some were slain. Widows are here, O god on the earth, with the scent of their men's blood in their nostrils. Mothers grieve their sons slain this day by invaders. *Is* this wark under the protection of the Lady of the Snowmist, the god who lives just above it? Is She less powerful than the Iron Lords, who asea slew her dove?"

Silence cramped all about him. Close and heavy it was,

and dark as rumor. People looked, stared, and held their breaths. Jarik had challenged the God on the Earth! Surely even for such a hero there was such a thing as being too independent, too brave, too daring! (*Has he great prowess and courage but no sense?*) And yet—those people of Kirrensark-wark now wondered, too, and they listened for the reply of Her.

More than one among their number expected to see this newcomer Jarik die then, and they wondered. He was mighty warrior and healer as well—and outlander. She was god. She had restored the firstman. Still, it was this Jarik—with Delath and that strange short-haired legging-clad *warrior*-woman from oversea—who had surely saved them all this day.

They watched; they waited.

Would She accept such a challenge? Would She even suffer it, countenance it? Would he die now, while they looked on? No one of Kirrensark-wark had ever seen Her kill. He had made such a challenge that either She—the god, the very god!—must accept and lose face in swallowing his undigestible words; or he must lose . . . more.

Mildly the mask said, "As all can see I have no face to lose." But no one laughed. And She said, just as mildly, "Did you fetch the White Rod of Osyr that was your mission for me, Jarik of the Black Sword?"

The voice rang, rang like silver. Like molten silver it flowed from within the helm-mask of Her.

Jarik was astonished! Jarik had forgot! "Yes!"

And he turned—turned from the god!—and went into the guesting-house next that of the firstman, where he had nighted. He returned with the short ivory staff that really did not seem so much; who, after all, could compare White Rod and Black Sword?

She stretched forth a hand gloved in scintillant fabric-imitating mail, and he had no choice. He bore the wand to her. Jarik *walked*, all noticed. Jarik did not run, even for the god. Did not even hurry. She took that wand of ivory, taken from an obsidian statue. She paced cat-like to Kirrensark's greathouse, and her armor did not chime, but rustled. With a swift gesture She drove the White Rod of Osyr into a niche between logs from which the chink had fallen.

She turned, and that voice of liquid silver flowed out to every ear.

"This is the sign of my protection. Leave it here always. It will tell me when danger threatens the community of Kirrensark, and I will come." And She turned to Jarik, and many, smiling, would have taken vow that She too smiled then. For She said, "You succeeded, Jarik of the Black Sword. You are indeed my champion!"

Jarik shocked them all again: "Unwillingly so," he said.

Grimly, he held out his arms, fists upturned and clenched, displaying his silver-banded wrists.

Snowmist said, "And never was I obliged to give you pain."

He knew that was not so, and assumed that She did. Or did the Bands of Snowmist do what they did of themselves, unto themselves, once they were in place? Who could be sure of the ways of gods and their creations? Since She had said that, however, he responded accordingly, as if he had not rebelled that day on the way to Osyr's Isle, and received the immediate physical agony of the bracers.

"I am a fool, my Lady," he said just as tight of lip, "but not an idiot. I do not place my hand twice in the fire."

She gazed at him. Sadly? Fondly? White-lipped with anger? Who could know, with Her in the mask, and eyeless? "Ah, but Jarik—you do." And She stretched forth a slim, gloved hand to him She called, not satirically but definitely with some hypocrisy, her champion.

Jarik held fast. "The bracers, Lady."

All of the people of the wark, young and old, wounded and unscathed, stared at Jarik. They saw a morbriner maniac in battle; sometimes a healer after; and one who challenged even Her, the god on the earth. They waited, hardly daring to draw breath lest they miss something. His instantaneous destruction for challenging Her, for instance.

That did not happen. While they watched, while Jarik watched, a mist shimmered into being around his extended arms. His arms quivered while he watched, and the hair twitched at the back of his neck. He felt a *frisson*, and he was not alone in that little skin-crawling shiver. Yet he felt little else. Only a coolness, as the Bands of Snowmist truly *became* mist. Wraith-like they trickled from his arms; trickled away. It was as if those bands of silver, or god-metal—

or mist?—had never been there. And yet they had. Jarik saw the evidence as he gazed at his forearms, turning them. They were not so tan as the backs of his hands and upper forearms, for on the sea he had not always worn his mailcoat and there had been much direct sunlight and no shade.

He looked at Her, and he blinked. Perhaps he was surprised to be freed.

"You kept your bargain with me, Jarik of the Black Sword. I have kept mine with you. I bade you return to me the White Rod of Osyr, and I would free you of the Bands of Snowmist. Now I would have you come with me." Again She extended a gloved hand to him, and surely within her mask She smiled. "And now proud Jarik who dares challenge even a god, will you come?"

Jarik's teeth teased his lip for a moment. "My . . . Lady," he said, and none could miss that his voice and stance had changed, were far less forceful and truculent. "I will come, Lady, for yourself promised agreement. I would ask a twofold boon, though, and give up all else if yourself agrees."

"Ah," she said, hardly missing his shift to the respectful pronoun. "Something of great importance, then. State it."

His eyes glanced toward one among those who watched, and back to Snowmist. "I would ask that Jilain Kerosyris go with us to Cloudpeak, to your keep."

The helmet nodded. "Jilain of Osyr's Isle. Agreed, Jarik, and you need give up nothing. I concur."

The hand extended. Jarik took it, and was reminded that the silver glove *was* metallic, though it was somehow cloth as well, and that it was cold. And then he staggered. Twice before had he made this transition, his hand in a god's, and this time it was a no less dizzying experience.

Upon his taking the mailed hand of Her, he knew a sudden tingling and darkness, split and shot fierily through by pinwheels behind his eyes. At the same instant he knew a great rushing and a sensation of nausea while his internal organs seemed to part and to float—as they did—while he . . . flew. Instantly. In the body, not as with the Guide, while his body remained behind. He flew; all of him. And they were there, and he was jarred so that he staggered when his feet again felt solid matter beneath them.

Now he knew that he was high, high up in the mountain that speared up above Kirrensark-wark, and inside it. In the keep of the Lady of the Snowmist. Recovering, he looked at Her. The helm-mask nodded, and then She was not there. She did not trickle away, in the manner of the bracers; She merely was there, and then She was not there.

Jarik had time only to glance about at surroundings he remembered and yet that remained an impossibility within the mountain's upper reaches; marvelous and magnificent.

Then She was back, and with Her was Jilain. Jilain was pale and as she alit, stumbling, her mouth dropped open. She found her footing and, after only a glance at the god and at Jarik, Jilain looked around her.

The soft light came from everywhere, without a single bright source. A pearly glow with the merest tinge of blue. Jilain looked about, turning slowly. The columns that rose from floor to ceiling of this great cavern were crafted to resemble trees, complete with bark and high-set branches. Shrubs and flowers seemed to grow from a carpet of grassy green, piled deep in an uncropped meadow. Uncropped, untrodden by grazing animals, unmanured. Every wall was painted with murals, from floor to ceiling. The scenes continued the illusion of a broad pastoral landscape outside, rather than the constricted space within the hollowed interior of a mountain near its peak. Deer seemed to graze amid a sprawling meadow dotted with wildflowers. On it trees and shrubs rose, and it rolled out and out to a distant mountain done in pinks and blues shading into that reddish-blue for which Jarik had no name, with white on top. The Lady of the Snowmist had contrived to bring the countryside into the mountain—and to strew it, too, with chairs and couches and many cushions of many hues, which were in gentle pastel shades. Summer shades, of the earth and sky. And the chamber sprawled large enough to support and continue the effect, yet not so vast as to create awe.

Karahshisar, the Lady of the Snowmist, lived within a mountaintop and surrounded herself not with raw cold stone but with beauty. She lived in beauty.

When her whereabouts had been explained to Jilain, she looked round about still again, and this time she murmured. Aloud she wondered about the godhead of Osyr,

who had no such magnificence about him. Snowmist said
nothing. She did take Jarik's hand again, and almost he
drew it away.

For a moment Lady Karahshisar was still, looking from
one of them to the other, with a hand of each in one of hers.
Then She nodded, and surely within her mask of iced snow
She smiled. She released them.

Jarik Blacksword looked then at Jilain of Kerosyr, and
knew that he loved her. And when she gazed on him the
same look was in her tawny eyes.

Settled on a chair-for-three Jarik had learned was a
couch, they acceded to her wish to hear it all. They told
Her the story, all of it.

Of the voyage to the Isle of Osyr the dead god statu-
esquely represented in black, and of Jarik's slaying the sorcerous guarding reptile in the temple.

Of his freeing her called the Pythoness, and the loveli-
ness of her, and the pitiful ugliness of her life, sewn shut
and chained as Osyr's bride.

Of his capture and confrontation with the Osyrrain, ruler
of those manless women, and of his beating and the murder
of the Pythoness by her own folk, her own enslavers, and of
Jarik's breaking then, and seizing the Osyrrain.

Of his long battle with Jilain they told, who had been
queen's champion of Kerosyr; first among the Guardians
of Osyr. Of the Osyrrain's treachery then, and then again
next day, and her death and Jilain's joining Jarik. Not
*Seadancer*; not the men; it was Jarik she joined.

Snowmist looked upon the scar each had put upon the
forehead of the other, and She knew the scars would last all
their lives. Already the scab had left Jarik's, to leave a visible Jin the pink of new under-skin.

And they told Her of the homeward voyage.

Aye, She affirmed that both the gull and the dove had
been her Sendings, to guide them. And yes, the hawk had
of course been sent by the Iron Lords, who obviously had
also dispatched the hawk-ship to intercept and stop them.
To slay them all, and prevent their reaching Kirrensark-
wark, and Cloudpeak.

"The Iron Lords also wanted the White Rod?" Jarik
asked.

Snowmist made a gesture. "Perhaps. More importantly,

they did not want me to have it."

It seemed to Jarik that nervousness came over Her then. A sort of apprehension came over the god. Was it—could it be fearfulness? A *god*?

"Jarik," the Lady of the Snowmist said. "The hawk-ship was not of Blackiron?"

"No! I saw those men, and I knew no one on that ship. Those of Blackiron are not warriors, either. Weapon-men crowded that ship sent for us." *Me! The Iron Lords tried to kill me*!?

"Then, Jarik . . . perhaps now you perceive that the Lords of Iron are not so pitifully pent up within their mountain and that little area beyond Dragonmount as they led you to believe."

He nodded, and thought: *And perhaps* they *did not send that ship at all*! But he said nothing. As was all too usual, there was too much, and the stories conflicted and presented the potential of lying gods.

At last, when She knew that he was going to make no comment, the god spoke. "And so now I have the White Rod of Osyr, which was wasted on Kerosyr but will serve the wark below: my people. And you Jarik have a woman—a woman indeed!—and the world has Jilain, who also was wasted there. And you Jilain have a man . . . although he remains not your mate, not even for a night."

"And so we shall remain," Jarik said stiffly, knowing that Jilain was looking at him. "She must be put from me, Lady Karahshisar. It is the second of the boons I would ask, both for her: That she be given knowledge, knowledge to survive and flourish, off Kerosyr. And then that she be put far from me."

"No!" Jilain burst forth, but Jarik would not look at her.

"And why do you ask this strange thing, Jarik?"

"Yourself must know, Lady, who seems to know more than possible of us. It is for her sake that she must be far from me."

"No! I will not go! You love me as much as I do you, Jarik—I saw it in your eyes and face and mouth and in your whole body!"

"Jarik, Jarik," the mask said. "There is no such bane on you as you believe. There is no bane on you that those you love or who love you must die, Jarik! It has but *happened*,

Jarik. True, yours has been no life of ease and will doubtless be no life of ease or merchant dealings—stop; do not interrupt!—nor will Jilain's life be one of distaff tending and cookery. Believe, Jarik. There is no death-bane on you or on Jilain, nor on any you love or who love you. Believe it!"

Jarik swallowed, and his eyes pleaded, begged that it be so. At the same time he began a pleading gesture that She tell him no lies to Jilain's peril.

A mailed hand rose to bid him hold his words. "Consider what has transpired. Each of you wears the other's mark, there above the eyes and between them. A strange betrothal exchange—but there it is! You have fought each other, and you have fought side by side. Together, you two broke the attack at sea, and destroyed the Iron Hawk of Destruction. No such bane exists as you imagine—already you two are as one!"

Jarik said, "Dare tell her that greater grief will not come on her in this life, because of me. It is already so!"

"Dare tell this one she cannot think and talk for herself!"

It was Jarik whom Snowmist answered, with heat. "I dare, you who challenges gods! Oh the magnificence of you mortal men; what your kind can have and be if *They* do not have their way! Jilain was not happy on Kerosyr! Is that not obvious? Can you not see or do you refuse to see because you refuse to look, you who challenges gods? She was also wasted there. With means I have I saw into the mind of Jarik. I saw a Man Who Was Two—and I knew that completion awaited that anomaly, on Kerosyr. You two complete *each other*! This is beauty, not ugliness or some thing of fear. It is done, Jarik. How can you resist your own feelings? How can you resist one who returns your love? You feel it within you, and it *shows*, Jarik Blacksword!"

"Because she cannot know happiness with me!"

Before the god could reply, Jilain spoke. "Some grief is coming upon this one now, Lady. There is hunger on this one. We were forced up and out early this morn, and foukht hard, all without breaking the fast of the nikht. And then you came, O God, and the fast is still unbroken."

"Ah," the mask said: "Yes. So. Then you shall eat. First, go and bathe and trade me those bloody clothes of war for those I shall provide. Food will be brought you. I shall call Metanira."

Jarik did not move. "Lady!" And when he knew She was looking at him even though he could see no eyes: "Why was I sent to the Isle of Osyr?"

"Why, for the White Rod, Jarik. And . . . in a way . . . so that you would meet and unite with Jilain."

"Then—does Yourself know all? What is in our minds, and what is in our futures as well?"

"Why Jarik . . . have you not seen into the future, your future?"

"I have . . . seen some—some things that happened, and some that did not, Lady. And that is not what I asked."

"When too much is asked, Jarik of the Black Sword, the answer will never satisfy because it will always be too little." The mask did not turn from him as She called her servant: "Metanira!"

# Eleven

*The waters of trust run as deep as the river of fear
through the dark caverns in the bone.*

—Marge Piercy

Jarik remembered Metanira. She and another came at once, even while he remembered that on his previous visit here the great chamber had been filled with attractive women and girls, all in pastel-hued gowns or tunics and all aflash with gems and silver. And now here was Metanira once more, while once more he still lacked answers. She he assumed was in her twenties was draped in a clinging sleeveless gown of palest shadeflower blue. Its skirt flowed all down her hips and legs to the floor as if it were a fabric woven of liquid sky. With her was that child he had seen here previously. A girl-child of a half-score years or fewer. Her eyes were the pale blue of his own and her hair nigh white, like Delath's.

Metanira smiled. The child did not.

Jarik was both tired and hungry. Yet he had also been cut off, and he was not serene of face as he rose. He and Jilain followed Metanira to that room that was beyond the dream of any wark-dweller in its luxury, and that yet was not *soft*. An exclamation sprang from Jilain's lips when she entered and saw the chamber.

His buskined feet on a carpet the hue of sheepgrass in June, Jarik glanced back. The girl was gone.

"I well remember how that coat of armor is removed, warrior," Metanira said, smiling. "Will you show me again?"

Jilain glanced rather sharply at Jarik, who was careful not to notice or to look at her. He removed weapons belt and then the warcoat, while Metanira watched. Jilain did not, but looked away. A seamless coat of multiply-interlinked chain was too heavy for normal drawing off over the head, and Jilain did not care for the sight of her man with his head low and his rump in the air while he wriggled, clinking, out of his mail.

When she looked his way again he was straightening, jerking his head to toss mussed hair away from his lean, rather bony face. His mail formed a gleaming little pile of black metal on the floor. It did not look big enough, now, to cover his broad-shouldered torso, however lean of hip and small of backside he was.

Rather than look at Jilain, Jarik removed his padded undercoat. A glance showed him the earthenware amphora he remembered, beautifully decorated in red and amber, orange and vermillion. He remembered the goblets of sweet yellowish-white wine he had been handed from it, on his previous visit to Snowmist Keep.

"Will you remove your leathern coat?" Metanira asked, of Jilain. Her voice seemed oddly . . . dull. She was almost startlingly blue of eye, with a deeply dimpled chin and fascinating hair, all wavy like spun, crinkled copper. Her expression was serene. *Stupid*, Jilain thought.

She looked at this one called "Metaneerah" with the smallest frown, shot a glance at Jarik—who was peering into that colorful jug—and nodded, slowly. All this was more than disconcerting. Jilain had hardly expected the "real world" Jarik and Kirrensark had spoken of to encompass so swiftly the fabulous keep of a living, talking god! Now Jarik was playing stranger again. She understood—in a way, or tried—but that did not help her. Pulling up the hem of her bronze-studded mailcoat of leather, she drew it up over her head.

*That* was a relief!

Under it she still wore the tunic given her last night, Lirushye Kirrensarkwife's ill-fitting one. It was well sweated, patchily dark here and there. So was the snugger one

Jarik wore, and she saw that his was still damp in places. Not ones to insist on much comfort, Jilain had noted of these off-Kerosyr people.

"Jarik," she said, and at last he looked at her. Her eyes swerved toward Metanira; returned their gaze to the man. "This one is in a very very strange place and is very uncomfortable, Jarik."

He nodded and started toward her. He stopped, in an obvious checking of natural impulse. She saw, and managed not to show him her disappointment and exasperation.

Jarik nodded. "I have been here but once, Jilain."

"And that one watched you remove clothing?"

"My name is Metanira," she said helpfully.

"No," Jarik said. "They watched me take off my mailcoat, for it fascinated them. Then they prepared a bath and told me they were to bathe me. I told them I would see to that myself. They said they would wait—and reminded me that She would be waiting, and they left. Then I undressed and washed. This time I shall wait while you enjoy their way of bathing. Perhaps you would like Metanira to help you."

Before Jilain could respond, Jarik spoke to Metanira. "Metaneerah, we will not bathe together. I will wait, or wash elsewhere." For Jarik had no wish to tell Jilain that on that other occasion both Metanira and another had returned to dry him, and that his body had reacted, to his embarrassment.

That servant of Snowmist looked at him as if struggling for comprehension. At last she nodded. "Yes. I shall draw your bath," she said to Jilain.

"But—" The woman of the island was ready to wring her hands, and it showed.

Jarik could not bear that she was so afflicted with confusion and frustration. He was not being cold; he was still uncertain and fearful of himself, for her. He wanted her, and so did not trust himself to see her naked, or let her see him so—and certainly he would not join her in that sensuously sybaritic tub of warmed water! Still, he was unable to bear her present discomfort. Jarik went to her and put his hands on her upper arms in a reassuringly firm grip. Instantly he was too aware of the warm skin and Jilain-flesh under the tunic.

"We are all right, Jilain. You will love the bath, and they will give you something wonderful to wear. Just—"

"This one cares nothing about things to *wear*!" His hands held her from him, and so her hands went to his waist. "This one wants to talk wit' you and hear you talk, Jarik! Why must one bat'e alone—stay!"

He had tried. He must be firm then, for both their sakes, and if she drew a wrong conclusion from it . . . then so be it. He felt too sure that he was right; too unsure of himself and the fate of anyone linked with it. "I will not," he said. It was hard for him to meet her eyes.

"But *why*?"

"Look," he said, and his eyes indicated Metanira, behind her. Thus he saved himself, for Jilain turned to look at the woman in the beautiful gown.

Jilain's eyes widened and her mouth came open. Near the far wall of the chamber, Metanira had drawn back a curtain to reveal a niche with smooth walls of pale yellow. Within the niche was a sunken place in the floor. It was faced with sky-colored god-metal or something similar and impossible, all smooth and shiny. Jarik tried not to look at Metanira's backside while she bent over the long oval depression. He knew what she was doing, though he had no idea how it was effected or accomplished. He knew too that it would give Jilain a start. Jutting from the wall above the sunken area was the arching neck and head of an eider, wrought in burnished copper that was like gold. From its open beak water now commenced to gush! From the wall!

"Oh!"

Jarik smiled at Jilain's unconscious little exclamation. Metanira did not turn but supervised the noisy gushing of clear water into the sunken tub. He remembered how before he had tried so hard to seem sophisticated; to accept. Now he felt so, for Jilain was become the naive barbarian who could only stare at this awesome yet not intimidating sorcery of a god.

The tub was filling rapidly with the noisy gush. Metanira turned.

"It will soon be full, and is neither hot nor cold. Shall I bathe you?"

Jilain's hand reached back blindly. "Jarik—"

"As you wish. Please enjoy it. I will be near. No one means us harm here, Jilain." *I think. I hope. Only I came here intending harm—I hope. But not to you, O my Jilish!*

She clamped his hand in hers. "Jarik—stay. Please stay. There is room for twa. See?"

"Our two naked bodies will not be in that tub together, Jilain."

"But—" She broke off, tried another tack: "Then stay, then. Stay, while one . . . washes herself. One will not mind—one will be happier!"

"I will not," Jarik said firmly, and extricated his hand from hers.

*Coward*, he told himself. *Send at me a score of warriors or even demons, and I am ready to face them. But I fear this woman I love—no; it is Jarik I fear, not her. I fear for her because I do love her. I will not, not! We must not . . . unite.*

Metanira terminated the water's flow. Water stood in the tub to a height of mid-calf, or nearly.

"Lady," she said, "please. The water is neither hot nor cold. Please undress. Shall I bathe you?"

"No!" Jilain swung to face Jarik—and he was gone. Staring at the doorway, a high esthetically delightful arch edged in pink and silver, she felt a stinging pressure behind her eyes. There lay his armor coat, she noticed. The Black Sword was gone. Oh yes. *He loves it above anything or anyone, that blighty soord!* Then, lips firm and head high, she turned to Metanira. "Yes."

Metanira made no comment on that swift change of this guest's wish, and her features maintained their serenely equable expression. She aided or "aided" Jilain in removing weapon belt and tunic—staring at the ruby called *llanket* without remarking on that remarkable part of Jilain's body—and tried to aid the other woman in stripping off the leggings. Jilain was even less accustomed to such cloying gear than to clothing on her upper body, for she had worn the leggings but twenty-four hours—for the first time in her life. In her attempt to get them off she staggered and realized that she had better sit down, or give conscious concentration to balance.

"Oh go," she said angrily. "Go and *help* Jarik! This one will see to her own needs. Who needs you? Who needs *him*?"

Without demurrer or indeed any sort of reply, dull-voiced Metanira left her.

* * *

Jarik had taken his weapon belt when he left that chamber because he was not comfortable without it; without the Black Sword. And because he was mindful of his true mission. He was agent of the Iron Lords, and the controlling bracers were gone from his wrists.

They had turned right into the chamber where he now left Jilain and Metanira. Accordingly he turned left on leaving. He walked up that corridor between pastel walls.

Several minutes later he came to the corridor's end; a wall of living stone. But this was not possible! Frowning, he pushed, strained, tugged, patted about the stone, peered at it. It was true rock. Yet he was sure it had not been here before, that they had turned rightward to enter that chamber where the bath awaited . . . No. He must be mistaken. He retraced his steps, still wearing the frown. How could it be that they had come that way and now he could not return in the same wise in that same direction? How was it that now immovable stone barred the way?

*I must be mistaken. That's all.* And back he went. The thoughts would not stop coming, though; they brought another answer, possible because it was impossible. *Because I am in the keep of a god*, he thought. *No one knows what limits there are to the powers of gods. Even those limits I think I know may be false, and not limits at all. Have the Iron Lords, gods, lied to me? Has She?*

He remembered words; were they words of the Guide? "If a man should make exception and contend that his statements and opinions are capable of admitting contrary qualities, his contention is unsound." Yes, he remembered that, and it affected him and his thinking and comprehension. Yet he also remembered another statement, from the same occasion: "There are intermediate hues between the contrarieties of black and white."

Then some things might be so and not so? Then good could shade into bad? A good person (or god!) was capable of doing bad—without being bad? Could there be *so* and *nearly so*; truth and not-quite-truth? Truth that shifted into falsity?

Then what about open corridors that became closed?

*Did the Iron Lords try to slay me out there on the sea, or did they perhaps not know I was on the ship? Is the White*

*Rod more important to them than I am, so that for it they were willing to kill me? Or . . . did they seek the death of someone else aboard* Seadancer? *Jilain? How could they possibly know of her*? (Did gods know everything—No; he was sure that they did not.) Kirrensark, perhaps? (*I am thy brother, murderer.*) Perhaps, though it was hard to see the importance of Kirrensark, even in Kirrensark-wark. Perhaps Coon, Jarik thought with a smile. Delath? (*I am thy brother, murderer.*)

By now it seemed to Jarik that he had been walking a long while between these pastel walls that made the corridor seem broader than it was. He frowned, and paused to glance back.

Fifteen paces behind him Jarik stared at a blank wall of living stone, in grey and sienna.

He wheeled. A few paces away, directly ahead, was another stone wall. It had not been there when he paused to look back. Just as fear grasped him and threatened to metamorphose into panic, he saw the leftward turn in the corridor. Feeling light-headed, he hurried to it and turned. Now the pale-walled hallway stretched out and out before him, an arrow-line luminously lit by no visible source or even central source that he could see. The distance was so great that the walls and floor and ceiling seemed to come together, so that the corridor's far end could be blotted from sight by his lifted palm.

He had not buckled on the weapon belt, and now he made sure the grip of his left hand was firm on his long scabbard. Though there was nothing to fight, certainly he was in the midst of ensorcelment, god-magic, and menaced. He would be ready.

Meanwhile he would continue walking. What other choice was there? Now he had somehow lost Jilain!

Well, he would not panic. He was being given a message: *In the keep of the god, do not wander.*

He paced along that corridor. Its floor was some sort of moss-imitating carpet, in a delicate orangey-green. Constantly he checked the wall on either side for doors or curtained doorways; consistently he found no sign of any break. The walls were blank and smooth, seemingly flowing beside him and out ahead. Apprehension was his companion and fear hovered, seeking to join him and pave the way for panic. He paced and paced, finding no door. He

was sure that in trying to return to Jilain and Metanira he
had walked six times as far as he had done in leaving them.
God-sorcery was at work. This place was a maze. And yet
how could that be, when he moved along a corridor straight
as a spear?

That thought made him pivot on his leading foot and
swing to look back the way he had come—the way he had
now walked many paces.

Twelve or thirteen paces behind him the corridor ended
in a blank stone wall. It was there; it had not been there.
He heard nothing. The barrier did not frown at him; it
seemed to sneer. Not even a fleck of mica twinkled on that
rugged wall of grey in several shades, veined with a bit of
sienna shading into red.

*This is not possible.*

*What shall I do? Walk on, and on, while walls appear be-
hind me and ahead of me yet never truly seek to trap me?*

Now he held his left hand close to his belly, his right on
the hilt of the Black Sword. Perhaps on impulse, perhaps in
fear, he began to walk backward. Two paces. Three. He
heard no sound save that of his movements. The soft coming down of his heel after his toe; the faint *jing* of metal on
his weapons belt. His own breathing—his own heartbeat!

"Jarik?"

He whirled and his blade was most of the way out of the
sheath by the time he was around. From a doorway to his
right Metanira emerged. She looked at the sword, which he
shoved angrily back into its scabbard with a *chok* sound.
He saw no wet patches on her long clingy garment.

"Will you come this way?"

She walked toward him, past him, and when he turned
he saw an open corridor. No stone wall, where one had
been only a few heartbeats before. Was this illusion, or
could the god shift reality; shift the interior stone of the
mountain to form immediate walls that kept him pent—
him, or any other who might invade Snowmist Keep?
(How could anyone invade the place, though? It was high
and high up Cloudpeak. Nor did he have any idea if there
was a normal means of ingress or not; three times gods had
taken him to two keeps of gods, and each time it had been
by their sorcerous method. Here-not here-there, all in a
rush and a few instants.)

He looked up and around. Was he being watched? Was

that possible? Following Metanira, he wondered if he would ever know answers to any of these questions. Truthful answers, mind; he felt now that not all he had heard from the Iron Lords was truth, as he knew that Snowmist had hardly answered all his questions. The Iron Lords had. Glibly? Did they reply so swiftly to his queries because he was after all only a mortal man, and not deserving of truth? *. . . dirt-grubbing hands of those stupid villagers . . .*

He would not diminish himself or admit anything by speaking, by seeking answers of this mere servant of a god. In silence and telling himself he was not awed, Jarik followed her. In no more than a dozen of her paces, she turned left. She passed through the center meeting of a twinned arras of some soft, almost furry fabric and held it back for him. Its color was that of pine trees.

Warily, he entered a chamber that surely had not been here minutes ago, when he had passed along a corridor bare of doorways. At first he thought he was in the same chamber. Then he noticed the amphora beside which stood a goblet of beaten silver indited with odd stick-like figures or designs unknown to him. The amphora in this chamber was of red, brown, and two shades of green.

"Does that contain the drink that is not ale?"

"Yes. Wine." A moment later she was handing him a goblet practically brimming and dancing with the golden-white liquid. A minute later he was handing back the goblet, empty. She filled it again. Abruptly Jarik recalled his previous sojourn here. The Lady of the Snowmist had urged him to drink wine. At last, suspicious, he had asked if it were drugged. And she had said simply, "Yes."

He was weary. He had fought a battle before breakfast and still had not eaten. And now he had emptied two cups of the wonderful wine of Snowmist. Despite a growing hunger, Jarik fell asleep in that room's tub, which was faced and floored in the god-metal or something like, the color of new doeskin leggings.

*If Torsy would just talk to me*, he found himself thinking, *I could worry about her a little and not have to worry about me. Being brave and a man is very hard when you're all by yourself and not even eight years old.*

He reflected on how he had been whiter than anyone else in Oceanside, or pinker rather, and not as big either.

They had called him puny, some of them. *Chairik's puny*, that's what they said. He had learned not to fight because when he did he got beat up.

After having to fight him to pull Jarik and Torsy out of the sea, though, Strode said, "That's the bravest boy I ever saw. He'da fought us all." Jarik heard those words, and he remembered. He would have fought them all too, but now on their ship he was hungry and hurting and he was gulping and sobbing and he and Torsy were all right, all right, and he seemed to spin through space, and through time, amid mists of red and grey and misty snow and

"Put down your sword, Jarik."

"I will not. I am cutting this tree with it." And that was in truth just what he had been doing, when Stath came to sneer at him some more. By now that late, late spurt had caught up with him, and Jarik's size had caught up with that of others, and passed them.

"Put down your sword or raise it against me, twice-foundling, doubtless bastard son and part-brother to a witling sow."

Everything Stath said was meant to insult, even indicating that Torsy was a sow, not a shoat, which meant that she was no maiden. Jarik's face went dark and he turned to face the other youth. His sword was in his hand and their eyes stared each into the other's. Jarik saw Stath swallow, saw him draw his sword with its hilt set with a carbanean, or bloodstone. The sword was shiny and well forged, the sword of the son of the firstman of Ishparshule-wark. The pommel of the sword Jarik held was the plain iron of the tang that, covered with wood and leather, was the grip. The guard was made of the horn of an elk—the elk Jarik had slain, alone in winter—and the blade, which had often been bent, was notched. He had indeed been chopping a tree, in anger against Stath, for he knew he could not attack him or fight him. Not the firstman's son. And Stath had followed him here, into the woods at the edge of the wark. Stath would not leave him alone.

"I am here to chop this tree, Stath." Jarik's voice trembled. So did his arm, and his face worked.

"Will you take it to your witling sister in trade for her favors?"

Stath had succeeded in his goading. No man could hear

such words and walk again with his head up unless he received apology or blood. Jarik charged, though neither of them had a buckler, the stout wooden shields of the men of Lokusta.

Stath struck away Jarik's blade in a ring of iron, and on the vicious backswing he sought to slash open Jarik's chest. That failed, for Jarik pounced back light as a spotted pup. Suddenly his blue eyes were glittering. They did not watch the sword flash across, its point only just missing him. He was not staring in concentration. He was not thinking. He was fighting. For the first time an armed Jarik faced an armed man—or youth; both were years from being twenty—and his brain stood aside to watch. Jarik had gone morbrin.

Swiftly he stepped back in and his own back-slash took Stath in the neck. The blade hewed into the ring-bones of the youth, and smashed one, so that Stath Ishparshule's son fell down dead in his blood and with his eyes staring.

That swiftly did life change again for Jarik, for he was exiled.

"And no one has ever taken up the Black Sword?" Jarik looked at it, that rustless sword standing above Blackiron Stone in the center of the fishers' wark called Blackiron.

"No one has had to," Turibark told him with his maddening patience. "There has been no need for the Sword, for any sword, in Blackiron."

"I would take it up," Jarik said; Jarik ever Outlander and ever rebellious and resistant to mandates. And so unsure, while he Sought and Sought.

"Do not even think such, Jarik!" he was told, for all around him were shocked. "It is forbidden!"

"You are all fools," Jarik snapped, and went from them. Doubtless they talked of slaying him or driving them from them, that day in Blackiron. But they swallowed it, and he stayed.

*I am a god on the earth, (something)son Jarik*, the Guide said.

"What have I seen, Guide?"

*It is your birthright and your conception, Jarik. You saw two that were as one, and when they became one they shattered and were nothing. You are a twoness that must be a oneness, and that can come about only by your taking on a third part, which will unify you into one.*

"*I do not understand!*"

*It will be agony to you that you do not understand*, the Guide told him, *and are two both at once, (something)son Jarik, and for that I am sorry. Yet the agony will continue when you are whole—three as one, though it will be a different sort of agony and you will know happiness. Some happiness.*

Jarik left Blackiron to go looking for Nevre and Torsy, who was his sister and yet who was not. He found them, in the woods. They were all over blood, both of them. They lay in blood, for they had been chopped with iron blades. Torsy lay on her back with her eyes open and Jarik saw the fly that walked on her cheek and trod on her eyeball, and Jarik saw that she did not blink. There was no need of Oak. There was nothing a healer could do for those two. Jarik went back to Blackiron and got the Black Sword, plucked it forth as easy as that, and no one dared say him nay. When he came upon Torsy's killers, over a day later, those three warriors were as half a man against him and the Black Sword chopped them all in their blood and they lay dead in their blood to a ravening maniac.

(*No wait, this is wrong; this must be a dream; they were men, just men, not the Iron Lords. I could not kill the Iron Lords!*) So the three got up and repaired themselves and they talked, the Iron Lords, with the outlander called Jarik. No eyes showed within the eyeslits of those foreboding iron masks. Nothing showed anywhere, except shining black iron. Some of it was chain and some of it was plate and curving great bosses, and all of it was black.

*You are too wise*, Jarik was told, and the voice was metallic and hollow, ringing dully within that iron mask under the iron helm.

Jarik said, Then those of Blackiron *were* slain because I took the Sword.

*Had the sword been there, Strodeson Jarik, it would have summoned us at the first sign of true danger.*

And

*You are of the people of the Hawk-ships, Jarik-Oak,* the Lord of Annihilation said, all hollow and metallic, when he had heard Jarik's story. *You are of the land—a large sprawling island actually—called Lokusta. You must know this.*

Jarik protested, No! They are murderers! Hawkship men are murderers! They slew my parents and my sister!

*Blackiron is part of the large isle called Lokusta. Endeavor to use your brain and not your juices, lad.* So spoke the Lord of Destruction, and then Lord Annihilation said, *Your foster parents. Your foster sister. You must have been a foundling, Jarik-Oak. Abandoned for some reason; some imperfection perhaps. Or because your parents had already more get than they could manage to feed.* And Destruction told him, *Once you have accomplished your mission and ours, we will return you here, Jarik our ally. You may remain so long as you wish. None will refuse you, none of these beautiful maidens and women who serve us. None of our servants will refuse any wish or desire that is yours. You will be Jarik, ally of the Lords of Iron, whom by slaying the Lady of the Snowmist you will have freed to protect all the people of the earth.*

Jarik blinked, smiled. He was important! An ally of the Iron Lords who were gods on the earth! He said, "On the morrow I will go forth in mail, with the Black Sword, on our mutual business."

*Done*, the Lord of Destruction said, hollowly and metallically, and the old Lord of Dread laughed aloud.

Thus Torsy. Thus Jarik. Thus Blackiron. Thus the Guide and thus the Iron Lords. *It will be agony to you that you do not understand*

Whose son? Whose son? Orrikson Jarik Strodeson Jarik and Jarik of the Black Sword—No! *Whose* son? Why?

Thus the Guide, whom he knew without knowing (and knew too that he was Osyr but was Osyr not dead?) and thus Blackiron that was gone to him and Torsy who was dead, dead, dead. And thus the Iron Lords, whom he knew.

But who were these? *Where am I? Why am I here and what place is this? It is agony to me that I do not understand but I must fight again, again, again . . .*

They were three, Jarik and these companions who were strangers. Somehow he knew that the stone and iron about them were beneath the earth. Beneath a fortress, a castle . . . what was that? What did "Rander" mean? Was this perhaps a god's keep?

*No. We are beneath the earth.*

By his side was such a man as Jarik had never seen. His hair was . . . black! Black as Jarik's Sword! It must surely be dyed for whoever heard of black hair—but black too were his mustache and his small pointed beard and almost black were his eyes. So dark, oh so dark. Onyxes or garnets set into his dark face. His skin! It was a deep copper—no, a deep bronze—no . . . his skin was, incredibly, *walnut*. Dark. Never had Jarik seen such a man as this one he knew was his ally. Or such a nose! It was a large nose, and neither straight nor pugged but crooked, high-bridged rather like the beak of a bird of prey, and the tip of his nose was definitely turned *down*! Further, he was a hand's length shorter than the ally on Jarik's other side, who was only a little shorter than Jarik. That other one was a woman not a woman. A god, surely. For she was covered all over in shining scintillant form-molding armor, all in blue, the blue of the sky. Over her head and face she wore a helmet and mask of the same metal, weirdly molded. At first glance she would seem a mail-covered woman with the cerulean head of a huge bird of prey! And she too was his ally, not his enemy. A god on the earth surely, though neither Snowmist nor Lord of Iron! And the man's upper lip was a little like a bow, Jilain's bow, for it curved sharply down in the center, under the tip of that long downturned nose.

*Where am I? Why am I here and what place is this agony that I do not understand but we three must fight again, again . . .*

They were allies three, underground in stone and behind that iron grille over there was a man, their prisoner, dimly seen in the flickery light of torches set in metal brace-cages mounted in the very stone of the walls. They faced stone steps, and down that stairway boiled men.

They were dark men like unto him on Jarik's left hand and they were strangely clothed. Men shorter than Jarik, but no less ferocious. They were mailed, in helm and scales of iron and of copper with some bronze, and on that one silver gleamed, just a bit of silver. They came one and two, and three four five they came, and six and a seventh. Seven came attacking down stone steps, attacking three ringed around with stone walls on a floor of hard, hard-packed earth, and Jarik and the shorter dark man and the woman in cerulean armor fought and chopped and leaped and hacked so that bright blood spattered stone walls and earthen floor and Jarik's hands and arms as they battled, three against seven and the mailed woman fighting no less than a man and seemingly invulnerable, and enemies fell to the weirdly mismatched three and

Jarik awoke.

Panting a little, he awoke in Snowmist Keep and knew that he had dreamed of his past. And that last dreadful combat, three against seven while one watched from behind bars . . . had he dreamed a fantasy, or was it part of history not yet written? Had he seen again a glimpse of the time to come? He did not know. Nor now, lying awake in Snowmist Keep with his belly rumbling, could he conceive of such a dark man, such a short man with such a nose and bow-curved mouth—and black hair!

Metanira came then. She bore him food to break a fast that was longer than he knew.

# Twelve

*But what a mystery this erring mind!*
*It wakes within a framework of various powers*
*A stranger in a new and wondrous land.*

— N. P. Willis

Jarik sat comfortably, dressed in an incredibly soft, flowing robe the color of the stone called samarine. His feet were bare. Within the robe, he wore Jilain's gift; the necklace of shells from the shores of Kerosyr. In a comfortable chair to his immediate left Jilain sat, her knees not quite touching his. Her legs were invisible under a full skirt that flowed in soft waves to her insteps. The skirt was the color of that quartz called silignant. Above it her tunic was sleeveless and low of scooped neck; its color that of the gemstone citrelain, which was less yellow than the hue of jonquils. At armholes and low "neck" it was bordered with white scallops resembling the petals of flowers. The garment, which was soft and would fall to mid-thigh were she standing, was loosely girt with a rope that seemed made of three slim strands of silver cloth, braided. Snowmist had provided her with a similar bracelet, delicately twisted of finer wire, which Jilain wore on her left wrist. Around her neck, not quite vanishing into the shaded valley between the upper curves of her breasts, was slung a typically Lokustan chunk of amber on a thong of sweat-darkened old leather. Jarik's pendant.

Jarik had found one of the delicately stretched and trebly-twisted silver bracelets on his own wrist, identical to Jilain's. He had removed it. He had no desire to wear any of Snowmist's silver, most especially not on his wrist.

Across from him in cozy proximity sat the Lady of the Snowmist, in her fulgurant armor of silver and white and grey. And her helm-mask. The pitcher of wine on the low table between them was of silver, as were the tall-stemmed goblets.

Jarik did not like the fact that he hardly remembered coming here, to the main chamber of her keep. It was lit, now, only in the area where they sat. Thus the sprawling size of that chamber was reduced to this warm "room" for conversation. Her chair was made so as to imitate a large tawny-grey stone, covered with moss. The low table seemed a big off-white toadstool. The padded chair in which Jarik sat was fashioned to imitate a huge carven tree stump. It was not.

The god spoke. "I shall answer your questions, Jarik, though I warn you that I have not the answers to all things!"

"Gods do not know everything?" Jilain asked, shifting, tucking up her legs on the mossy bank she seemed to be sitting on. It was not a mossy bank.

"No, Jilain. Gods do not know everything."

Jarik knew what his first question must be. "Are you my mother?"

"No, Jarik. You are not my son."

"Am I one of the abandoned boy babes of Kerosyr?"

"I think not."

"This one thinks not also. No boy babes are *abandoned*, on Osyr's Isle."

Jarik looked at her. "Always? You know this? Before you were born and when you were a child . . . all were slain?"

Jilain nodded, looking down. "One is sure. There have never been that many. Not that many men ever came to Kerosyr."

Jarik dropped that. "I am of normal parentage, then?"

"I think not, Jarik."

"Think not?"

"No, then," Snowmist said. "You are not of normal parentage, Jarik of the Black Sword. One of your parents, Jarik—and I know not which one nor who it was or the other parent either—was of our kind."

"Gods? Your . . . kin? Kin of yourself and the Iron Lords?"

"In a way, Jarik. Aye—my 'kin,' then."

"One . . . then . . . Jairik is . . . half . . . half *god*?"

"Aye, Jilain. And half man. And neither of either. And both of each, as he is the Man Who Is Two. Yet he is more nearly whole now than when he journeyed to Osyr's Isle."

Jarik asked, "How is that?"

"You have Jilain, Jarik."

"And Jilain has him!" Jilain added.

"Aye," Milady Snowmist said. "And he has too the Black Sword, and the blood of my race, and the respect of Kirrensark's wark, and the love of a woman, and of a woman-god. You are a fortunate man, Jarik."

"Fortunate!" he burst forth, while Jilain put her head on one side and asked, "You love Jairik, Milady God?"

"I have loved him, Jilain, and lain with him."

"*What*?!"

"*You*?!"

To their simultaneous exclamations Snowmist replied, "Twice."

"*Twice*!" Jarik echoed. "But—"

"Twice," the silvery mask repeated. "Ere your man was yours, Jilain, he was mine. After your man was yours—yet not yet yours in the flesh—he was mine still again."

While Jarik looked horrified, the muscles of Jilain's face tightened, as did her lips. A bit less showed of her hazel eyes as she stared at that expressionless mask—and at the superb womanly shape below.

Jarik said, almost gasping, "Just—now?"

The mask faced him full on. "Aye, Jarik."

"I have been drugged again?" He was suddenly on his feet with a rustle of the handsome, medium blue robe. His hands were knotted.

"Yes. And you have my promise: never again will you be drugged by me or my servants, Jarik of the Black Sword."

"Wonderful! Oh, wonderful! How *fine* of you, whoring god! And do you like unconscious bed-partners the best?" He stood tall and yet leaned toward the seated god, across the low table that rose only to his mid-shin.

"Jarik," Jilain said, "wait," and her hand slipped over his fist. He jerked it away and only glanced at her; it was a dark glance of anger. No; of outrage.

"Jarik Blacksword," the Lady of the Snowmist said, and there was strength and the confidence of power in her voice. "I said to you that I would answer your questions. Now you know that I spoke true, and still do. I could easily have kept that to myself."

"I did not ask if you had lain with me—used me!" he raged at Her. "Such a question would not have occurred to me!"

"I wanted you to know."

He stared at Her, whirled away, walked away. *If I had the Black Sword.* . . . Perhaps, however, it was best that he did not. He would surely have driven it into Her—or tried. And there were more questions to be asked. So many questions. He stalked about, working off his rage and outrage. Jilain followed him with her eyes. The helm-mask of the god did not turn. *Would that I could call the Black Sword to me but bid it linger at a little distance*, he thought, *rather than come straight to my hand.*

He returned to the lighted area that was so like a comfortable, intimate little gathering in some woodsy glen, and he resumed his seat on the brown chair facing her.

"The youths you bring here, Lady," he said tightly. "They are for . . . night-mates?"

"Aye."

"You lie with them, and get yourself with child?"

"Aye."

Impulsively Jilain said, "Gods and—and humans can, can breed? Produce children?"

The mask said, "Aye, Jilain."

Jarik glanced at Jilain, and spoke to Snowmist. "And then you make those youths forget. As I have forgot."

"You were asleep, Jarik. You are different, as I found out very swiftly! Aye, I make them forget—and reward them with lifelong health."

Jilain said in a low voice of awe, "Such is yours to confer?"

"It is. It—"

"Why then do these yout's not live forever? Is not perfect healt' the key to immortality?"

"No, Jilain," the god said, and her voice sounded indulgent; an aged parent explaining to a child, without impatience or condescension. "You will age. All humans . . . we all age. Eventually the body reaches its limit of aging, so that brain and muscle and bone can age no more. Then comes death."

Jarik had relaxed somewhat, and explained to Jilain. "It is that those youths who are Chosen—so it is called in the warks, and once I dreamed of it—enjoy perfect health all the days of their life. Until the day they die, at advanced age."

"Then—then what is the cause of their deat'?"

An argent armored arm gestured with a faintly metallic rustle. "Advanced age," said the Lady of the Snowmist.

Still uncomprehending—for who could?—Jilain repeated herself. "And perfect lifelong healt' is yours to confer, god on the eart'?"

"It is. It . . . costs me. Of myself, I mean; not of property or anything measurable in silver or gold or kine or horses."

"And this you have done with me. When first yourself bade me come here, brought me here . . ."

"Yes, Jarik. It was because you are well made, and had performed a fine heroic deed, entered a battle that was not a battle but an attempt at murdering Kirrensark; a matter that was none of your concern. And you entered into it anyhow, and you prevailed. Thus you represented good . . . stock; a good man."

"To make a *god*?" Jilain said, almost squeaking, while Jarik said, "I? A good man? *I*?" And he made a sneering face that ill became him.

A god on the earth sighed. "Good for fathering a babe to take on a responsibility most awesome and awful, yes. True, you will never be a 'good man' as others use that phrase, Jarik Blacksword who has been Jarik other-names. How can you be, who have seen and experienced so much terror and evil, and are marked by it, with scars on the mind?"

Jarik stared, tight-lipped, at nothing. "And so twice we have been night-mates, Lady God, and I remember nothing of it."

"It is true. Once, you said just now, you wanted much to

be Chosen, as those of the warks call it. I know it confers popularity on those I bring here, along with health. When did that change, Jarik Blacksword? Your feeling about being so chosen, I mean? When did it become 'use'?"

"I was only a boy then. I knew nothing of gods. I needed. . . . I had not been enslaved by you, then. I did not know you then, Lady God."

"Jarik: You do not know me now."

After a long silence Jilain said, "Jarik . . . this one thinks that is true."

"It is true," the Lady of the Snowmist said. "And your seed has found the egg in me, Jarik Blacksword. You will father a god. It has begun."

"A god?"

"I did not mean that it might not be a girl, Jarik. One has but to look on Jilain, and reflect on what she is, to know that some distinctions between the sexes are not worth the bother of different words. Some say god*dess.* Some would find it necessary to call Jilain 'warrior*ess.*' We know what we are. Call me 'he;' call Jilain 'brother' or 'he' and see if it matters. It will not diminish us—those of us who *know* what we are." The womanly mask looked at the woman. "I and Jilain are god and warrior, are we not?"

Jilain nodded; Jarik shrugged.

"And if I call you 'brother,' Jilain? And if you call Jarik 'sister'?"

Jilain Kerosyris smiled. Jarik, looking at her, noticed for the first time that the scab was gone from her forehead. Pink baby-skin showed there where he had cut her, in an overturned V. Jilain said, "This one has done that. It did not disturb Jairik, or Strave the archer, either."

The expressionless helmet-mask nodded.

Ridiculously, Jarik felt compelled to look at Jilain and say, "We are sisters, warrior."

Jilain's smile was bright sunlight bursting forth. "We are sisters, warrior!"

Then Jilain looked at the Lady of the Snowmist, and her expression became quite serious. "Never has this one envied gods, Lady God. Now she does. One envies the Lady of the Snowmist, god on the eart' and alive as well— but not because She is a god!"

They all knew that a face smiled then, within a mask. "I know, Jilain. I know."

Jarik sat forward. "I see and understand. And now we are come to a problem. Yourself knows it," he said, and only She noticed that he had resumed the respectful pronoun. "I was sent here by the Iron Lords, Lady God, to do death on you. I made bargain with them."

"I know. So you did. 'Twas an unseemly bargain and fool's errand. They have reason to seek my death; you do not. You were easily taken advantage of, by those three. And now I have subverted you to my wishes, body and brain! And it would appear that the Iron Lords sought to do death on you, out on the sea."

Jarik said, "Was Jilain that hawk sought to slay."

"*After* it had slain the whit' dove, and *after* this one had taken toll of three helmsmen!"

Jarik looked at her, bright-eyed, and Jilain gazed back, wide-eyed and serene. "This one had never slain, Jairik. This one was . . . *impelled* to slay the Osyrain, in honor. For the honor of Osyr and His Guardians. After that . . . one saw a way, asea, to lessen the number of deat's by slaying the most important man on that other ship. Then one had to do it again. And of course again. It was not . . . hard."

He stared, and then looked away in pain, realizing that since their paths had crossed, Jilain had slain again and again.

And then she shocked him, for she said that which he felt, though she added a qualifier he did not bother with: "There can be nothing wrong in slaying in defense of honor or oneself or others," Jilain said.

*But I introduced you to it,* Jarik thought. *And I—I enjoy it, the killing. O ye gods and Guide hear and help me—I enjoy it.*

It was then he heard Jilain say quietly, "Too, this one has found that she enjoys it. The adventuring, the danger, the . . . slaying."

"Killing to no purpose save greed or mere uncontrolled anger is murder," the god on the earth said, "and is not worthy of humans or gods. Killing to purpose and without remorse is part of the undeniable heritage of your kind and mine. It is stupid to call it wrong, for it is natural to us both. Not all deserve the gift and reward of life. Murderers, for instance."

The man and the woman gazed at her in silence for a

time, and then Snowmist spoke on.

"At any rate. My brothers the Lords of Iron prepared you well, did they—since you did not slay me at all but served me well! Perhaps they are not worth serving, Jarik Blacksword? Perhaps you were mistaken in allegiances?"

"I have no allegiances," Jarik said, from habit, because he was Jarik. "Nor do I *serve* the Iron Lords. We made a bargain. They left me the Black Sword when surely they could have taken it, and they put me at Kirrensark-wark, that I might exact my vengeance. In turn I agreed to slay you, Lady God—who they said keeps them penned atop Iron Mountain and within that little area about it and Blackiron, that they might not extend their protection to others as they protect that wark called Blackiron."

"And yet," She said, who was a god on the earth and yet with mortal human blood in her veins, "they were able to send the iron hawk far asea after you, and a shipload of killers as well."

Jarik's face remained tight. He mused miserably, still all cloudy of mind: *Aye. But what is true and who is right? Osyr did not strike me dead, as the Pythoness believed he would, that cold black statue. Even learning that I came here to slay Her, the Lady of the Snowmist did not do death on me. And—assuredly that hawk asea was from the Lords of Iron, who most certainly did tell me that their power was limited by Her to that small area along the coast, other side Dragonmount. Who is to know truth from lies? —fact from fiction or fancy, reality from illusion or pretense or . . . the same sort of blindness that is on those of Kerosyr: the blindness from lack of knowledge? No, no . . . I know only that I vowed vengeance on a man and did not take it, and had even more reason to kill another man and now cannot. And I know that I vowed to slay Her, this silv'ry god on the earth; I made a bargain with other gods, her kith, and have not kept it. And She has* used *me!*

"You said that you had lived for vengeance and promised to do murder. But Kirrensark lives, on whom you sought vengeance, Jarik. And you and he are fighting-comrades and—friends? And I too live, unmurdered."

"Aye," he said, dull of voice. "In all my life, as I see it now clear, I have done naught. I have accomplished but one goal I set out to reach. The Rod of Osyr. But that was not *my* goal; *I* did not want it or want to fetch it either! I obtained it and brought it to you—brought it to the enemy of the Iron Lords I made bargain with!"

Jilain's rose-pink skirt rippled as she swung her legs off her chair to the floor, and leaned close to lay a hand on his arm.

"Jarik . . ."

Calmly Snowmist's voice overrode them both. "There have been other accomplishments, Jarik Blacksword. For one thing, you have the Sword. And—"

"I have not the Black Sword! It was taken from me in your keep!"

"We both know that you set it aside and no one took it from you, Jarik Blacksword, just as we both know that no one can take that Sword from you and keep it, when you want it!"

He looked at her. "And if I call it to me? No stone wall will prevent its coming?"

"No, but that is not of—" She broke off, for she saw that he had stiffened and closed his eyes. With a sigh that was less than godly, She leaned back and waited. It was She who had shown him that property of the Black Sword. It was She who had told him it was his, peculiarly and specifically his; attuned to him. It was She who had shown him that he could call the Sword to him, not the Iron Lords. They had been content to let him keep it, since he was a needful gullible to send forth on their errand of assassination. But they had not apprised him of all the Sword's worth and properties! No, not Nershehir, Seyulshehir and Eskeshehir!

Jarik heard Jilain draw in her breath, with a hiss. He opened his eyes and turned his head in time to see the Black Sword come floating to him, hilt foremost. A thing of iron-like god-metal that winglessly winged to him on a course straight as a bow-sped arrow. He did not put out his hand to take it, because of Her and, like a faithful dog, sleek and black and obedient and loving, it lay down at his feet.

*Then* Jarik gazed at the eyeslits of the mask of the Lady of the Snowmist.

"No, Lady God. My taking the Sword was little accomplishment. My taking it brought about the deaths of three in the village of Blackiron and perhaps another as well. For with the Sword in my hands it did not warn the Iron Lords that Blackiron was under Hawker attack, until I returned there with it."

"Still I dispute your determined persistence in wallowing in misery, Jarik Blacksword," She said. "Considering your words 'in all my life'—Jarik, Jarik! It has been a very short life indeed. You have hardly begun this your life."

Jarik felt tension tighten him. He was far from comfortable and far from trusting. Perhaps now, he thought, they had come to the real reason for his being here, and the real meaning of the words She had just spoken. For who could trust this Lady of the—who could trust the words of gods?

"And there is much life ahead," Jilain Kerosyris said, "and many accomplishments!"

"Is there?" he asked, staring at the helm-and-mask of a god with the powers of a god. "Or is my life to end now and here?"

"It is not!" The argent voice of the Lady of the Snowmist was vehement. "No! Nor is the end of your life any time soon, if I can prevent it, Jarik Blacksword!"

"And if this one can prevent it!"

# Thirteen

*Yes, 'tis my dire misfortune now*
*To hang between two ties,*
*To hold within my furrowed brow*
*The earth's clay, and the skies.*

—*Victor Hugo*

Jarik had leaned back in a release of tension—some of it. "And what will yourself do now, Lady God, now that yourself has the White Rod of Osyr?"

"It is accomplishing its purpose. It *has* accomplished its purpose."

"Has?" Jilain echoed.

The Lady of the Snowmist leaned forward with much rustling scintillance of body-hugging armor, and set an elbow on her mailed knee. She lifted a finger that She did not quite point at that orphan of the storm She guested.

"The Rod of Osyr is not necessary to me, Jarik, although now it will serve Kirrensark-wark below. It is our gift to them, and they are good and deserving."

He remembered the words of the Iron Lords about the people of their protectorate: . . .*dirt-grubbing hands of those stupid villagers below*. . . and he could not help comparing. He wished desperately that he could be sure. Why had not the Guide, who told him so much and so little, told him also whom to trust, among gods who said conflicting things to him?

135

"Though I should not want that wand in the hands of *Others*," She was saying on. "No, the White Rod was merely the means to send you to the Isle of Osyr, with purpose."

He was frowning in new incomprehension. "Why?"

"That you might return with Jilain, Jarik Blacksword, and be made whole thereby . . . or nearly."

Both of them stared at Her, and at last Jilain hesitantly said, "Our meeting was ordained? Fore-known? Yourself knew?"

The god straightened. "No. I knew that Jarik of the Black Sword was only partially a man, and that his potential was—is—enormous. *His* importance—*your importance*, Jarik. And I saw that there was that on the isle called Osyr's that would make him more a man, more nearly whole; hale. Now consider. How could that have been accomplished by stealing that white wand of a god? Or the golden chain? How could it have been of personal importance to you, Jarik, to slay the python-guard or lie with the Pythoness? Or to bring about the death of the queen called Osyrrain—"

"This one did that! This one slew her, for Osyr and for Jairik."

"It would not have happened," he said, "if I had not been there . . . to bring about more deaths, and to disrupt your life."

"Jarik!" Abruptly the mailed god flexed to her feet to stand over him in the magnificence that was simultaneously womanly and godly. "Jarik! Your way is that of the coward! No—*do not rise in anger, you*! Hear me. The coward's way: First you knock yourself down, and then you apply kicks to that groveling victim of yours—you! Think on that! Do you enjoy being miserable? Be in no haste to deny it, but first use your brain!"

Both of them stared up at Her, who seemed now twice the height of any man, looming over them all slim and womanly in silver and grey and the color of snow asparkle in the sun.

"At any rate," She said, "it is surely obvious: that which was of great importance to the life of Jarik Blacksword on that island was . . . you, Jilain."

Jarik wanted very much to stand and not have to stare up

and up at the god standing so near, but just now he dared not. "You order me to remain seated, my lady Snowmist, and so I do, but I like not this craning my neck! Now why sh—"

"Not even for a god, Jarik Blacksword?" She said, and they could hear the smile in her voice.

This time it was Jarik who ignored her words, as She had earlier ignored words of his. "Now why should you have care to whatever is of great importance to me, Lady God?"

The Lady of the Snowmist turned and walked behind the seeming great moss-covered stone that was her chair, and She swung to place both hands on its back so that he knew She was staring intensely at him.

"Because, Jarik, you are important to the War. And that makes you of inestimable importance to me—and to all the world."

Now Jarik stood. "The . . . the war? Which war—what war?"

"The War that has continued for centuries, Jarik Blacksword, and which remains still in the balance. The War in which I am but one of the soldiers—as are the Iron Lords."

"What," Jilain Kerosyris asked, "is war?"

"Oh my child!" And armor rustled and flashed with swift movements then, for the god on the earth hurried to Jilain and bent to embrace her. Jilain was stiff in astonishment, and yet even then she was aware: the armor was chill to the touch, but somehow did not feel hard and cold and cruel, this metal covering people wore to protect them from other people.

Snowmist straightened; paced; resumed her seat so as to face them both.

"Jarik? That question you can answer."

Jarik pulled a deep breath and let it out slowly. He turned to the woman who was so innocent—and who was such a warrior, and fighter, and killer.

"Out on the sea, Jilain, we fought a small battle—small, because you won it before it was joined. This morning in the wark we fought in a battle. A battle is a mass fight with something at stake, and a battle is but a part of a war. A war is between two great groups of individuals, and . . . were another to seek to own Kerosyr, possess it by taking

it, and the Guardians of Osyr fought, that would be war."
He looked from her as she nodded—frowning. "And Lady,
there are ever wars in the world, are there not? It is the way
of us and even of some insects. Wars for this or that land or,
or principle, food or growing- or grazing-land. But a war
that has you said lasted for *centuries* . . . how can that be?
What are the stakes—what the cause?"

"The stakes, Jarik Blacksword, are you."

"I?"

"A war over *Jairik*?"

"Aye. And you, Jilain, and Kirrensark too, and those on
the ship who attacked you, and the Guardians also. For the
stakes in this War are all humankind."

Jilain touched herself between her breasts. "All of us?"

Jarik seemed to sag. "I . . . see. By taking it, by arming
myself with—with this," he said, leaning down to close his
hand around the hilt and lift the Black Sword, "I stepped
all unwittingly into a War between gods . . . between yourself and the Iron Lords!"

"You see well, Jarik. You are perceptive. It is true, but
there is more too. More than you can see. There is more
than you know, for there is more than *I* know. To begin
with, there are *others*. Other gods, beyond only the Lords
of Iron and me. There are other gods. The time has come
to extend this ancient War. To wage war among the gods
on the earth, rather than fight skirmishes and wage a holding action. *They* are taking it beyond that point. We must
seek to do that which must be done."

"We?" Jarik asked, and Jilain said, "Whick is what?—
that whick must be done, this one means?"

"Aye, Jarik, *we*. The War in which the plots of Iron
Lords are but one part of the conflict, one war-front among
many. That which must be done, Jilain . . . oh my dear,
that is the paradox and the problem! What must be accomplished is the destruction of the Forces of Destruction."

The phrase rang leadenly in the air of Snowmist Keep.
*The Forces of Destruction.*

Frowning, Jarik said, "Yourself speaks of the Iron
Lords? Only a part of a conflict? I know those gods, Lady
Karahshisar, in their armor and masks of black iron, whose
swords spit fire to consume living men and dead alike.
Yourself said the Forces of Destruction. The Iron Lords,

then? For their names are Dread, and Annihilation, and
. . . the Lord of Destruction.''

"I speak of them Jarik, aye. *And* of a king enthroned . . .
at least one, though there may be more subverted, for I
know far from all there is to know. And others, others. The
Forces of Destruction; gods and humans combined and allied. Their purpose is to destroy.''

*Peaceful Kerosyr basking in the sun in the middle of the
sea*, Jilain thought, and was not sure whether the thought
was wistful or no.

Jarik smiled, grimly and satirically. "A king enthroned.
And perhaps others, you say. I have never seen a king.
Kirrensark, and Ishparshule and Ahl and other wark-
lordlings . . . yourself, neither a queen nor a king; the Iron
Lords who are gods like unto yourself and not kings, for
they have no kingdom; a stone god of a few people on a little island and a queen over a few women on that single little
isle sleeping on the sea. But no king have I seen.''

"I would that you would, Jarik of the Black Sword!'' The
tone of Her was intense, the silver of her voice gone hard
and ringing. "Aye, I would that you would see a king!''

"And there are others?'' he said, grasping for the concept, seeking her meaning and wondering at its width.
"Others, you said, in this . . . this Forces of Destruction?''

"Aye.'' She held up her mailed hands, and ticked them
off on her fingers, as She called their names:

"The Lords of Fire, who are three in number.

"And the Lord and Lady Cerulean—which is the color
of the sky, and of cold fire.

"The Fog Lords, whose number I know not.

"And Lady Tiger, who controls both the Baron of Indwell and Milord Rhune of Bluehills.

"The King of Taris, and his satrap the Lord Emos
Severak, of Vasteris, in Taris. And Trilithon Teg.''

"So many,'' Jilain breathed, for the world must be large
indeed.

"I know none of those names!'' Jarik said, and knew that
there was much world, and that he had seen little of it.

"Aye,'' She said. "And they have foes, those who are
pitted against them. Be thankful for that! Their foes are on
the side of you, Jarik, and you, Jilain, I swear it on my life;
for those others would destroy all of your kind; all of the

anthro-men. For there are other kinds of . . . men, and women."

"Other kinds of humans?" Jilain said, glancing at Jarik and wondering what another kind might be like.

The god-helm shook. "I did not say that, Jilain. I said other kinds of men and women. I did not say that they were humans."

And while Jilain felt a chill at that, Jarik was nodding, his fingers toying with the red-wrapped hilt of the Black Sword.

"I have heard it said that there are such," he said. "Experiments of the gods, it is said."

"That, Jarik O Jarik of the Black Sword and the two minds, is far more precisely true than you know. Experiments of the gods. Yes."

Jilain said, "And opposed by others? Allies of . . . yours, Lady God?"

"Yes, Jilain. We are the Gem Lords, who are two;

"Milady Shirajsha of the Web of Silver;

"The Flame Lords and the Queen of the Golden Flame . . .

"And she who is called Chance and who is not really one of us at all, but is with us and humankind in this struggle;

"Aye, and the Barons of Hilltower and of Dort, and in a way,

"Lord Sadik, for he will not join our enemies and is thus in sore danger from them. And . . . earthly champions. One called Torsy, who is dead. Aye, Jarik, even Torsy whom you called sister. She would have been important and yet has been important, to you, and perhaps that was her importance. One Rander, I think, though he knows it not. He is younger even than you two and may indeed come to naught, or to death from *them*. And Kirrensark Long-haft. Aye, oh aye. He whom *they*, the Others, tried to subvert nigh twenty years ago. They will try for Rander, not yet Blade.

"And the queen of a land I will not name; her name is Xanthis."

The Lady of the Snowmist paused then, gazing upon them from within her helm-mask of gleaming argent god-metal. "And there are Jarik of the Black Sword and Jilain of Osyr Isle—called Demonslayer now, eh!—who are two and yet one, and yet still another, for you Jarik are two unto yourself! Oh and aye, make no mistake about that other part of you. Oak the InSightful, Oak the Scry-healer, is important!"

"I!" Jarik echoed, loudly.

"And this one!"

"Both. Yes. And we must talk, and make a bargain. For I know that Jarik Blacksword is a man who keeps his bargains! Come, and I shall tell you more, and show you somewhat."

It was then. She rose and turned to lead them to another place to "show them somewhat" and it was then that Jarik Blacksword, reminded that he was a man who kept his bargains, confused, unhappy, aware of a bargain unkept, mistrusting; it was then that he kept that bargain he had made with the Lords of Iron.

# Fourteen

*Then Dimness passed upon me, and that song*
*Was sounding o'er me when I woke*
*To be a pilgrim on the Nether earth.*

—*Dean Alford*

On the instant of her turning away, Jarik rose with the Black Sword in his hand and all in that same swift movement plunged its glass-smooth blade through the silvery armor and the body of Her who had used and reduced and subverted him and sore confused him, and that after he had made bargain to do death on Her. The Lady Karahshisar of the Snowmist he stabbed deep and hard now, and he was at pains to angle the blade downward into her womb, where quickened his own seed.

He heard the beginning of Jilain's outcry and
There was Darkness.

\* \* \* \* \* \*

"Jarik!" Jilain screamed, with the hideous sound of pain and terror in her voice, and Jarik clapped spurs to his horse, for those horrid ugly creatures were carrying her into the necrotic grey fog that was their home.

And he overtook them and struck again and again with his shining iron sword, so that snarling animal heads flew from bodies that were neither beast nor human and which gushed blood that spurted over hands furred and clawed like those of beasts. Such a taloned hand or "hand" tore down his leg, though he felt only the blow of its impact and the sudden cold in his leg without taking note of the frightful wounds that poured forth his blood in a scarlet sheet while he struck away the arm of the creature. Overtaken, seeing the blood of their horrid rearmost brethren spilled, the other animal-men panicked as beasts might, which had less than the brains of men. A taloned hairy paw leapt out, hooked, and arced down so that Jilain's face was ripped into a scarlet ruin while another of the creatures bit away the fingers of her right hand and a third—at the same time as Jarik, shrieking as one gone entirely mad, struck his blade deep into its furred back—tore off the left breast of Jilain Kerosyris and hurling it from him thrust his snouted beast's muzzle into the wound to tear out her heart with its teeth. *Lady Snowmist,* Jarik Blacksword thought in agony, calling on the only god he had, *if only I had the Black Sword*! And then the masters of those creatures of the fog, those *un*-men of the fog, came gliding forth like wraiths from the domain of ever-shifting grey and while Jilain died and one of the *un*-men tore away Jarik's right arm so that his shoulder fountained blood and was terribly cold, the creators who were the Lords of Fog of Akkharia in their grey masks, laughed in swirling gusts that were like the fog itself.

"Jarik!" Jilain called. "What are these—what are they?"

"The Iron Lords," Jarik told her, and he smiled. "The Lord of Destruction! And the Lord of Annihilation! And the Lord of Dread! The Lords of Iron, Jil, whom I serve! My allies—our allies!"

"*Well done, Jarik,*" boomed forth the metallically ringing voice of the Lord of Destruction, from within the mask of gleaming blue-black iron that was a part of his iron helmet that was not iron.

"*Well done, Jarik*!" rang the metal-echoic voice of the Lord of Dread, from within his mask-helm of black iron that was not iron, but he did not say "Jarish."

"*You have slain our sister Karahshisar, Jarik, and well done,*" called the Lord of Annihilation, and his hollowly, metallically echoing voice was full and soaring with the happiness of triumph. *"The Lady of the Snowmist is no more!"*

"Aye!" Jarik Blacksword said in jubilance and with pride, catching up Jilain's hand in his left and fondling the hilt of the Black Sword with his right, his hand of deeds. "It is done. The bitch died not hard by the Black Sword, and so did the seedling within Her for it was mine and I've no desire to be siring a son born of our enemy!"

Annihilation said low, *"You . . . lay with her? With Karahshisar?"*

"Aye, or so She said, Milords of Iron—twice. For She had want of a child of mine." And Jarik's chest stood forth and joy and pride were sunshine on his face.

*"Hoho brothers,"* the Lord of Annihilation called in a voice that might have emanated from a well walled with iron, *"the feisty little earth-grub of an anthro-man has lain with a God on the Earth! Twice, it says! Hoho Jarik, and then you did death on her, is it? Slow about accomplishing your mission for Us, were you? In no hurry to slay Our enemy, were you?"*

"I—"

*"Hear him, hear it!"* Annihilation interrupted. *" 'Aye,' it said! Hoho little Jarik, stupid little mortal with the dirt-grubbing hands, then surely turnabout is fair prey, and We appreciate the pretty little girl, anthro-girl there by your side, ally Jarik, and We shall all have her . . . twice, yes twice!"*

Jilain cried out, "Jarish!"

And Jarik cried out "No!" and drew the Black Sword of the Iron Lords against those Iron Lords themselves, the very gods themselves.

But they only laughed and pointed, the gleaming Lords of Iron, and Annihilation drew his own sword of dread black metal that indeed was not iron, and he extended it so that its tip was levelled at Jarik. On the point of making attack, Jarik saw only a shimmering in the air, and then the gushing licking hungry flame, and he felt the terrible heat. He knew then that he had burst into flame exactly as those three Hawkers the Iron Lords had slain, in seconds, that day in Blackiron. And Jarik Blacksword knew that he was dead of the Iron Lords his allies, though he had carried out their mission and kept his bargain with them. One last thing he heard, in Jilain's voice:

"Jarish!"

and

"Jarik!" she called. "They charge!"

And she sent another arrow into another of them before letting go her bow to draw forth her sword even as he did, rising behind her while scores of the men-at-arms of Indwell came leaping at them. Battle was ferocious then, with the Black Sword and the weaving flashing blade of Jilain taking heavy toll. There were many and many, and so Jarik chose no specific enemy, no victim, but merely slashed and chopped and slashed, back and forth with all the force of his mailed arm, tearing his blade free of this shoulder and shearing through that neck as though its helmet's curtain of mail was not there, back and forth and back like one utterly mad, blind, the battle-rage on him and possessing his soul and his arm. A hurled ax sundered his shield and he knew without pain other than that of the jarring blow that his arm was broken. It dropped to his side. Still he swung and swung the other, his arm of deeds in great back and forth slashes while his useless arm flopped and flapped like a stricken sail. Blood streamed out in a ribbon of red from the mirror-smooth blade of the Black Sword, and heads flew. And when two blades at once smashed into her buckler so that it was splintered and she knocked off balance, Jilain Kerosyris staggered sidewise, very much in the wrong direction, and the Black Sword sent her head arolling on the backswing. And back dashed that awful blade even while she stood geysering blood and shuddering, headless, and the battle-blind Jarik saw her only after she had toppled and lay partway across one of his feet. Then did he shriek out his rage and horror. He faltered but an instant while still the enemy came and came. He resumed his slashing, not again and again but all in one great back-and-forth horizontal 8 that struck down enemy after enemy. And still they came, the minions of the Lord of Indwell who was the minion of those gods on the earth forming the Forces of Destruction, and Jarik staggered at a blow and felt the blow and the blast of cold when his left arm was chopped away, and he fell to a knee when his left leg was chopped away by an ax like a slice of the moon, and still he swung and slashed until his helm was splintered above by an ax that did not cease its shearing downward smash until it was wedged in his lower teeth.

The fifth *un*-man fell, and then the sixth, and Jilain nocked her final arrow and drew string and let fly. Then did a seventh fall. She rose then to whirl smiling upon Jarik, who was bound and watching helplessly while she came in a wake of *un*-human blood to his rescue.

"There, *un*, my love! All are dead," she said, "and we—"

Then a great burst of blood started from her mouth, at the same time as her shining leather coat bulged at the chest and was sundered as the gory leaf-shape of a spearhead burst through. Blood sprayed Jarik and it was only after that that he heard the sound of the spear striking her back. With a hideous look in her eyes and with her mouth fountaining scarlet she toppled, falling forward—and the spearhead standing from her bilobed chest drove into the face of the love and companion she had sought to save, and dying Jarik knew that he should not have done death on the Lady of the Snowmist, for he saw the blue-armored figure beyond and above the beloved, dead head lying on his shoulder, and Jarik knew that this was the Lord Cerulean, a god on the earth, and enemy of Elye Isparanana who was Karahshisar—whom Jarik had slain in keeping a bargain with the Forces of Destruction.

And he believed.

"Die slowly, little man," the Lord Cerulean said hollow-metallically from within his gleaming blue helmet-mask that was fashioned into the head of a great hawk. "Die slowly, soil-grubbing anthro-man, for it was you who brought death on the Lady Cerulean! Die slowly—and mayhap you will last long enough to hear news that the very last of your kind has been destroyed, annihilated, extirpated from the face of this planet!"

*The last? But—but I Saw myself fighting side by side with Her who must be the Lady Cerulean, a god on the*
Darkness.

"Jarik!" Jilain called, in a voice of great sorrow.

But he heard only dimly and too he paid no heed, for the beautiful, beautiful Lady Tiger was bending over him, smiling, all soft and seductive and beautiful and for him, him; what cared he now that her strange minions—neither tigers nor men and yet both in one—were enjoying the body of his Jilain; was he not after all about to enjoy the supreme experience of being night-mate of the beautiful beautiful, the incomparable Lady Tiger?

"If only the Iron Lords had not taken back the Sword, and we had the Lady Karahshisar's guidance," Jilain made lament; and then she was shrieking, shrieking; but Jarik, in a private heaven inhabited only by himself and Lady Tiger, could not be concerned over such trifles . . .

and

In the keep of the Lady of the Snowmist the healer called Oak bent over a fallen god, seeking desperately to heal while Metanira and another named Wildflower stood close and aided him and Jilain Kerosyris stood well away, out of the light, where he had bidden her go and take that hideous terrible murdering Black Sword that was a thing of sorcery and murder, and Metanira glanced around and screamed.

Oak looked up, and his hands went as if frozen while he, too, stared.

Snowmist Keep had been breached and broached. A figure stood there, and though it showed no eyes, it was surely looking at Oak bent over a wounded and fallen god, seeking to heal Her. The invader was armored all in scintillant black that even over there in a dimmer area of the chamber was like black water running in sunlight. Boots of the same shod him and rose up his calves; from the boot-tops blossomed leggings of that armor to vanish beneath the skirt of his black coat of the same, its long sleeves feeding into gauntlets that rose to mid-forearm and were reinforced by small plates of blue-black iron, like the horn of Jilain's helmet and bow. Like cloth the armor was, and at the same time like woven metal; the same as that armor of Snowmist's, save that it was black, black. An unornamented black helm that Oak knew was not iron covered his head, with a curtain of the black-lizard-glistening armor covering three sides of his head. The mask attached to the helm rendered him featureless while curving back on either side under that arras of woven mail that might have come from an invulnerable black snake. The mask, of that blue-black iron which Oak knew was not iron, was pierced by eyeslits and a grim slitted mouth that was like a gash, without lips. Nothing could be seen within. A strange iron not-iron "nose," too, was mounted on that boding helm-mask.

Oak saw no mouth. Oak saw no eyes. Oak saw nothing of that grim tall figure's flesh or features; only its form which was that of a man. And in one of those mail-gauntleted hands it bore a sword that looked identical to Jarik's; black and shining and glassy, reflective as water or gemstones of jet or the wings of deathbirds in the rain.

"*So!*" The voice came from that dreadsome mask all hollowly and metallically, echoing within the chamber formed by mask and helm. "*So our servant Jarik kept his bargain to do death on our dear kith, Karahshisar, and well done—and you, Scry-healer, now seek to save her, do you?*"

"How—how came you here, Lord Destruction?" Oak asked, for Jarik's memories told him that he recognized the voice of this god on the earth. "Yourselves told Jarik that Snowmist kept you close confined, other side Dragonmount."

"*And Jarik believed!*" The Lord of Destruction paced closer. The two servants cowered and Oak felt fear. "*How can she keep us there now, though? Eh? Eh? Stabbed her deep, did he not?*"

Oak looked down at the body he labored over. "Deep, aye. But not dead. Dying. Unless . . ."

"*Stop, Oak. She—is—to—die!*"

Oak stared at the featureless mask; stared at the two horizontal slits where eyes should have been. "I cannot do that. I must do what I do. It is what I do. You know that, Iron Lord. Jarik slays, and Oak heals—or seeks to heal!" And to one of the two servants of Snowmist so near to hand: "Wildflower. Hand me that wad of cloth."

Wildflower, wide-eyed, pretty and young and fearful, looked at him, and chewed her pretty lower lip, and glanced at the Iron Lord who had appeared in Snowmist Keep. Oak stared, and she turned to do his bidding. The Lord of Destruction raised his god-sword of the god-metal and the god-power then, and pointed it at that pretty young woman with the daffodil hair, and she had not even time to shriek as she burst into flame, all over. She perished in seconds in roaring flame that also caught the wadding Oak used to staunch blood-flow. Metanira sprang back, for her skirt had commenced to smoke though she stood a long pace from the pillar of roaring yellow and white flame that had been her comrade.

Then the Lord of Destruction moved his arm, and the tip of his fire-spouting black sword was leveled directly at Oak.

Almost ridiculously as he was about to die, Oak's thought was on the irony: this body and these minds were to be slain because of him, the healer, rather than because of that bloody killer Jarik, who surely deserved it!

Then—

The three long ships disgorged hundreds of men with axes and spears and swords and bright-painted bucklers. Sunlight flashed brightly, as if happily, off the bosses of brass and iron and copper on their mailcoats as they came charging up the long hill that separated the beach from the wark of Kirrensark. Kirrensark's people, barely a hundred now and hardly recovered from the voyage followed so closely by the dawn battle with Ahl, awaited them. They took toll on those attackers with the stones they rolled down into their howling mass. From the tops of the masts of the trio of hawk-prowed ships swooped birds of prey not hawks and yet great hawk-like birds whose wings did not move; birds that glinted and shone and gleamed blue-black in the bright sunlight of day.

Jarik and Jilain burst from the Cloudpeak keep of the dead Lady of the Snowmist. They rushed down the mountainside as fast as they dared and were able. Below, men were dying. Aye, and the women and the children too, of Kirrensark-wark. Flames leaped high in an obscene dance of flickering horror; rushed up from houses and out-buildings alike, while the attackers ravened among weary defenders whose number they halved, and halved again.

By the time Jilain and Jarik reached the scene of leaping dancing orange flame and rolling dark smoke, even the screams had ceased, for all were dead. Winded and weary, Jarik and Jilain nevertheless made attack. And too each slew a goodly number of the howling enemy before her legs were cut from under her and a thrown ax smashed in the face of Jarik Blacksword who had slain the Lady of the Snowmist and left Kirrensark's wark open to attack by these human minions among the Forces of Destruction.

"*Ah, Gods may not slay Gods,*" the Lord of Dread said. *It is a law of the universe. Too, long long ago the Lady of the Snowmist wove a powerful spell, that keeps Us here, con-fined. We cannot leave this place to extend our benevolent protection to others as We wish, for she prevents us.*"

Jarik asked, "She is a sorcerer!"

"*She is a god.*"

"As are you, Iron Lords?"

"*Even as We are, Jarik,*" the Lord of Annihilation said. "*And it is hardly unknown that too often the gods must ask the aid of mortal men.*"

"*We want you to slay her, Jarik,*" the Lord of Destruction said.

"*You must slay her,*" Dread said in his rumbly voice. "*Slay the Lady of the Snowmist. Slay her slay—*"

*slay slay slay slay slay slay*

"Done, done, all done," the Lady Shirajsha said, shaking her head dolorously so that the firelight struck flashes of silvery grey from her frosty mask. Despair and self-pity formed a cloak about her mind, so that it was no longer an organ of cerebration at all. "I am all that survives—and you, of course, Jarik One-arm who were once Jarik Blacksword and once a man. First it was poor Karahshisar, and after that the Iron Lords sent death on that Lokustan of hers, Kirrensark, and the Gem Lords came for the Rod of Osyr, who died before any of us and who stayed dead, poor Osyr who was Osyshehir. Oh yes—after that the Iron Lords burned you so, Jarik, and raped your poor dear what-was-her-name so that she was never the same, and it was probably a kindness when the minions of the Fog Lords slew her and uh . . . where was I? Gone, gone, all gone, all of them, all of us gods come to your earth, my kind as well as our allies among your kind, and you, poor wreck of a, uh, Jarik, Jarik, and I, poor little Shircha who was once so beauteous; we can only wait here until *they* come for us. Ours to see it happen, Jarik, poor Jarik One-arm; the extirpation of your kind from this entire lovely young planet of yours and its population replaced with *their* half-formed, half-brained, part-beast creations, who or which will all be slaves to the Forces of Destruction become the Forces of Rule, throughout eternity! For they shall live and rule forever and ever. *We* sought men who were as we are, women who were as we are; thinking, with the tempering of emotion. *They* sought rule over the beast-men who would do only what they were told. And now *they* have won, Jarik One-arm who was once a hero once a champion of the Forces of Man and a man and, for that brief flashing silv'ry instant, a hero in the War! Well, well, Jarik. Not I! No! Perhaps what remains of your kind will go all stupid now and say 'not me,' do you think, Jarik poor Jarik what was I say—No! Not I. They will not have poor once-pretty little Shircha. They will not come and make me watch the ultimate Destruction and the rise and spread over this lovely world of *their* creations those obscenities their creatures, the New Creatures, the un-Men, aye and seek to impregnate me even me in hopes of gaining something viable, a bit of new blood. No! Shirajsha shall not wait for that. No, no, not the Lady Shirajsha, not little beautiful Shircha of the Web of Silver! I shan't wait for them to come in triumph to us and do things to us and make us watch the Annihilation of all your kind from this entire lovely world we thought held such promise! No Jarik, poor Jarik One-arm, all is lost now and you can wait alone, alone, for I am too much the coward to wait for them to wait for them to come triumphant to us and make us watch all that and do things to us and laugh at us. Ah, ah, that would hurt, hurt, to be laughed at, for I am after all . . . I am . . ."

And the Lady of the Silver Web, who was the Last, lifted her long slim knife of pure shining greyed silver save that it neither bent nor broke nor pitted nor nicked nor even turned dark, and though still wearing her grey-silvery mask of webbing she commenced to saw through her neck so that the hot red blood ran and then began to gush, in jetting spurts that shone in the firelight like molten rubies, *llankets* spurting over him who had been Jarik Blacksword and who had destroyed them all and made the world safe and free for the Iron Lords and the reign of the beast-men, forever.

"*You must slay her,*" Dread said in his rumbly voice. "*Slay the Lady of the Snowmist. Slay her slay—*"

slay slay slay slay slay slay

"*We are convinced,*" the Lord of Destruction said, "*that it was at her bidding that you were abandoned to die, as an infant. Perhaps she foresaw that it was you who would come in time to slay her slay her slay her.*"

"Then She is not your sister and not my god!" Jarik cried in his pride and his needy needful needing. "She is an enemy. I will keep the Sword. Yourselves leave me the Sword, and will lead me to Kirrensark of the hawk-ships. In return, I shall slay the Lady of the Snowmist, evil Karahshisar. My enemy—our enemy."

"*Aye*," the Lord of Dread said, and the great iron helmet with its attached iron mask nodded.

"How . . . can it be accomplished," Jarik asked, "the death of a god?"

*"The Black Sword will slay her, Jarik—and those she raises to menace you, though you must have as much care as ever, warrior."*

*warrior warrior warrior slay*

Jarik said, "The Black Sword would slay yourselves, then."

Kirrensark Long-haft asked, "Seek you to provoke me, Jarik Blacksword?"

"I came here to kill you, Kirrensark," Jarik told him.

"I have seen into your mind . . . minds, No-man's son Jarik of the Black Sword-and-Oak the Healer! You have no secrets from me."

*slay slay*

"Yourself has several secrets from me, Lady Karahshisar. Why did you bid that I be abandoned by my parents so that I never saw them and do not know even who they are? Were?"

"I did not."

"Who am I?"

"I do not know," the Lady of the Snowmist said. "I have seen into your mind. You do not know who you are. You are an enigma, a Mystery. Know and be sure, Jarik-and-Oak, that neither do the Iron Lords know—and that they have some fear of you."

"Fear?"

"Fear."

"Fear!"

"Aye, Jarik. Fear, of you."

"Are you my mother?"

"No."

"Am I one of the abandoned boy-babes of Kerosyr?"

"No," the Lady of the Snowmist said.

"Are you my father, Orrik of Akkharia who reared me?"

"No."

"Father . . . I mean Orrik . . . why do you leave me? Where are you going?"

"To die, Jarik the thrice-obtuse."

"Strode of Ishparshule-wark, are you my father, who was rearing me and my . . . my sister, Torsy?"

"She is not your sister, stupid."

"*Are you my father?*"

"Of course not. No. Now go. Go and wander in exile. Wander and wonder, Jarik the Treacherous. God-slayer!"

*Oak! Oak my brother, heal me! Be born and heal us!*

"Are you my sister, Torsy, who was reared with me as my sister?"

"No."

"Torsy! I love you—I need you—why do you leave me? Where are you going?"

"To die, Jarik the Helpless."

"Ah then, Lords of Iron. The Black Sword would slay yourselves."

"*Jarik, Jarik! Jarik the Unthinking! Think you We would place the means to slay Us into the hands of those stupid villagers? Or of a dirt-grubbing little night crawler such as you?*"

"What becomes of the youths yourselves bring up here from Blackiron, from time to time?"

"*They become Iron Lords. We steal their bodies.*"

"Lady God—what becomes of those youths yourself does bring up here from Kirrensark-wark and Ishparshule-wark, from time to time?"

"Each is potentially the father of the next Lady of the Snowmist, for I must continue."

"But what if something happens to yourself ere a new Milady Snowmist is . . . grown, Milady Snowmist?"

"Then you and your kind on this world are in a lot of trouble, you murderous wart."

"I—you—yourself does steal their seed?"

PAIN

"Steal?" the Lady of the Snowmist repeated, with heat. "No, I do not steal, Jarik. In return I reward them with life-long health—and the wark rewards them with high popularity."

"It . . . is true. You do not steal, Lady of the Snowmist. *They* do."

"Aye. Then why have you slain me, you blood-handed friendless brain-sick barbarian bastard?"

*Heal me, Oak! Heal us!*

"Because I keep my bargains, my lady Karahshisar, and I made bargain with the Lords of Iron, your loving brothers who steal the bodies of others and live in them, covered all in iron that is more than iron. And the bargain was that I would come here and do death on yourself. And I keep my bargains. And you made me a slave. A man has his pride! Besides, you did also confuse me, and make me uncomfortable. And what you say is true, my lady God; my hands are indeed covered all with blood, and obviously too it is true that I am a barbarian. And sure I must be a bastard, for I know not who birthed me or fathered me either. Art thou my mother?"

*Heal me, Oak. Heal us, Healer.*

"No. How could I be your mother? I bear your seed in my womb."

"My—you what?"

"*I bear your sword in my womb.*"

"Are you my mother?"

"No! How could I be your mother, grubber in the soil? I am a god!"

*Heal m*

PAIN

"But . . . surely no god can be slain by an earth-grubbing mortal."

"Ah! It is true, Jarik!"

"Then . . ."

"Then I cannot be dead, can I Jarik of the Black Sword, sore confused Jarik Blacksword. I am not dead, then. You have of the gods a second chance, as few men have. Here it is. We must talk, and make a bargain. For I know that Jarik of the Black Sword, Jarik-who-is-Oak, is a man who keeps his bargains, pretending that it is a matter of honor and importance and that he hath pride. Come, I shall tell you more, and show you somewhat."

And She turned, and paused, as if waiting, a frozen waterfall of shimmering silver. And then the Lady of the Snowmist looked back at him. "Ah. Are you not going to kill me this time, then?"

"I! No! I was too hasty—I must know more, more!"

"There is much to know. Much you do not know."

"Aye!"

"You know nothing, Jarik."

"It is true."

"You know not even who you are."

"It is true, Lady God. I am no one, for I know not who I am."

"You do! You are Jarik of the Black Sword. Jarik Blacksword."

"It is not enough!"

"You are Jarik Blacksword, and Oak, who has the In-Sight and scries that he may see the hurt in others, and how to mend it, and he mends it when he can. You are Jarik Blacksword and Oak the Scry-healer, aye—and you are Jilain of the Isle, too!"

"Jilain?"

"What is it, Jarish?"

"She . . . She is not dead?"

"Of course I am not dead! You have been dreaming. You have been seeing the possibilities of a future, of futures that might be—that might have been. You have been seeing such all your life, and must know that some are true visions into the time to come and some are visions of Might-be. You are that too, then. You have that ability, for which many would give much, and without so much whining and self-pity. You are still Jarik Blacksword, and Oak the Scry-healer, and Jilain Kerosyris, all at once."

"But—"

"But! What sort of stupid beginning is that, for human converse?"

"B—that is what I am now, Lady God. It is what I have become. It is not enough!"

Jilain's voice came, "Only children must identify with who birthed them, Jarik. Men and women are what they become of themselves. How can this one know who her father was?"

"!"

"It is far more than many are, Jarik Blacksword," the god said.

"It is not enough. What care I of many? I am not many—I am I."

"This one is this one!"

"It is far more," the god said, "than many know of themselves, Jarik of the Black Sword."

"Talk to me not of others! It is not enough! Talk to me of me! I must know more. I must know who I am. Who my father was. My mother. My *people*."

"Jarik," Jilain said softly, "it does not matter to this one . . ."

"It matters to me!" Jarik's voice rose high, threatened to crack. "This one must know!"

"The answer lies within the world, Jarik Blacksword," the Lady of the Snowmist said, very quietly. "It lies out there, waiting to be found. By you, in the world that must be lived in. In the world that is, and the world that is not to be and is not yet . . . if we save it, Jarik. If we wrest it and protect it from the Forces of Destruction."

"And Dread, and Annihilation!" he said, and his voice was lower.

"If we save it from those who would create dread, yes. If we save it from those who would destroy, who would annihilate your kind, yes, and then people—'people'—this entire world with slaves. Slaves who are men raised from animals, beasts who are more than beasts and men who are less than men."

"We," Jarik said, very quietly indeed. "Yourself said we, Lady God."

"Aye, Jarik Blacksword. So I did. We. For you must know that the Iron Lords are not your allies, or worthy employers or gods for the following. They keep no bargains. They steal bodies. They lie. They do murder and send others to do murder. They wish to destroy all Jariks—all anthro-men."

"They are . . . *They*."

"Aye, Jarik Blacksword. And we are we."

"Yes," Jarik said, softly and slowly, pondering as he spoke and staring ahead as though he saw across some vast distance, and through it. "No, *they* are not my allies. *They* put the lie upon me. *They* burned me, raped Jilain—"

"Jarik!" Jilain cried in a voice of fear; it was fear for him.

"No no, Jarik," the Lady of the Snowmist said, "that has not happened. That was but a vision of the possible future. A time-to-come that you might create, if you remain allied with the Forces of Destruction. For presently you are. You have had other such visions of the time to come and the time that Might-be, have you not?"

*The time to come? The* possible *future*, he mused. And he

pondered. *The time that is to be . . . that might be. Aye—*
*how awful it was, that vision and others! Visions. The time*
*that might be. If I slew Her, those are then the consequences.*
*If I—but She might have put those thoughts, those visions,*
*into my mind! (Minds.) I am not sure! How can I ever be*
*sure?—Oak! Heal us!*

"Nevertheless," he said, for he knew that he must talk,
listen, keep talking, continue this conversation (why?);
"they were lying to me. They tricked me. I need be keeping
no bargain with those men in the masks of black iron. And
stolen bodies."

"Jarik!" Jilain's vice cried in excitement and pleasure.
"Oh, Jarish!"

*Oak! Oh, Oak!*

Snowmist said, "Then you will surely join us. For now
you know at least of the War, the War that is among the
gods on the earth—how can you walk away from it?"

"We cannot, Jarik," Jilain said, and he noticed that he
much liked her voice; surely taken from a dove.

"We cannot walk away," Jarik Blacksword said, "Lady
Karahshisar. Yourself speaks truth, Lady God. We will
join yourself now in the War."

And Jarik held forth his arms, and turned up his palms,
open and empty. "Lady; Lady God . . . restore thy bracers
to my wrists."

The god said, "It is not necessary, Jarik. They were to
protect me from you. And to . . . ensure the obedience to
me of an agent of the Iron Lords. For *they* would kill us
all."

Jarik chewed at his lip.

"They were a comfort to me, Lady, Lady Karahshisar.
They were a—a security. Wearing them, I *belonged.* I mat-
tered. I have never belonged, not in all my life. Wherever I
was, I was a foundling. A visitor. Adopted. A guest; one
apart. *Found on the beach.* That is my true name. My
name! There is no mother, not even the name of a father
for my name." His arms were still outstretched; he moved
them a bit, as though in supplication.

Jarik said, "Restore the bracers of Silver Mist."

And Jilain, too, stretched forth her arms, palms open
and upturned. And they two stood there thus, suppliants
to a god in a silvery mask, and her in armor, a god born of

mortal man—and birthed by a god.

And the mist came, like silver and day-fog and pearls, and it was chill when it touched their hands and their wrists and began to circle there to wreathe them. It crept about their upturned wrists in little tendrils, all smoky and wraithlike, and the tendrils spread and joined and became opaque, and then solid, so that there were bracers locked on their wrists then, thin and long and without lock or fastener or seam. The Bands of Snowmist. Up from wrist along forearm they extended, and they were longer than twice the length of Jarik's smallest finger.

And Jarik Blacksword was comforted by their presence, by their temperature that was his own. By the security of their presence on his thick forearms of a man of weapons. They made him part of her company. Part of Her. Part of the company of the gods on the earth who had created (?) his kind and sought to protect them that they might inherit the earth; a part of the company of gods, the Forces of Man. He belonged.

"You have joined me now, Jarik Blacksword." So spoke the Lady of the Snowmist.

"Aye."

"And you, Jilain Kerosyris."

"Aye. We are joined, this one and Jarik and yourself."

"Then," the Lady of the Snowmist said, "you cannot slay me." And her voice sounded weak.

"No," Jarik said quickly. "I cannot slay yourself, Lady God. It is all well then, isn't it. I could not slay you with the bracers on me—I could not slay yourself with*out* them, now! I could not slay *you*! I could not have slain you! *I could not have done it*! Tell me that I did not—Oak! Oak, heal us—Oak, Healer, *heal her*!"

And then Jarik opened his eyes at last, and looked down, and there before him on a table all padded and draped in white splashed with crimson darkening into brown lay the body of the Lady Karahshisar of the Snowmist, whom he had stabbed with the Black Sword of the Iron Lords because he had pride, and was confused, and felt bound by a bargain dishonorably made with the dishonorable. And he knew that at last these dreams were done.

This, Jarik knew, was reality.

# Fifteen

*"It is not true to say that everything that may be good or bad must be either good or bad. There are intermediate hues between the contrarieties of black and white."*

—the Guide

"Oak! Will She—"

"Oak?" Jarik assimilated, realized, understood—insofar as that other identity was understandable. He turned to look at the speaker, who was Jilain. "I am Jarik."

"Oh." She blinked, pausing to make the transition within her head and to begin anew. He saw that she wore a different tunic, without skirt or leggings. This one was a pale green containing more blue than yellow, again sleeveless and low of round neck. It ended midway down her thighs. She wore nothing else save the amber pendant he had given her.

"Oh," she said again. "Jarik! You have been Oak. Once you—you had stabbed the Lady of the Snowmist, you became Oak, all at once. You gave orders—Oak did, that is. You—Oak saw how She might be healed, he said, in his—in your mind and in hers. But . . . you never remember being Oak, Jarik?"

Jarik stared at her, feeling weary. "No." He looked about, feeling no less disoriented than he had during that succession of visions.

They were in a different place. A different area, since he saw that they were still within Cloudpeak, within the keep of the Lady of the Snowmist. And She was there.

On the white-padded and white-draped table before him, beneath a large strange focusing light that was many-faceted and *closed*, a lamp that breathed no air and showed no flame or flicker—there lay Her he had stabbed. The Lady of the Snowmist remained masked, but naked. In a way; She was wound about with a huge bandage that encased Her as previously her armor had done. This time that "armor" of pastel cloth extended only from loins to ribcage.

*Only*! He closed his eyes in anguish. Squeezed them tightly. Never had he seen such a bandage. How could She live with such a wound? What had he done—and what had Oak done in consequence?

"I . . . I don't . . . no, no, I never remember. But . . . so many things have happened to—have happened since then! Was it all in my mind? Seemed to happen, then. I was . . . I was in other places. In the time-to-be, or the time that might be?" He shook his head. What horrors he had seen and endured! Then, "Jilain! Are you all right?"

Her face changed, went soft. She made as if to touch him, but did not. "Of course, Jarik. Worried, just worried for you. One is so glad you—you are back. Oak is, Oak is so *surly* when he is busy! And he stays busy. Oak is totally . . . totally dedicated, single-minded."

"Yes," Jarik said, so quietly that he only just breathed the word. "Oak is my good side. The good part of Jarik Blacksword."

"Oh Jarik! You are not evil!"

Jarik's eyes turned to stone and were bleak as the sky before the coming of the blizzard. "I disagree. But—so many things happened! Was it all a dream? All of that? Dreams? The Iron Lords? Those warriors of . . . Baron, uh, Indwell? The Fog Lords and their, their *creatures*?" A shiver ran through him and his fingers worked. "All those words; all I have learned? Just dreams and visions, while Oak worked and my mind, thrust aside, sought . . . sought something to occupy me?" He shook his head; touched it. He felt stubble without paying it any mind. "Ever do I dream, while Oak works. Lady Tiger?" Again he shuddered. "What a woman! And poor dotty Shirajsha! Driven into the return of childhood upon her brain by all the horror, the destruction to come, the War lost . . . because of me? Was none of that real?"

He looked about, and his eyes were those of a trapped animal seeking the light, and a way out.

Then he remembered to look at his own wrists. There were no bracers. His arms looked obscenely naked. Aye, and he felt so. This was not freedom, not with his wrists bare and this guilt upon him like a weight of solid iron! He turned his eyes again toward the warrior woman across the long white table from him. A tear was shivering on her cheek, twinkling there like a droplet of dew suspended beneath a leaf.

"How long . . . how long has it been, Jilain?"

"Since you put sword into Her," she said, and saw him flinch at the phrase. "Most of a nikht, and two full days. Did you know that most of the women we see here are not here at all?—That you fought illusions that other time you were here? She tested you; She. Did you see the little girl that other time you were here, Jarik?"

He remembered. "Yes. I saw a child, a girl. Very pale."

"She has never been out of the mountain. She was born here. She is her daukhter, Jarik; the girl is the daukhter of the Lady of the Snowmist. She has tried and tried to talk to Oak. Oak hears nothing when he works, or ignores all else and everyone else. Unless he needs something of us."

Jarik nodded. Then he asked, frowning, "Needs?"

"Tools. Certain tools he demanded of the girl. He demanded that water be cooked, heated until it steamed. At first, at the very first, he demanded help in getting Her out of her armor, and then he demanded this one's skirt and railed when one was slow in removing it. Soon he had need of this one's tunic, too. And he used his own robe—that beautiful robe She gave you, Jarik. All those things are bloody, and more too. We all jumped to obey Oak, and fetched and carried for Oak, and accepted Oak's surliness and his impatience and railing. He is so competent, Oak is—and no fit companion for anyone!"

Again Jarik only nodded. *I am no fit companion for that noble healer*, he reflected, but the thought was fleeting. He was still working on acclimation. It seemed so long ago, that he had—had done this, to the god. A downward glance showed him that he wore a loose and almost sleeveless tunic. It was white, and it bore much rusty brown splotching. The stains were hard, with a slight metallic sheen. Blood, he knew. The blood of a god. The blood of Her. He had spilled it, and now he wore it. He gazed at Jilain, blinking.

"I hope—I hope that danger never comes on me when I am Oak, and so busy!"

"This one will be there," the champion of Kerosyr said. "This one will defend you when you are Oak, Jarik."

"You were not given another skirt, I see," he said inanely, for he noticed without quite noticing that his brain was slow and lazy and not ready to function.

Jilain shrugged. "Skirts were not made for Jilain," she said. "This one was not made for skirts. Besides, all that cloth would have tripped one, when *he* came."

"He? Oh—Oak."

She gave him a look of concern and confusion. "You do not remember? You remember nothing of this time when you were Oak?"

"I remember much. All of it is unreal, though. So far! I think."

He set a hand to his forehead, and found that his hair was bound back with a strip of cloth, tied behind. Dreams, illusions, visions! *What was reality?* Why was he so convinced that all of it was real or as if real? That what She had said was true, and what Shirajsha had said? That his dreams or visions had shown him truth? There were two factions of gods. They were divided and at odds over the future of humankind . . . that is, whether humankind should *have* a future on the earth! And the Iron Lords represented the other side. The Forces of Destruction. . . .

"Jarik?"

He waved his hand, lifted his head. He looked at Jilain.

"This one did not refer to Oak, Jarik, when she referred to *him* who came. It was one of *them.* The dread gods. An Iron Lord."

"*What?*"

She nodded. "An Iron Lord came here, Jarik. We—"

He stared, looked all around, stared again at her. One of the Lords of Iron. *Here!*

"Metanira and one named Wildflower were helping Oak," Jilain said. "This one stood well away, over there. Oak had bidden one get far away with it—the Black Soord. Then *he* came. He merely . . . appeared. One moment he was not here, and the next moment he was. He said that

She must not be saved, that She must die. You—Oak said that you must try to save Her. Oak bade Wildflower fetch—something. For his healing. One forgets what—"

"Cloth," Jarik said dully, staring not at Jilain, but through her. "Wadding, to stem the flow of her blood."

"Yes! Jarik—you do remember?"

"I . . . don't know." *Do I*? *That happened!* "Did he—did he kill her? Wildflower, I mean?"

"Yes. Horribly. Yet all in an instant. She became . . . flame. Metanira was paces away, and the garment she wore is scorched. He did it with his soord. Just such a soord as yours, Jarik, like the Black Soord—it *is* a black soord! Then he, he moved, just a little, pivoting a little, to point that horrible thing at you, that fire-soord!"

*Oh ye gods and Guide! Yes! Yes, I remember. But then—why am I alive?*

"And?" Jarik looked down at himself. "Why am I . . . what did he do then? *Jil what happened then?*"

"This one stood stricken into a statue by what she had seen, by the very sikht of that iron god of gloom and menace. The Iron Lord had not seen this one, and she stood frozen. But then one saw what he intended. He was going to kill *you*, the same way, in a burst of flame so that Oak might not save Her and that She would not live. Then this one came alive. Oh it is shame on a Guardian that this one was so slow to move, almost too late to act! It did not occur to one then that she mikht not stop a god. One had to—had to act! One was thinking nothing at all. One just . . . charged, with the Black Soord stretched out like a spear because time was so short and it went rikht into him."

"Into . . . Jilain? Through, *through the god armor.* My Black Sword, which had been theirs?"

"Yes. Into him, into the Iron Lord. He . . . he writhed on the point and—see? Up there. That darkness is char and scorch, where his soord spat fire without direction."

"You . . . saved . . . me. That was *real*, and you—then he vanished, is that it?"

She shook her blue-tressed head. "He was alive, twisting on the blade so that one could hardly hold it, and then his soord fell from his hand, that big black-mailed hand. It fell onto the floor, right there, and no flame came out of it. Then one yanked the Soord—*your* Black Soord—out of him, and whipped it back to strike hard, overhand-sidearm and with all one's might. The First Stroke, Guardians are taught to call it and to practice, and the best stroke of all, with the moost power behind it. The Black Soord chopped deep, Jarik. That Iron Lord fell down and was dead. Is dead."

"*Dead*!"

"Yes."

"You . . . *slew* . . . an Iron Lord?"

"Aye, Jarik."

He looked about, while his brain seemed to reel and his vision swam. Yet he could see, and he saw no Iron Lord. "Where . . ."

"We took him away, Jarik. Elsewhere, to another chamber. Oak would not suffer the body to lie there, and so Metanira and the child and this one carried him to another chamber. There he lies. Each of us has driven that Black Soord through the armor of gods into gods, Jarik. While we carried him away, Oak was already busy with Her. That Iron Lord is dead, Jarik. And see!" She showed him a hilt with an inch or so of iron blade. It had been snapped off. "With this, one tried to pry into his armor! Iron *breaks* on that armor, Jarik."

"Yes . . ." He stared at her, and then he lurched and hurried from behind the long table on which Snowmist lay, and Jarik seized and embraced Jilain. The truncated dagger fell forgotten. She strained to him and her arms enwrapped him. Through both their tunics he felt the hardness of the crimson gemstone tipping her breast—which was unusually firm itself, with the underlying muscle—and he did not mind, at all. They hugged each other and never had anything felt so good. Jarik was sure that he could stand and hold Jilain and be held by Jilain for hours, days. For ever.

"One thokht . . . ummm. One thokht that this was never going to happen," she murmured, pressing close and holding him so tightly as if she sought to blend their two bodies into one inseparable unit.

"So did I," he said, and for a long while then they said nothing but only strained together. Holding and feeling; being.

After a long while and yet far, far too soon, he became aware of his weariness. Cramps seemed fighting him for possession of his body. His calves were beset by quivers.

"Have I . . . has Oak slept?" That he murmured with his lips close to her ear.

She shook her head against his. "No. Oh, you drowsed and napped a bit now and then—standing rikht there, once. You have never left Her. Now and again you would growl 'water' or 'beer' and, twice, 'food!' We brokht you— Oak—what he asked. You drank and ate without pleasure, merely to sustain your body. Oak poured *wine* on Her and on bandages!" She hugged him in a renewed straining to him, making "umm" sounds. "Oak is not pleasant, Jarik. He does not want to talk. Only to do, and no one knows what he is doing but he. He ignores everything but his task. He wants only to escry, and heal, and to hover."

"And I? Oak *is* a healer. You prefer the company of Jarik, who stabbed a god in the back?"

He held her tightly, lest she decide to pull away from one who had done such a deed. His arms were going leaden and his calves quivered in weariness and the long strain of standing; his head was light and his brain hardly functioning at peak. He tried to ignore all that, and he held onto Jilain.

She remained against him, holding him. "You had made an agreement, Jarik. You had given your *woord*," Jilain said, and for her that was all of it. Among the Guardians, statements were promises. Promises were vows. Vows were *helderen*: unbreakable, as if sacred. One did what one said one would do; to do that which one had said one would not do was inconceivable. The queen of the Guardians had broken such a promise—and Jilain Kerosyris had slain her and harangued the other Guardians to choose an honorable ruler.

Jarik clung to her and stared at nothing. Every warrior had a blind spot, beyond the shield-edge. For Jilain, Jarik realized, it was a larger area. Where he, Jarik, was concerned, Jilain Kerosyris was blind.

"*I . . . love . . . you,*" he said or tried to say, and could not get the words past his throat.

She moved a little, and the ruby on her breast, the *llanket*, hurt him. He did not mind. She had not heard him, though, and he was sorry about that. He would tell her. It was so hard, being Jarik—and trying to be more than Jarik was just as hard.

"The child," she said. "The child, Jarik, said that you

had to do it. Umm, your back feels good to these hands. She understood. She is very wise, Jarik, that child. She is not . . . normal. A god's child. She says that she understands, Jarik. She holds no malice—and she says that *She* would understand.'' Jilain nodded at the body of Karahshisar, very pale and still, a god on the earth who lay wounded, unconscious, massively bandaged. Jarik could not see the indicative nod; he felt it. "The girl knows that you made a bargain, and were sore confused, and felt that you had to keep your agreement with the Iron Lords. She said that it makes you—proves you—what *She* thokht—thinks you are.''

"Yes,'' he said, with his jaws clamped so tightly that the bones hurt. His hands moved on her back and felt the firmness of muscle, the central depression that was only that, not a hollow. He could feel no vertebrae, and knew they were there. He held, he was held by, a warrior. A very fast and very strong woman, and she loved him. He loved her.

"Yes,'' he said again in that grim voice. "I keep bargains. Like a child, bound by a foolish oath. Oh yes. I kept my bargain with the Iron Lords!'' He was rigid, and she stroked his back. "The Iron Lords, who sent their iron hawk to kill me and to kill you, and who came, one of them, even here—after they had told me they could not—and sought to murder me. Because inside me there is a healer!''

"Oh Jarik.'' And they were silent, holding.

She said, "But Oak made no bargain, Jarik. He tried to save Her, and he is *you*, Jarik. You must not forget. Oak is you! This one is a part of you, Jarik—but Oak *is* you. Oh! Jarik!''

That she said suddenly, with a movement, and reluctantly Jarik let her step back a pace. He felt a breath of chill across his chest, where her warmth and his had for many minutes reflected each other. He saw that her tawny eyes were wide, and the thick black brows above expressed a new concern, just recollected.

Suddenly he heard himself say, "Jilish.'' And she was back against him, with both of them clinging and straining together.

"Jarish,'' she murmured. "Jair-iiishh . . .''

After a time he had to ask: "What was it, Jilai—Jilish? What did you suddenly remember?''

"What? Oh! One said that Oak is yourself, and heals, and one remembered: did you save Her, Jarik? Is She alive? Will She live?"

Keeping an arm around Jilain as she kept one about him, Jarik turned to look down upon Karahshisar. Naked and bandaged, She looked frail and very, very human, despite the mask. He noticed how small She was, how delicately made. It was Jarik's eyes that looked at Her, though, not Oak's. Jarik was helpless. Oak would not have let Jarik return if She were not all right, would he?

*Of course. Perhaps Oak would . . . go away, if She could not be saved, if She was dead or doomed. I do not know!*

He said it: "I don't know, Jilain."

"Oh wait—Jarik! Oak is gone! She must be going to live, then! Else he would have—oh." Jilain had thought of it too and she broke off, not wanting to voice it. She touched the still god. "Warm. She lives, Jarik. She is warm, but not hot; for a time She had a terrible fever, which Oak foukht and foukht until he sweated so much we thokht he had caught it. Now . . . Oak mikht leave if She were dead, but. . . . Anyhow, She is alive, and without fever. Her breathing feels normal or nearly. And Oak has left. She must be well, Jarish. Sleeping while she knits. She is healing."

Jarik blinked. She felt the sudden squeeze of his hand as he felt a reeling sensation. Suddenly one hand sprang out to brace him against the table of the wounded god, while he leaned heavily on Jilain. Sore fearful, she held him with both hands, her expression of worry for him.

"Yes," he said softly. "She will live. She will . . . be alive. She . . . the Lady of the Snowmist will . . . will never move again." And tears streaked the face of Jarik Blacksword, who had sought to slay Her, and the face of Oak the Healer, who had saved Her and sought to make Her knit.

The worry had left Jilain's face and now she looked sharply at him, her head on one side. "Jarik? You know this? Jarik? Oak?"

"We are here. I know it, yes. I am Oak. I am Jarik. We are not 'I, Jarik' and 'he, Oak'; or 'I, Oak' and 'he, Jarik.' We are one. I have seen with Oak's eyes and known with Oak's knowledge. Uh!" He leaned even more heavily on her and on the table. "I must rest."

And he collapsed.

# Sixteen

*When a man is convinced that all is darkness, he will cling to that conviction even in the brightest sunlight.*

—Moris Keniston

*Adversity attracts the man of character. He seeks out the bitter joy of responsibility.*

—C. de Gaulle

Jarik awoke. He had not dreamed. That, he mused, was a blessing of the g—

*Lady Karahshisar.* A god on the earth. A God on the Earth! A god; the Lady of the Snowmist. She would live. She would even talk. (Jarik found that he lay on a bed, and that he was pleasantly naked.) But the Black Sword had girded through Her, deep into Her, from behind. It had slashed the spinal cord as it drove, and Oak could not repair that. She was paralyzed, irremediably and forever. Or until She . . . died. (And somewhere an Iron Lord lay dead. Was it the Lord of Destruction? Ironic, since She referred to the *others* as the Forces of Destruction, if the one called Destruction was dead!)

(Thirst. Pox and blight—my lips are dry as hay in high summer!)

The girl. Perhaps the child—

His stomach made gurgling noises like a mountain stream at the time of thawing, and then it rumbled. He was ravenous. His stomach was a cavern—and yet he felt that if he pressed finger to navel, he could feel backbone.

Turning, he started to rise. This bed was in still another room; the amphora nearby was yellow, lightning-decorated in brown and seemingly splashed with blue dew-drops. And he was naked, though a coverlet was partway over him. Jilain? he wondered. Metanira? It occurred to him then that this time he had slept in Snowmist Keep, and She had not lain with him.

In the thought was neither happiness nor triumph.

Beside the bed stood a long-legged table of some blond wood. On it was food, meat and lentils and cabbage; and a perfect goblet of silver beside a pitcher of some beautifully decorated and glazed pottery that was glazed warm brown and red and orange. The aroma of meat made his nostrils twitch and his mouth fair spurt its saliva. Again his stomach complained. He sat more nearly erect and reached for the meat, and then he saw her.

She was nowhere near his height; not even the height of Metanira, whose crown came to his lower lip. She was very slim, and in her tight-fitting garment of white and silver there was no bud of womanhood on her and less to her hips than of his. She was masked in silver, but not helmeted; her hair was blond, with less gold in it than his and less white than Delath's.

*No more than ten*, Jarik mused.

*Not old enough.*

"You are not old enough, are you." It was not a question, and his tone was one of resignation.

"Eat. No. I am not. At the time of womanhood, I will be the Lady of the Snowmist. Eat." It was a girl's voice and yet not a child's. So serious; so grave, and wise.

"This has never happened before. The . . . necessity before the successor was ready, I mean."

"No. Hear me, Jarik of the Black Sword. I have said eat and you must eat. There is time for talking."

He took his gaze from her mask, for he was abashed—by a girl of ten!—and did not wish to face even eyes that he could not see. Pushing meat into his mouth, he chewed. *I am the servant of Her, and She will never move again. I am her ally and servant, and this one, this grave child in the min-iature mask of Her, will be Her. I shall serve her until She is*

*ready to don the armor and helm-mask of the Lady of the
Snowmist, for then she will be Her.*

"We understand, Jarik Blacksword. My mother and I
understand. You are forgiven. You *are forgiven*. You are
not to kick yourself when you are down."

He twitched at those words, nearly dropping another
morsel of meat. They were *her* words. He jerked up his
head to stare at the mask above the juvenile body that, almost, could have been of either sex or no sex.

"Who are you?"

"You know who I am, Jarik Blacksword. You know who
I will be. I am not yet, though, and need time. We need
time, Jarik Blacksword, for me to grow. Call me
Karahshisar."

"She named you that?"

"Eat. There can be no other name."

Again he averted his eyes. He continued eating, forcing
down lumps of food and seeking to liquefy the growing
leaden mass in his belly by drinking water from the pitcher,
not wine from the jar. The girl remained; daughter of the
Lady God on the earth.

*The Lady of the Snowmist is dead; long live the Lady of
the Snowmist.*

But She was not dead. Feeling that as an even heavier tax
on his mind and on his growing conscience, on his very soul
than before, Jarik ate. And he wished that there had been
punishment, hatred, rather than forgiveness. Forgiveness
was a burden little less than guilt. How could it be justified?
*Murder is only an ugly word, invented to describe a specific
type of death.* "For all things there must be recompense,"
Jilain had said, on the Isle of Osyr. "Sometimes it is long in
coming. How can truths differ from land to land?"

So the Guide had said, and so Jilain had said. Recompense. Murder.

How could it be justified or forgiven? How, he reflected
miserably while he ate that which he did not taste or enjoy,
could what he had done be justified or understood or
excused?

*Recompense. Recompense. Payment. For all things there
must be payment.*

Jarik finished eating. The food was not gone; he finished
anyhow. And he straightened, turning to face the girl who

would be Snowmist. He extended both arms, palms up and open. He gazed at the mask, meeting steadily eyes he could not see.

"I cannot place the bracers of mist there, Jarik Blacksword. I have not yet the power."

With a sigh, he dropped his hands. He would be her servant and protector and guardian; he would wear that sign of Her.

"She is awake," the younger Karahshisar said. "She would see you."

*How can I bear it*, he thought, and rose anyhow, forgetting his nakedness when the coverlet slid from him. She gestured.

"Your robe, Jarik Blacksword."

Woodenly, nodding, paying no attention to the color of the ready robe, he took it up and drew it on. He tied the cord, which was wrapped and sewn with the fabric of the robe. She turned then, and he followed her along the dim stone hallway.

"Can She—talk?"

"Five days have passed," she said over her shoulder. "She is able to speak, weakly."

Turning to pass through a doorway, she brought him again to the chamber of the white-draped table, and that pitiful bandaged woman who had been a god. His eyes glistened when Jarik went to the side of that sickbed, and extended his wrists for the symbolism and the actuality of the bracers. His stance and his plea were unmistakable.

Wearing only her mask and the bandage, the god on the earth spoke. Her voice was weak as that of a sleepy child and seemed to come from afar; from the very domain of the lonely Dark Brother; from the other side Death.

"Jarik? I can . . . not take your hands . . ."

When he started to speak, his voice rose and caught on a sob. He broke off, swallowed, took a brace of breaths, and tried again.

"I tried to slay yourself. I did this to yourself. Yourself cannot move—I will move for yourself! I will be your arms and legs, Lady God. I will be your sword. Restore the bracers, Lady God."

"My right arm," She said, little above a whisper. "And in it the Black Sword of the Lords of Iron. Yes, Jarik. Thus

you become a . . . warrior for the Forces of . . . Man. But
. . . the bracers, Jarik, th . . . they are unnecessary now,
aren't they. We do not have need of—"

"I must wear them!"

She was silent for a time, breathing shallowly and with
care, so that he was glad for the mask, that he could not see
her pain when She drew breath. He shot a glance at her
daughter; *How dare you forgive this*! Then Snowmist was
speaking, interrupted by pauses of almost cadenced length
during which She summoned strength for the next
utterance.

"Leave me with my daughter then. I must instruct her.
Send us Metanira, and Sutthaya."

"They—those two are real, Lady God? When first I was
here, and foolishly sought to attack yourself outright and
yourself prevented me, yourself . . . vanished. A huge ax-
man attacked me then, and after that a—a thing, a demon-
thing. I slew them—or did I?"

"Call me by the normal pronoun, Jarik. You remind me
that I have treated you most ill. For believe me, Jarik, gods
are arrogant! It is hard to remember how we affect mortals,
how easy it is for us to hurt, and to gain the concept that it
does not matter. Mortals matter, Jarik. You matter. What
you ask about—that does not matter. You saw them; you
fought and slew them. I observed your prowess. The rest
does not matter."

"It does matter! Were they real? Did they exist?"

"No, Jarik. They were not real. They could not have
harmed you, physically. I give you truth: I have never
sought to harm you, Jarik Blacksword."

Jarik fought to keep back his tears, and he would not
raise a hand to wipe them away when they escaped his eyes
and began tracing down his cheeks. Nor did it occur to him
to feel unmanly, he who had felt unmanly at age eight, because he had wept. He nodded. He put out a hand to touch
Her; did not. What he had eaten was an iron ball in his belly. Nodding again, he turned from Her.

A girl with very long hair, all honey and fall leaves, was
waiting for him. Her hair fell to her waist, which was small.
She was small all over, and her face the oval shape of some
shields. She was quite pale in her long clingy gown of deep
rose.

"Will you come with me, Jarik Blacksword? To Jilain."

Jilain! "Yes!" And he followed, staring over her head rather than at the shifting of her backside within the gown, and wondering: *Is she real*? He did not reach out to touch her, as they went along a pastel-walled corridor and rightward, into a smallish chamber. Here awaited Jilain, and she smiled in brilliance. They embraced, and stood looking down at the mailed figure at her feet.

An Iron Lord.

He lay on his back, masked face upturned. By his side lay the Black Sword—no. It was *a* black sword. For its hilt too was black, plain, dullish and fluted for gripping fingers, rather than the red stripping with which Jarik had wound his own hilt; leather well chewed into softness.

"Well, Lord of Iron," Jarik said low, staring and remembering.

"Do you know whick one it is, Jarik?"

"No. They are identical—I mean, their armor is. I learned to know them only by voice."

"He will not be speaking," Jilain said, as bleakly as Jarik might have said it.

"No." Jarik squeezed her, staring down almost as if in a trance. "No. Jilain Kerosyris slew him—an Iron Lord!—to protect Jarik. I am your brother, warrior."

"This one is your sister, warrior."

With a sudden small smile, Jarik said, "This one is *your* sister, warrior."

On him her hand responded warmly, and then he squatted. He straightened with the sword of this dead Iron Lord. He held it, looking at it, studying blade and hilt while he turned the weapon in his hands. He saw in it no difference from his own; no means by which it might be coaxed to emit flame. He had hoped to find some such, but he had not expected to. Stepping across that mailed corpse of a god, he looked upon the wound that had killed him. Jilain had chopped well into the god's side, through the black armor. There Jarik saw twisted metal, and torn cloth, and flesh and bone stained by blood.

He glanced over to find that the long-haired girl was still present. "What is your name?"

"Seyulthye," she said, and after a moment Jarik realized that he had heard part of the name of the Lord of Dread.

He did not like that, but assumed that the name had come from one of Dread's kith: Milady Snowmist.

"Hold this," he said, pressing the god's sword on Jilain, and he squatted again to pull off one big mailed gauntlet of black. Under that stiff great-glove with its well-articulated joints was a hand . . . a hand gloved in a most strange and exotic cloth. It was at once shimmery silver and yet dark, very tightly woven. He remembered how once he had put his hand into one of these; into a hand covered with metallic cloth, and he had found it cold.

*Colder now*, he thought with a grim sort of callousness that helped mask some of the eerie feeling and the unworthy elation: here lay a god on the earth. Dead. Killed. A sprawled collection of armor, without identity. A god!

Not without some feeling of nervousness and that innate feeling that would come to be labeled "sacrilege," Jarik began drawing off the glove. He discovered that it ran well up the arm, under the black armor. That added to his indefinable disquietude, but did not subtract from his determination. He had to see.

He uncovered a hand, and it seemed no less than human. It was unusually pale, slightly bent of fingers, and cold in death. Not an old hand. It was a seemingly normal human hand. This Iron Lord had been no less human than Snowmist. And no less god, Jarik felt sure.

"Have you tried to remove any of this armor?"

"The helmet. One broke her dagger on it. Not otherwise, no. We did not have do with this soord, either."

"Hmm. I just realized. The armor could be useful, Jil! The helm, even the mask. Axes, swords, spears—none will mar this metal of the gods. These gauntlets and undergloves, too."

He removed the two from the other hand. Two big stiff-cuffed gauntlets with reinforced fingers between the easily-bent knuckles; two sleek mesh gloves he could conceal in one loosely fisted hand.

He moved up to the head of the fallen god. In helm and attached mask of iron-not-iron, it seemed monolithic, an inviolate refuge behind which hid a face to be seen by no human. With both hands Jarik turned the head to the left, then to the right. He saw no mark of Jilain's attempt at prising off this heavy black helmet. He did find what he sought. Seam and hinge. In a few moments he had the secret, and had opened the helmet of the Iron Lord.

He felt a little frisson run through him and his armpits were damp. Squatting beside the fallen god, Jarik glanced up at Jilain—who watched as if entranced, almost breathlessly—and at Seyulthye, who looked young and lovely and stupid.

He helmet was made in two pieces and hinged so as to overlap smoothly on both sides. The closure was on the left. Jarik removed the helmet. He *felt* it, a palpable boyish fear or dread, and he heard the intake of Jilain's breath. He swallowed, hard.

Wide open eyes, grey-blue, stared up at him and for a moment horror seized Jarik with an almost substantive grip. Then he dropped the helm—with little noise, on this carpet crafted to imitate moss—and hurriedly closed those cold dead eyes. He straightened then, and when his hand found Jilain's, it was seeking his. Blindly; neither of them could look away from that face of death. An immortal god, proven mortal. Strangely, Jarik felt small, not huge, looking down upon a god.

"You have slain a god," he said, almost whispering.

"He looks very human," she said, "dead."

He did, and the head looked small, merging from the neck-ring of that armor of the god-metal. He was very pale, this one who had been an Iron Lord, with lean cheeks and a good nose. There was no hair on the face except brows and lashes, which were very light, and the blond hair of the head had been cut weirdly short, so that the ears showed.

"Lyd," Jarik said, "Hawkbeak's son of Blackiron. The age is about right."

"What?"

"Sixteen years ago—before ever I was there—the Iron Lords took from Blackiron one Lyd, son of Hawkbeak. A fisherman. Lyd was eighteen, well-built and well-favored of face. Does this fellow look about that age? Thirty, uh, four?"

"Younger. And so pale."

"Gods do not go forth without their armor, and no sun shines inside mountains. It has to be," Jarik said reflectively. "Young and pale because for sixteen years he has had no wind on his face, and no sun! No travail and no true worry. Besides, Lyd was the most recent, and this man is surely not older. This was once a youth of Blackiron, Jilain. Lyd, who was son of Hawkbeak. Also his name was Nershehir; the Lord of Annihilation."

She gazed upon Lyd/Nershehir/Annihilation, in silence.

"You have annihilated Annihilation," Jarik said, feeling no desire to cope with the remembrance: in his dream-vision the invader of Snowmist Keep had been Eskeshehir, the Lord of Destruction. Perhaps he had been mistaken— or Oak had. And somehow the figure at his feet was little less imposing and no less ominous, now that he had a name.

Jarik bent to pick up the helmet. Even with the attached mask it was not so heavy as his own helm, which was of considerably less substance—seemingly.

"Seyulthye," he said confidently, "do you divine the secret of this armor's removal, and remove it. We must dispose of this days-old corpse, and we want all it wears."

She nodded. She would obey, whether because he had given her an order with such confidence, or because obeying was what she did.

Of a sudden Jarik frowned. "Seyulthye—are you real?"

"Real?" She looked at him blankly.

"Where are your parents? Where do you come from?"

"I know none of that."

"Get the armor off this, Seyulthye."

"Yes."

"After that," Jarik said, squeezing Jilain's hand in signal to be silent, "Jilain would like you to bathe her, make love to her, and be still while she sticks pins into you."

Seyulthye's face hardly changed. "Pins?"

"Jarik? This one will *not*—"

"Jilain: I want to be out of this room."

He took up gauntlets and gloves and, with him carrying also the helm-mask and Jilain the sword, he tugged her out of that chamber of death. She willingly accompanied him, while Seyulthye went unconcernedly to the armored god.

They were well down the hall, with Jilain just starting to question him about the ridiculous things he had said to Seyulthye, when that girl's shriek brought them around in a whirl. They saw a light of solar brightness flashing from the doorway they had just left, and then smoke was pouring out.

When, coughing, they could see within, they found that the dead Iron Lord and nearly every trace of Seyulthye had been consumed by a sudden flashing flame of such heat that the room was black: floor, ceiling, and every wall. They felt the heat; the flame was gone. That swiftly had the armor of a god destroyed itself and its dead wearer.

Unless—no. Jarik shook his head. No. The man was dead. The god was dead. And not even gods, he knew from experience with both Snowmist and the Lord of Iron, could rejuvenate the dead. The dead were beyond the abilities of Oak and of gods.

Blight! Who could have known that the armor of the god was so constructed as to self-destroy when tampered with?

"Thus do gods prevent mortals from coming into possession of god-armor," Jarik said, for saying something was necessary. There was no blood, and it was obvious that no blood had ever run within what was left of Seyulthye. She had been real, yes. A technical point, that: she had been real, but not human. She had been a creation of a god.

"Now," Jarik murmured, "I think I know why Metanira's voice seems so . . . so dull. And why she repeats phrases, like the most stupid of children. She is *real* enough. But, somehow, Milady Snowmist must have *made* her."

"As She . . . made Seyulthye?"

"Yes."

"We are in the midst of much sorcery, Jairik."

"I think we are surrounded by something beyond sorcery, Jil. If gods are supreme, then all must be by their sufferance, including sorcery. Thus their sorcery must be beyond sorcery."

"Yet they cannot do everything. Anything they wish or might wish, one means."

"Evidently not. Since now we know that the Iron Lords could travel here—"

"We know that one could, Jair. Ugh, one likes the sound of 'Jil' but not of 'Jair'!"

He was impressed with her logic. All right. The Lord of Annihilation had proven that the Lord of Annihilation could enter Snowmist Keep. Perhaps there was some reason Destruction and Dread could not. At any rate, Jarik and Jilain did not know. They did know that only Annihilation had invaded. *Don't we?*

"Since we know now that at least one Iron Lord could travel here and enter this keep, we know that either they lied to me about that—or that She kept them away with, uh, some sort of . . . spell?" Gods did not cast spells, he thought; gods just Did Things.

"That seems logical to this one, Jarik. She had means to keep them from here. But those means depended upon Her. Somehow She had to . . . maintain the—the force, or spell, whatever it is. Oh! We are like unto children talking about . . . well, whatever children have no idea of. At any rate, when She lay unconscious, that Iron Lord could broach the keep. It—he did. Now She is conscious again, and the others cannot come. His brothers? No no; they are all villagers, aren't they. *Were*, that is. Somehow this is harder to talk about than to think on, Jarish!"

"I think we are short some words, yes. How to apply words to that which we don't know and don't understand if we do know or mightn't understand if we were to know?"

"Jairik . . . would you please just not say such things as that? It is what this one said: trying to talk about it is harder than trying to think about it." After a moment she said, staring at nothing with narrowed eyes: "Very well. Suppose we say that gods have means to keep anyone from broaching their keeps, even other gods. But they must consciously maintain those defenses. As if someone had to stand and hold a gate, rather than lock it!"

He nodded. The Guardians had lived in a walled village, the first ever he had seen. There had been a gate.

"So, when the Lady God lay unconscious, an Iron Lord was able to enter. As if the gate stood open, no? So one did—and what that did accomplish was to show us all that they *are* Her enemies, and that they have no thokht about killing you."

"I'd say Destruction and Dread have plenty of thoughts about killing me, right now. And you!"

"It also accomplished the death of one, and we learned from that! But one had a question: how? How did that Iron Lord enter this mountain?"

"There is no use asking questions that are unanswerable," Jarik said, remembering the words of an Iron Lord to that same effect. "Perhaps She can tell us. We must ask. We need to know so much!"

"All we can, yes! A War, She has said. And it has begun! Another question. How is it that he is destroyed?"

"Annihilated," Jarik amended, almost smiling. "That one I can . . . well, I can suggest a possibility. They have the armor. It is of some metal stronger than iron—iron breaks on it! Thus they are invulnerable to us, to the weapons of mortal humans, as they call us." *Now we know how mortal they are*, he thought, and again he almost smiled. "For some reason though, they made a newer, better metal. They forged it into swords, so that gods could strike through the armor of gods."

"Wait—here is an improvement on that thokht, Jairik. *They* have the god-metal; all the gods. They wear it. The Iron Lords, though, uh . . . discovered? Created?—the new metal. The soords of black are theirs, Jarik, and we have no knowledge that Lady Snowmist has any such."

"Hm! Yes, I see that, and it is sensible." Abruptly Jarik banged a fist into his palm. "Blight! We now have another sword of *theirs*. Will it cut through the god-metal, though? We don't know—and Annihilation's armor is all gone, with his body."

"You have the gloves," Jilain pointed out, "and that ugly helmet with the mask attached."

"Yes, and I don't care to try taking a cut at it with Annihilation's sword. Those gloves and helmet can be useful to us, surely."

"Oh. Of course. Well, we can find out. Then both of us would have black soords, wouldn't we!"

"Just what I was thinking. You know what else I have been thinking?"

"Noo, Jairik; what else have you been thinking?"

"About this," he said, and slid both hands up into the tunic she wore.

# Seventeen

*Below that superficial surface mind was the wide dark reach
of all that he was . . .*

—Vardis Fisher

The girl of ten came to them as Jarik and Jilain
were talking, in low voices. They were clothed, although
en deshabille. They rose, their eyes questioning that
masked face. She gestured and seated herself on a straight
unpadded chair. In silence but with eloquently questioning
eyes, they resumed the couch that faced that chair.

"Might we have something of the god-metal," Jarik began, "that we may learn whether the sword of the Lord of
Annihilation pierces through it?"

The masked head tipped slightly in a way that reminded
him of Jilain. "It will. You named the invader. You know
that it was he? Nershehir called Annihilation?"

"Yes. I have his helm and mask. I know that Dread is
old, about ready for . . . for a new body." Merely voicing
that concept gave him an unpleasant chill, as if someone
had bared his back and run a finger right up the middle.
"Destruction is not so old, and Annihilation the youngest.
Sixteen years ago he took a new body from Harnstarl,
eighteen years of age. The face we uncovered looks—that
is, looked even younger. It must have been Annihilation—
Nershehir."

The masked head tilted again. "That is very good

deducing," she said, in that child's voice that was still too old for a girl of ten.

"We mortal humans are not stupid," Jarik said. "We just do not know as much as gods!"

The mask nodded. "It is our hope that you will continue intelligent, Jarik Blacksword. As it is *their* wish that the earth be peopled only by ignorant, slavish beast-people. Be assured that the sword will slice iron and pierce our metal, Jarik, just as your own does."

"Do you—does She have such weapons?"

"No, and I came here to tell you things. If we do nothing but listen to your questions, they may not be said. Will you listen?"

Again a ten-year-old girl had fronted and abashed Jarik Blacksword, and again he took it . . . precisely because she was not merely a girl of ten.

"We have much interest in those things you have to tell," Jilain assured her.

She told them then, in the voice of a child that was so controlled that it was almost that of an adult. For ten years, she had been raised to become a god. Now she told them that those ten years had become more than a lifetime:

All of the memories, all the knowledge of the adult Karahshisar had been transferred into the mind of the child Karahshisar. She had lived three months past ten years, and now had knowledge and memories of several lifetimes, and more as well.

"All this," Jilain burst out, "in so short a time!"

"We have . . . tampered. We keep promising that we will cease, and then we do it again. You have been here fifteen days."

"Fif—!"

She lifted a hand, and they fell silent, automatically reaching each for the other's hand. Ah, she was strange, this child who was a woman, this woman who was yet a child, who was in turn a goddess. In her now were collected the memories of century upon century of existence. They were no burden, she told them; she did not remember everything at once, any more than any old person did. The knowledge was with her; the memories were available to her. To . . . Her.

Yes, she possessed full knowledge of Jarik Blacksword.

No no—that is, she knew all that the Lady of the Snowmist knew of him, for she was the Lady of the Snowmist; she was She. She did not know who he was, of what union, of what people. He was Beach-gift, the foundling.

He held out his wrists, then, and she put about them the sorcerous thralldom of the bracers and, at Jilain's request, the silvery mist curled and encircled her wrists, too. There it became solid.

"How—how is it that you have her memories?" Jarik asked. His forearms were crossed; he was tracing the fingers of each hand over the bracer on the opposite wrist.

"It is done. We are . . . our minds are conjoined. You know that I—She . . . we can come into your mind, though not at will. Not at this moment. Do not fear that, Jilain, Jarik! This is part of the War, Jarik Blacksword and Jilain Kerosyris. It is part of the difference between the two groups of us, the gods on the earth. We who think of ourselves as the Forces of Man, and those *Others* of our kith: the Forces of Destruction. We are old, all of us. Ancient we are, and not of this earth. *They* simply take bodies, use bodies, to live on and on. The individual whose body is thus taken is slain, though not physically."

She saw how Jarik frowned deeply, and hunched forward, and she amplified: "When Oak is in your body, are you truly Jarik? No. You are in a way not present. In a way you are dead. The way the *Others* do it, this supplanting of the mind is permanent. The original brain is no more; that person is no more."

Jarik shivered. So did Jilain, and her fingers tightened on his. They stared at the masked pre-adolescent who possessed the memories and knowledge of many centuries of age.

"Hence the masks," she said. "The faces of the gods change. The faces of those in both groups of . . . antagonists. They, the *Others,* take bodies. The living bodies of fine sturdy young men. They supplant their very minds within them. The young men live on only in the body, the shell; they live on as *Them.* Yet they are dead in truth, for they are no longer individuals with any awareness whatever. Their brains are forever suppressed, gone; replaced by those of the *Others.* An Iron Lord, or a Fog Lord, or Lady

Cerulean, or . . . any of *Them*."

Jarik stared and listened, and he remembered. *I would not be an Iron Lord*, he had told that ominous trio, and at the time he had known and understood less than he did now!

"*We* birth anew," Karahshisar was saying. "Naturally, as beforetimes on . . . in the place we came from, to your world. We reproduce as you do, whose remotest ancestors we created—or rather developed, by means of our knowledge, from the ape-like hominids."

"Sorcery," Jilain breathed.

"A word for it; so is 'science.' They were far more than apes, and yet far less than human, those most remote ancestors of your kind."

"There are worlds," Jarik said slowly, "other than this." He sought confirmation, without quite asking a question.

Sadness was almost a palpable fourth presence in the chamber; he had felt need for the sound of his own voice. Now that he had heard it, it provided small comfort. And too, he knew that he had voiced the manifestly obvious. He had striven never again to do that, since the Lord of Dread had taught it him, by example. His brain stumbled. How long ago it seemed, that interview with the Lords of Iron! He had been but a boy . . . and yet it had been less than a season agone, not quite two months.

*Twa moont's,* he thought, for he was most aware of Jilain of Osyr's Isle. She was a part of why he was so much older, and a different person from that boyish and impressionable Jarik the Iron Lords had tricked—doubtless sneering and smirking at him behind their masks!

And now the Lords of Iron were but two. *Twa!*

The child nodded. "I have said it. Now the Lady Karahshisar has had to compromise. A new factor appeared, and it is not a random one though she did not know. It is you, Jarik. You, Jilain, are the random factor. We—"

"What does that mean?" Jarik asked.

"It means that because of you, some things that might have happened will not, and some things that might not have happened will—and have! In your case, Jilain, it means that some things that would have happened, even with Jarik present, will not. Have not."

"I saw a vision," Jarik said dully. "An attack by sea. I was attacked by an iron hawk. It slew me. I know that I died, in that vision. Then it happened—and Jilain changed all that."

"That sounds a sensible explanation," Karahshisar said, and she lifted a small hand. "*But*. We can no more explain your periodic spells of prescience than we can know whether they are of what will be or what might be, *unless*—. Do you understand that?"

"No."

"Neither do we. The Lady Karahshisar, as I said, has been forced to compromise. She has transferred all the content of her mind, *all*, to me; her daughter. And she still living."

"Your father," Jarik said on a sudden thought. "He is a man? A human, like me?"

"Of course. A youth—at the time of mating—of the wark of . . . I shall not tell you. Of the wark of Ishparshule, or of Kirrensark, or perhaps of Ahl, or another. I shall not tell you. It is not important."

*Not important. The identity of her father is not important! Yet to me it is so important to know who my father is!*

"Do not ask his wark or his name, Jarik Blacksword. He is dead, now, that mortal who fathered me. I never knew or thought about it, you see. These memories are new. A father was not important. You and I share in that, Jilain."

"Yes," Jilain said, nodding thoughtfully. "Yes . . . Lady."

Jarik made no comment, but stored away what he had heard. *Dead? But the youths brought here by the Lady God return to their homes in perfect health. Then he must have been slain, or died by accident. An animal, perhaps. Or . . . it is not true that he is dead, and she does not want me to know. Perhaps only that I might not occupy myself in wondering and seeking below for the father of this young Lady of the Snowmist. Someone I knew, possibly—or know!*

Jarik wondered. Would he ever, ever be certain of what he was told by these gods on the earth?—of what was true and what was not; of what was illusion and what was reality? Now even She, She, told him that She did not know which of his pre-visions was of something to come, and which of something that *might* happen. Unless, She had said. Unless something else happened, to change that.

Jarik sighed. It would be nice, being someone else someplace else—with Jilain!—and knowing nothing of gods and their strife and their lies!

"So it has always been," the masked child said. "God into god into god, like the seed into the flower, and into the seed again and yet again into the new flower that comes from that seed and produces within itself a seed for its successor. As a wayfarer pauses now and again for brief rest or lodging, so we who are a-travel along the road of existence find in each rebirth but a fleeting rest."

"Then birt'," Jilain said, frowning over the concept, "is . . . is only old matter dressed in some new figure similar to the old. Like a new . . . tunic."

The child Karahshisar nodded. "It is but the outer form that changes, aye. Thus: immortality, perpetual continuation. The purpose of existence is to continue to exist. That being impossible, the purpose of existence is to replace the self; to reproduce. Called ever by the same name we are, for it is only the stamped seal that changes. The wax remains the same. It is an unending cycle, a ring, the ring of return-and-remain. Through countless cycles of time it continues, through the passing on of the entire content of the mind into the new vessel." She touched her chest with a hand that wore the scintillant silvery glove of Snowmist. "The new body. Each new flower is different, as each new Karahshisar is different. And yet we are all the same. Hence again: the mask. The face that only you and those here have seen will never be seen again."

This time she sat still, without making the human gesture of lifting a hand to touch her mask of frosty silver-white. For she was not human. Not quite.

"And—we? Is it so with us?" Jarik asked.

"We will not now talk of that," she said, a god; and though she was but a child of ten years and three months, there was an end to that.

After a few moments given to thought, Jarik spoke again. "And She? The Lady God. Has She still her memories, though she has shared them with yourself?"

"In our way of transmitting memories and knowledge from Snowmist to Snowmist, Jarik, the contents of the mind are not like diseases, that you might pass on to another while keeping yourself."

"Oh," Jilain said, uttering the sound as a little gasp.

"You have said No, that She no longer has memory?"

And the mask told them, in low tones that did not tremble with emotion. On the table in that other chamber within Cloudspeak now lay a lovely, bandaged, masked vegetable. She who had been the Lady of the Snowmist was moveless and mindless.

*The god is dead; long live the god.*

Jilain whispered, through lips gone dry. "Why does She not . . . die?"

"It is our choice," the child Snowmist said. "We may . . . it is possible that we may peradventure have need of . . . the body."

Jarik looked at her: the Lady of the Snowmist, a god on the earth, and she was ten years old. He stared at the floor. A concept was teasing his mind, fleeting in and out and round, like mist. He could not quite catch it. Unknown to himself, his fingers were amove, tightening about those of Jilain, so that she knew some pain. She made no sign or sound.

"Metanira will see to her," Snowmist said. "Metanira serves. Metanira is not human, not really. She is . . . made, constructed, a simulacrum. The Lady of the Snowmist constructed Metanira and Sutthaya and others, long ago. For . . . company. They do what they are bidden, and that only."

That hardly satisfactory bit of explanation helped to explain several other things. "And they *cannot* do aught else?" Jilain asked quietly.

"That is true," Snowmist said. "They do only what they are bidden to do, and that is all they *can* do."

That mist-like concept was still playing wind-tag with Jarik's mind. If such as Seyulthye could be *made* . . . others could surely be made . . . one to fill the armor of Her? So that none might know she was . . .

But then, he thought, who would know, anyhow? She was seldom seen; gods were seldom seen. And how possibly could a creature that did only the bidding of others fill the armor of Snowmist, and function in it?

*The god is dead; long live the god.*

Another tremor disturbed Jilain's body. Her hand and Jarik's clung like the hands of nervous children in the darkness. "Do they—do they think they are as we? Human?"

"If they thought," the girl who was Snowmist said emotionlessly, "they would think that they were human. They do not consider that they are human or not human. They do not truly think. They do not choose. They accept. They are. They will see to the needs of my—my other body."

Noting her use of the words "my other body," Jarik was as if shaken from a torpor. He had merely accepted. Now he knew that he was indeed looking upon the Lady of the Snowmist. This girl of ten summers was one of the gods on the earth.

*Unworthy Jarik—unworthy Iron Lords! Unworthy—and futile! For Them, I slew the Lady of the Snowmist. Now I am hearing the Lady of the Snowmist. She lies there in that other room; She is here. She is a woman—a god, in adult form; She is this girl-not-girl. She is a . . . a vegetable . . . She is this warm, breathing, thinking, talking child, with every memory She has always . . . had.*

*Once again I have failed—and this time I am glad, glad!*

It seemed to him then that he blinked, and the girl sitting opposite him was clad all in silver and grey and white, and on her head, her masked head, a cap rested. A cap of silvery mesh that sprouted two lovely white wings . . .

"It has been a week since our conversation about Her, and about me, and I am glad that you both have kept in condition and . . . that you have at last joined."

Jarik and Jilain sat dumbfounded at that. They exchanged glances that showed clearly neither of them had any idea of the passage of a week—and no memory of those things of which She spoke. Before they could speak and ask their questions, She did.

"The time has come," She said, with a most businesslike air. "We must go to work." And the two before Her were profoundly attentive. "I've no time to tell you more, save that there are other forms of men. Other forms of men exist that are not human, not really men. They were developed—only a little—from beasts other than the apelike creatures that were already more apes when we—when we came among them. These beasts are the lower animals. The Others, the Forces of Destruction, wish to destroy us, and you. The anthro-men; the humans, men and women alike. Thus will the Iron Lords and their allies rule supreme, over a planet of slaves. Slaves. Creatures like men and yet like animals, who with their tiny brains will do the bidding of their masters and strive not. *They* see this as a good existence. *They* have human allies in this. Yes; there are anthro-men who aid the Iron Lords and the Ceruleans and the rest of the *Others* . . . unwittingly aid *Them* to bring about their own destruction, along with yours, and all humans."

Jarik's mind worked at the gallop, and yet it was as though he galloped through a field strewn with boulders and gulleys, or through a forest nigh impenetrable. He glanced at Jilain and noticed that she was naked. He said nothing.

Jilain said, "Why—why does your kind wish to have us here, as we are? Striving, troublous, petty, uncontrollable; dangerous—"

"Because you are those things! We do not seek pets, Jilain Kerosyris. Dogs do as their masters tell them. They do not think. They are punished and rewarded, and thus are trained. They do no more, save the mindless performing of a few instinctual acts. You are like us! Created in our image! Imbued in the beginning, the long long ago that was *your* beginning, with consciousness. The . . . disembodied consciousness of other people of our wor—our kind. You continue us, here. For we were many, a great race, and the gods on the earth are all that survive. We are few. Through you, in you as in our children, our kind survives and lives on to rise once again. We ourselves cannot last forever. Osyr is dead. Nershehir is dead. Many others perished, at the Beginning. It is what we desire for you; what all humans desire: That our kind survive in the universe."

Jarik saw paradoxes, still. He and Jilain had just been told that a week had passed, and that they had not been idle. Where were those memories? Metanira and Sutthaya and Seyulthye were *made,* without minds—to serve Snowmist, not the Forces of Destruction. (Weren't they?)

Were they? He started to speak—

"But give close heed!" She said, almost sharply. The Child of the Snowmist leaned a bit forward, raising a finger on a hand that was forever invisible in the rustly mail-mesh of a god.

"There is work to be done! A War has begun. You have joined us and there is a War to be fought. Battles must be fought, and one is imminent. Explanations must wait," She said, not pausing or commenting while both humans before Her nodded, the young woman and the young man who knew so little even while their brains reeled with new knowledge, knowledge possessed by no other humans. "Are you ready to work, for your own kind against the Forces of Destruction?"

"Aye."

"Aye!"

"It will mean fighting humans, men; your very own kind. It means risking death and dealing death. And too it will mean facing and fighting the gods on the earth. The risk is enormous."

Both nodded; Jilain repeated her "Aye."

Jarik did not speak; he would not admit that he enjoyed fighting and killing, and could hardly believe that Jilain did. It merely made them human, but neither knew. He was one of those strange humans who did not seek to deny instinct.

"Good. For it has begun," the Lady of the Snowmist said. "We must begin. An attack has been launched, as none has been in two centuries."

"Attack? On—what? Where?"

She continued as if uninterrupted. "*They* have grown to fear us, suddenly—or to feel more confident in themselves and their human forces. I believe the former. Even now the seas are filled with hawk-ships, attacking everywhere; men slay and rape, pillage and burn the world; men who do not know they are tools, wielded and as if driven by the Forces of Destruction. On many coasts are hawk-prowed ships drawn up. Myriads of people will be slain. The earth will be soaked with blood, and in many places a foreign people will run through the land as though it is theirs. The progress we planned for this world will be slowed. The progress of humankind, which we planned and which we wish. All this, by *men* . . . men in the control of *Those* who will replace them in time with animal creatures; *un*-men. And these men are all unawares of that! All unaware that they are devastating and humiliating lands at the behest of gods who wish only their ultimate extirpation. And they are natural for the task set them. They are of cold lands, where the growing season is short and winters are long. Naturally they will settle in many of the places they raid, and whose men they wipe out, whose civilizations they disrupt. Then they will live there, and become of that land, and there birth their children. And all the while they will unwittingly be on the business of the Forces of Destruction."

*Lokustans,* Jarik thought. *Hawkers. My people.*

*No! I have no p—*

*I have! I have people! They are Jilain, and Snowmist; my people are the Forces of Man! All those I do not even know! Yes! Jarik has people; I belong. These are my people.*

The Lady of the Snowmist rose, and She was the height of a child of ten. "And," She said, "we are besieged."

The words disrupted Jarik's exultant thinking and his exaltation. He sprang to his feet and his own word exploded from him: "What?"

"Come."

They followed the child, followed Her along the corridor of living stone in pastels and into the Great Hall that Jarik and Jilain had first seen. Now they saw, with trepidation, more. What had seemed a lambrequin of some magnificence, a wall hanging of silvery thread or mesh laced all through with pale blue, was something else. It was something of the gods. An eerie, ever-shifting and somehow vertical *pool* that set horripilation on their limbs. Tiny feet seemed to run up the backs of Jilain and Jarik, who were naked and had hardly noticed. They stared at that which was incredible and they saw it shift, moving mistily.

In that impossible pool a picture swirled into view, and coalesced like the freezing of silvery water.

And then they knew that they were seeing outside.

They saw the wark of Kirrensark on its high promontory and they saw the vast greenish plain of the sea . . .

And they beheld too the three hawk-prowed ships that were putting in toward the strand below the community. Perched atop the mast of each hawk-ship was a gleaming blue-black bird of prey. Jarik's hair trembled and quivered on his nape. *He knew this scene.* He remembered a dream so recent . . . a dream!

The child-Lady spoke. "Swiftly: we know things that They do not know. Undoubtedly the other Iron Lords know that Nershehir is dead. They may believe that I destroyed him, as They must know he came here. They do not know about me; my present weakness. They cannot know all there is to know of Jilain! Perhaps They know that you are willingly one of us now, Jarik, and perhaps They do not. They do not know that we have two of their own swords in the hands of two warriors who surely have no equal in the world."

Through this Jarik and Jilain stared at the vision-pool—and they stood tall.

"It must be Jilain who goes now into this battle," the Lady of the Snowmist said, who was ten years old, and who was centuries of age. "In my . . . in the other body's armor."

"Her armor!" Jarik gasped.

"*My* armor. The armor of the Lady of the Snowmist, Jarik Blacksword. Jilain: It is impregnable save to *our* metal or weapons. The weapons of the Forces of Destruction."

"The Iron Lords?" Jarik asked.

"Yes," She answered impatiently, and went on to Jilain: "You will find that when you wear it your strength is increased. It will not interfere with your natural speed, that armor, but you will discover that you are stronger. Will you do this?"

(*The Black Sword,* Jarik was reflecting, and wondered what she possessed, this girl he could not call Lady Karahshisar, this girl who was Snowmist Herself. What did She possess, that would cleave through the black iron-not-iron of the Lords of Destruction and of Dread? *Anything?* So he thought; nothing. It was the Forces of Destruction that had made that improvement, Jarik felt. What the Forces of Man had was—Jarik. And Jilain. And two of the swords, and—what was She saying?)

"Yes!" Jilain said, and her voice was not as the dove's, but loud and full of excitement.

Jarik spoke with firmness. "Jilain will not go alone, armor or no." And once more he caught up and clutched the warm hand of Jilain Kerosyris in his. "I will go to meet those killers. I have my own good mail, and even two gauntlets that may not be cut, and the Black Sword. And my skill."

Abruptly it occurred to him that he had not tried on the

helmet of the Iron Lord—because he had dreaded having it on his head. Now he did not know whether it would fit—and how much it might interfere with his vision in combat, when nothing must interfere with vision.

"And the helm-mask you have been practicing in," She said, while he felt Jilain's hand flex and clutch in his hand. "Better, though, that you remain here, Jarik of the Black Sword. You will be needed elsewhere, and elsewise. The War is only beginning. This will be a mere battle."

*She is telling him that he is more important than this one,* Jilain thought. *Aye—and gladly one will go, for him.*

But Jarik would not have it. He insisted.

Jarik argued with the girl Snowmist and with Jilain. He prevailed, too, and stood watching this magical depiction of the approach of those warrior-bristling ships while Jilain went away with the girl Karahshisar.

He frowned, seeing sails different from those he had seen before. Seeing helmets that ran up into spearhead shapes; leafshapes atop the helms of warriors! Seeing shields that were oval, not round, and wildly painted in many colors. Seeing—But he heard footsteps; a rustling . . .

When they returned, he was staggered, body and mind. For it was young Karahshisar who came, the new Snowmist, and with her . . . the Lady of the Snowmist!

Magnificent she was, in her silvery armor that snugged to her woman's body and held arms and hips and legs like silver skin; in her helm with the delicate wings and the mask that made her faceless; in the silver-metal gauntlets with the white stripe at each high flared cuff. Supple chain or god-mail she was, from neck to ankles to wrists. Mesh-faced gauntlets and boots she wore; and the helmet, and the mask of Her. Like no warrior save the Iron Lords, she was covered completely in armor. And at her side swung a long scabbard, and from its mouth stood a fluted hilt and simple guard of black. Again, a sword like unto no other, save that of the Iron Lords—and Jarik.

*No! There were others!*

Of a sudden Jarik remembered his dreams, his precognitive visions. He remembered the womanly figure that had stood beside him in some sort of stone prison, and she all in blue god-armor. Had that told him that this Lady

Cerulean She spoke of was not of the Forces of Destruction but of Man, or that she—She—would join them; would join Jarik Blacksword? And then he remembered the identically mailed, masked, helmeted Lord Cerulean, who had slain Jilain from behind and hoped that Jarik would die slowly.

And then She lifted a gauntleted hand, and drew the helmet up and off, and it was not She. It was the fine-boned face and tan (not dog's!) eyes of Jilain that he looked upon, Jilain of the Isle of Osyr.

*It is as if the armor of a god was made for her!*

Jilain smiled. Swallowing, Jarik returned a weak smile. He had fought against her and with her, side by side, and he had realized that he loved her. He had had the thought many more times than once: *What a woman! What a warrior! What a woman!* He had not realized, however, how magnificent was Jilain.

She had her bow, her own curved and recurved bow, and the sword of the Lord of Annihilation. And she reminded Jarik, Jilain of the Snowmist armor, and he turned to find that Metanira had fetched his superb linked chaincoat given him by the Iron Lords, now his enemies. (Then his enemies!) He got into it, with Jilain's aid, for when Metanira would have helped him the armored woman banished her. And he buckled on the Black Sword, with its long handle wrapped tightly all about with soft red leather. And no, he decided on the instant, he would not wear the helm of a dead Iron Lord, for he would not cover his face with that mask. (*I do not care to be an Iron Lord,* he had dared tell those gods on the earth.) However while Metanira held the big flared gauntlets of black, he drew on the supple, skintight undergloves of metallic mesh. He would wear those gloves, yes. No cut of a sword or ax on the knuckles would cause Jarik Blacksword to abandon his purpose or drop his Black Sword!

Suddenly he shot forth an arm to point at Jilain. "The sword you wear! Say that it is yours!"

"Ja—Jarish . . ."

"*Say it,* Jilain, my Jilish of the Snowmist armor!"

She circled the black pommel and hilt with her silver-mailed hand. "This is my soord. This soord is this one's."

"Snowmist! Lady Karahshisar—look into your memo-

ries and see what She—what yourself said to me, when the
Black Sword was not by my side. Say to Jilain those
words!"

The mask looked at Jarik, and saw the excited, fanatical
light in his eyes. Jarik was not one to be crossed or denied,
not now. Snowmist knew it—this Snowmist knew it. Jarik
Blacksword was dangerous, ever dangerous. For one or two
or Three Who Were One, he would never be wholly sane.

"That sword is yours, Jilain. You took it up, and you
shall use it. It will not leave you. It is yours."

Grinning, Jarik paced to Jilain, and with his gaze on her
eyes, laid hand on her sword. "I would borrow this," he
said, and drew it forth, and walked away from her. He spun
back, still grinning, holding the black sword that had been
that of the Lord of Annihilation and was now Jilain's of
Osyr's Isle. "Want it!" Jarik said. "Think that you want it!
Will it to you!"

He felt no tug, and time stretched forth, and the sword
did not leave his grasp or try to do.

"She has not used it," the Lady of the Snowmist said at
last.

Jarik's shoulders sagged a bit and he looked crestfallen,
boyish. "It is not yet hers? But once she has used it, blood-
ed it—"

Karahshisar nodded, standing by Jilain's side and
dwarfed by her, so that she was indeed a child in silver and
white and grey. "Yes. Then it will come to you, Jilain. As
Jarik's sword comes to him."

Jarik returned the sword, then, and two warriors faced
the masked child.

"Can you take us down there," Jarik asked, "as She
did—as yourself did, in the other body?" He chafed at his
stumbling over concept and words.

"Say 'She' for the other body, Jarik, if it is easier.
And—I do not know. The traveling as I do it—ah, now I
slip. The traveling as *she* did it is accomplished in the mind,
with the mind, not with a spell or what is normally considered magic or sorcery or even that god-"magic" which is
science. I . . . I have no experience with this mind, this
body. Let me try . . ."

And the child vanished.

After the initial shock of her instantaneous leavetaking,
Jarik and Jilain gazed into the vertical Pool of Scrying.

They saw mad activity below: all of Kirrensark-wark was preparing for the imminent invasion. Then—

"Ah! See!" Jilain pointed excitedly.

Of course he saw; at the storage-house farthest from the long house of Kirrensark the firstman, where no people milled, She appeared: the child who was the Lady of the Snowmist. The two up in her keep stared while she glanced about Herself—and then she vanished from the scrying pool before them—

—to reappear in the vast mountain keep with them. She nodded exuberantly, sighed with a rising and falling of breastless girl-chest, and extended a hand.

"Come, Jilain."

Jarik stayed the woman beside him. "No. I go first, lest you choose to leave me once she is down there, and I go mad with watching."

The mask gazed at him. "How much distrust we have taught you."

Jarik forewent comment on that. "Can you carry me to the smokehouse behind the house of Kirrensark himself?"

"Aye."

Thus spoke the child, and as Jarik started to turn toward Jilain to say he knew not what before they went into battle, Snowmist caught his hand and he was gone amid the rushing and the floating of his stomach, and then he staggered a bit. That was because his feet had impacted earth; he was beside Kirrensark's smokehouse. All about him the crisp air was chill and full of shouts and the sounds of preparations for battle.

For a moment the diminutive figure in the mask of silver looked at him, and Jarik thought that She was going to say something, deliver some injunction or word of encouragement. He needed none. Perhaps his face showed that, and perhaps She merely decided that all had been said. She vanished and he knew She had returned into Cloudpeak, for Jilain.

# Eighteen

*"Railing against war makes as much sense to me as a man screaming in reproach of his own testicles. War is a fact. I believe it is as much a part of man as sex. Creation and destruction are sprung from the same pod and grow into a single tree—Man. No war would be like no sex—an affront to one's self, a gouging out of the eyes because the color of daylight displeases."*

—Jeffrey Weinper, Pfc.
K.I.A. Vietnam, 8.iv.68

Jarik thrust himself away from the furze-roofed smokehouse and stepped out of its shade. Into the clamor and frenetic bustle of a community preparing for war he prowled, a wolf come among them with cold blue eyes and a sword like night itself. A child ran dodging past. She held an eight-foot spear close to the head. The shaft's end dragged and bounced behind. Someone's leather jerkin hung on her, falling past knees to chubby calves.

*On an errand for father,* Jarik mused, just as a harried woman in long dirty-blue skirt rushed from the other side of the smokehouse. She narrowly missed Jarik without ever seeing him. Behind her she half-dragged a squalling child of three or so. In her other hand she lugged a well-made bucket bristling with arrowheads. The mess of age-greyed homespun over her shoulder, Jarik realized, would become bandages.

He did not know who she was. He knew few people of

196

Kirrensark-wark, and could identify perhaps as many as four women here—two of them of Kirrensark's family.

A boy of twelve or so, already shouldery and snake-hipped, dagger-girt, his head like a haystack sprouting a nose, saw the man in black mail.

"It's Jarik!" he shouted, pointing.

Someone else called out and also pointed, and soon even cheers rose amid the excitement at his unaccountable reappearance. Children wanted to run to the hero Jarik with his Black Sword, so long gone from among them. Most were barked or screeched at by this or that adult, who ordered them to continue with their errands. So many people on so many errands, their directions often conflicting so that constantly their paths crisscrossed, imparted to the community the chaotic aspect of a kicked anthill.

Mothers sought to hold back smaller children, the while they wiped at drooping strands of hair. Already they were harried and sweaty, the women of Kirrensark's wark. Jarik sought as assiduously to ignore them, for he did not care to be bothered. Children were not among his favorite creatures, if he had any.

Besides, he kept fancying that he saw potential little Jariks.

*The Hawkers have come to Kirrensark-wark*, he thought, *at those who once came a-hawking from Kirrensark-wark to Tomash-ten of Akkharia. I wanted to fight them then, even at age eight. This time I will. For Her and the Forces of Man and these children, not Kirrensark or all his wark. Let these invaders with their pointy helms create no orphan Torsys or orphan Jariks among the children of this wark!*

He came face to face with a helmeted Delath Berserker then, at a nearness of four paces of a tall man. Bronze seemed to glow with its own dull fire on Delath's age-darkened leather jerkin. Their eyes met and both men stopped. Bright eyes, with no morbriner rage on them as yet. Orphan and his foster-mother's slayer; Oak's slayer and thus midwife to his strange birth within Jarik. Seconds passed, and each was long, while the two stood studying each other.

Delath was waiting; Jarik was deciding.

"Jarik," the white-hair said at last. His voice was flat. Jarik heard neither warmth nor deliberate coldness. He thought that Delath's helmet, drilled to accommodate its decoration of an oblong of fly-housing amber, looked silly.

"We have wondered about you, Jarik Blacksword."

Jarik, too, spoke natural words. "We have visited long with the god," he said, knowing that he stated the manifestly obvious. It occurred to him just then that gods were gods and mortals were mortals, and sometimes among mortals the manifestly obvious was either necessary or a human courtesy. "Then She saw this coming attack."

"Ah." After a silent moment Delath added, "She will be coming?"

Jarik evaded. "There are only three shiploads of attackers, Delath. Can they require more than you, and Jilain, and me?"

Delath gazed at him a moment before glancing about. "Jilain is here, too?"

"She will be."

And again they were silent—amid a vast almost manic disruption, negation, denial of silence. Staring at each other. At last Jarik's chest swelled and fell in a long sigh. Linked chain rustled. He had decided, about him and Delath.

"She will be. We will take them, battle-brother."

Delath nodded, and nodded again. "We may never be friends," he said, knowing what he had heard, knowing the decision Jarik had come to. "But I am your brother, warrior."

"Ah!" It was a woman's voice that intruded. "They come flying, those eerie birds that flap not their wings."

Delath's wife, Jarik remembered—or was it his sister? They had been introduced on that festive evening of homecoming. It seemed two or three nights ago, that night over two weeks past. Jarik glanced up, following her skyward glare.

Two of the birds of sorcery came in from the ships, on unflapping wings. They glinted, for the sun was high and bright on this cool day. The birds of *them*. Of the Others. The Forces of Destruction. They came to spy, to reconnoiter, and Jarik Blacksword knew it. Of a sudden it occurred to him to disguise his presence here.

"I am Jarik," he said to the woman, who had as much silver as snow in her hair as copper and straw, and who was girthy as a rainbarrel. "Will you loan me your cloak, now, and quickly?"

With a look that showed incomprehension without question, she complied.

Jarik muffled himself. The birds came soaring over, looming above flowing shadows like night-demons that soiled the land. A god-bird's shadow fell onto the round face of a white-haired child, and was gone from it. Jarik was right about the hawks' purpose; they made no attack. Nor did they espy the Black Sword in Kirrensark-wark, or Jarik either. And the three ships swept in toward the land while Kirrensark's people prepared like impossibly noisy ants.

*This anthill shall not be kicked,* a man thought, and under a woman's cloak a knuckly hand closed on the red pommel of a sword of night.

Jarik made his way toward the edge of the brow of land fronting the sea. He paced, hooded now, voluminously cloaked, a prowling wolf among them with glacial eyes. All around him people were readying for their resistance, for none thought that trio of strangers' ships came to talk or trade. Arrows went *zizzz* up at iron hawks, and missed. The hawks reconnoitered without swooping, without attacking. Men and women alike struggled with large stones. And then a big man with grey in his big beard wheeled and his blue eyes met Jarik's. On him was a round, gently domed helm, sided with wings copied from the helm of Snowmist. On him a big leathern jerkin all set with amber studs and carbuncles and mean-looking bosses of bronze standing forth in beveled points.

"Jarik! Well met!"

"Think you that you can beat them off, Kiddensok?"

The voice was cold; Oak's voice and Oak's arrogant healer's gaze. A frown shadowed over Kirrensark's face. "Jarik?"

"Oh, aye, Jarik. Jarik who saved your life from Ahl's assassins, Kiddensok. Jarik who saved your wark from Ahl's attack—with Jilain and Delath," he added, mindful of Delath beside him. "Jarik, aye. Shall I fight still again for you, Kiddensok?"

Kirrensark looked as if he wanted to speak; appeared to be trying. His face was stricken and his beard worked with the movements of his mouth.

"It seems to me that if my Black Sword fights again for you and your wark, Kiddensok, this place should not be called Kiddensok-wahk." As he uttered those words Jarik watched resignation come over the big firstman's face, not fear; and again he was not made happy to be impressed with this big old leader. Kirrensark must think the younger man meant he wished to change the community's name to Jarik-wark, which it could be only on the death of its present firstman. Yet Kirrensark showed resignation but neither consternation nor fear.

Horns winding in unearthly sounds, the attackers were bringing their ships in to shore, over two hundred feet below the wark.

"You destroyed my first home, Kiddensok, that day the man beside me destroyed my stepmother and unborn brother. It stood on a bluff above a strand, above the sea, just as this wark does." Jarik swept an arm to take in the community visibly becoming a spear-bristling, helmet-glinting armed camp. "That farming community of Akkharia was called Tomash-ten: Oceanside. Would be a good name for this wark, if it survives this new onslaught, wouldn't it? Oceanside."

A new tension held the three men, as Jarik had offered a bargain and was awaiting an answer. Kirrensark drew breath—

"THEY COME!"

That shout from the hilltop barricade was unnecessary. The ululating cry blown up by the sea-wind was announcement enough. Three ships bearing foreign attackers were making landing. It began.

Atop the bluff sprawled the wark, its buildings cozily clustered near the incline's brow. Yet not to its edge. There, all along the very beginning of the downhill slope to strand and sea, a bulwark of stones had been raised. They were piled there, not fitted as a wall. Some of them only the strongest of men could have borne there on legs like the low branches of oaks. Others were huger, and had to have been rolled into place, by several stout men at once. Others were head-size and larger. They formed a bulwark, a sea-wall standing atop the natural wall of the land.

They were not mortared.

In a mass of flashing iron and pointed shields below dagger-like spires that seemed to dance atop helmeted heads, attackers ran yelling from their surf-beached craft. They flowed in a living tide over the sand to begin mounting the hill, and their number was scores and scores.

Behind them, others of their dark ilk sent up a humming cloud of arrows in an effort to force back the defenders. The sheet of slim wooden shafts whirred darkly and sang in the air—while stones, grinding upon stones as they were shoved, provided a contrapuntal basso. Down upon the attackers rumbled the stones of the wark's "seawall" defense. Warcries became screams. Men were knocked flying by bounding stones far bigger than they; were crushed like scarlet bugs beneath rolling grinding chunks of rock; were struck by flying granitic missiles so that they spun and fell to writhe in pain.

One of those three ships died, smashed by two rolling bounding boulders at once, and both bigger than five men interlinked.

Yet the tumblers of those stones were sore harassed by arrows, and more than one Lokustan was struck down by a missile lofted blindly from below. Someone's daughter, turning to rush from the barricade to her yelling little sister, went stiff and huge-eyed when an anonymous arrow dropped into her back behind the left shoulder. Only a few paces away a man grunted at impact, stared at the feathered staff standing from his chest, and yanked it forth. When he saw no blood, he bellowed a laugh and threw it over the stones.

Men still came up the slope, shrieking rage and brandishing oval shields and spears and war-axes. Every shield was brightly painted and nearly every helm was not domed, but drawn up into a nasty-looking point that seemed an elongated onion sprouting a shortened spearhead.

They were not Lokustans. They were not Akkharians. They were not Kerosyrans.

They were like no men their quarry had ever seen, in this time when the world was small indeed, and peopled with gods still quarreling over their creations.

These were in general shorter men than the Lokustans, and much darker, as if they were born not pink but perhaps the hue of Jilain's eyes or of new-tanned doeskin, to be sun-darkened not into bronze or tan but brown or very old copper. Mystic amber gleamed on none of them. Many wore bits of blue, though, and pieces and touches of blue, and had the heads of blue hawks scratched and painted on their long shields.

*They are not of Lokusta or Akkharia,* Jarik thought staring, *and they are not of the Iron Lords! Yet the same black hawks accompany them. It has begun indeed. These must be minions of those gods She called Lord and Lady Cerulean— Lady Cerulean, whom I vision-saw fighting at my side against just such men as these.* (Didn't I?)

*But not this day. Not this day.*

And . . . how could men be so dark? Could their land have so much sun?

Whatever their source, those men were paying heavy toll to rolling falling bounding bouncing stones and boulders, and now their outré allies came hurrying to their aid on extended wings.

A hawk—black, even blue-black in the sun, but not blue—swooped and dived to strike a man who was throwing his weight against a big mica-glinting chunk of rock. Arrows missed the bird or ricocheted from it; the man cried out. Both hands flew up and he toppled backward, even as the bird seemingly rebounded straight up. Its victim's cohorts saw the hideous red ruin that had been his face.

The great bird, bigger than raven or true hawk, wheeled in air with never a flap of its nighted wings, and it dived.

A man earned shame by hurling himself from its path with a scream. At the same time several arrows missed the diving hawk and a spear glanced ineffectively from its gleaming body. One of the arrows arched. It fell and fell until on the hillside an attacker gasped and looked stupidly at his hand, into which a nearly spent arrow had driven a half-inch.

Above, a second warkman was hurling himself *at* the hawk, leaping from stone to stone and through the air with rustly chiming of his black armorcoat of links. His sword, in hue the same as the armor and the iron hawk that was not iron, flashed a blade some said was so sleekly smooth a walking fly would fall off its flat. The mindless bird drove on at its intended victim. This was a tree-like man on stumpy legs with calves like big rocks, who pried at a boulder with an oaken pole thick as his thighs.

The yelling, leaping Jarik struck, so that the Black Sword clove through the demon-bird. It fell in pieces down the slope and men cheered—even while another such unnatural bird of prey banged off a defender's helm with such force as to turn his head two-thirds way round. With a broken neck and sundered vertebrae slicing through his trachea, he fell. He lay kicking and did not rise. After a while he stopped kicking.

More and more arrows came whizzing up over the dwindling pile of stones. Some found human targets while men continued to ascend from the ships. Scattered here and there along the rampart, the wark's archers acted as marksmen, rather than loosing in volleys. As specific targets they picked the foremost attackers and those beyond the reach of tumbled stones and boulders. Only seventeen men of the wark wielded bows, and nearly half of them missed nearly as often as they hit. Of the hits, half again failed to inflict incapacitating wounds. Strave Hot-eye, felling his sixth target with his tenth arrow, wished for Jilain Demonslayer.

Bent solely on attack and menaced only by defenders directly ahead and above, the foreigners had no need of rearguard. They had abandoned their ships on the sand without leaving any of their force to guard them. What need?

On one of those ships *appeared* now a shining, magnificently martial figure, a scintillant statue of silver to which life and movement had been vouchsafed. So swiftly had the child borne her there and departed that no one saw Her. No one was watching the vessels anyhow. What need?

They took note now, the defenders; for the attackers did not look back. Lokustans cried out her presence, and cheered, and among them only one man knew that this was not the Lady of the Snowmist come to save her own. Jarik knew that he looked upon a most mortal woman, in the armor of Her. She bore the serpentinely curved bow any man of *Seadancer* recognized: the bow of Jilain Demonslayer of Kerosyris. She began to use it at once.

The foremost of the attackers on the hillside above the strand threw up his hands and arced backward, seemingly trying to curl over the arrow in his back. Those of his fellows who noticed cursed their own archers—the rearmost of which was at that moment dropping with a shaft in the back. Moments later another man on the slope fell suddenly flat, his fingers clutching earth with breaking nails. An arrow stood above him as his only monument. Invader archers cursed each other, and another died with a cry. While a boulder plowed down over and through three, then four men, another man on the slope squealed in the way of a hog at slaughter time. With an arrow in the back of his neck he fell twisting to roll down and down. Perhaps it was Milady Chance who caused another dark man to turn—so that Jilain's hard-driven shaft smashed into his face and dropped him kicking.

An invader archer turned and saw the source of that arrow-death among his own. Just as he started to point and yell, an arrow from Jilain's bow rushed into his mouth and burst out the back of his head.

Activity atop the incline nearly ceased as wark-defenders stared in awe and exultation at the toll of . . . Her? Another climber fell to an arrow loosed by her only Jarik knew was not She.

Gane the Dogged turned frowning to him. "Jarik—"

"Yes. It is Jilain. Come—the two of us should be able to budge this piece of mountain, and tumble it and the one atop it as well."

They could not, but with the aid of a third man they sent trundling hurtling death down into the invaders. Meanwhile an eighth arrow missed an attacker because he lost his footing, dodging a rushing stone, and slid several feet back and down. A ninth arrow found its bloody home in an eighth foreigner, and a ninth man soon fell to Jilain's tenth arrow. That it took him through the thigh rendered him no less ineffectual as a climber or warrior.

By now many men on that hillside were turning fearfully, to see and dodge rather than be struck down from behind by feather-rustling shafts from their own ship. They did not know about their four archers who now lay with Jilain's arrows in them, but the fall of six men on the slope to whizzing death from behind was grievously demoralizing. Now an attacker shouted and pointed, and another saw her, and another.

Strave saw an advantage, and shouted immediately.

"Onto the rocks and put two volleys into those archers down there! If ten don't fall I'll bite your ugly noses!"

Up pounced his archers, while below, three and then four discovered that they could not drive their shafts through the silver-shining armor of the apparent god on their own ship. Now warriors wheeled to charge back. They swarmed at their own ship against the single enemy that had seized it to become more deadly than rolling, flying stones. Their yelling whelmed the keening of seventeen arrows from above. Those shafts fell among their own bowmen, who perforce lost interest in Jilain.

She turned her attention to her nearer and more personal menace. Her unseen sniping was at an end. Others resumed forging up the slope while Jilain's arrows downed one of those running at her, then two, four. . . .

Somehow three attackers gained the very brow of the hill and aided each other in clutching the massy grey-and-umber stone there. Gane of Kirrensark-wark clambered atop it to hack down at them. Delath, thinking he had lost his senses, dragged Gane back. Spluttering in anger, Gane told the other man what he was about. He heard the white-haired man's yells, then, and loaned his shoulder to Delath's chosen chore. The stone budged. Dark hands slapped onto it as it teetered. An attacker screamed as it started to move, and then another, and for a moment Gane looked up into blazing eyes dark as oak bark. Then boulder and Hawkers were gone, in a rumbling rolling horror that jellied those men in their armor and smashed down one, then two of their comrades.

During those same swift seemingly eternal moments an iron hawk took off Gane's helmet and some hair and scalp with it. Delath's ax struck the hawk so hard that the bird careened to strike sparks off one of the permanent boulders. As it started again upward a man came hurtling through the air, a dark streak in black chain-armor. Just as black, his sword smashed the god-hawk so that it was hurled many feet down the hill—to vanish with a loud cracking sound and a burst of white and yellow fire. A nearby attacker screamed, dropping his weapon to clap hands to his eyes. He fell and went rolling and sliding down the slope.

Jarik, having destroyed the second of three demon-birds, was carried by his own momentum to fall against

Delath. The older man helped him up, and for a moment their eyes met.

"Nicely done, Jarik!"

"Let the past be dead as that fell bird, Delath."

"I am ever your brother, warrior."

Meanwhile the third hawk, as if aware of the deadly menace both to its kind and to the men it aided, was streaking for the ship on which Jilain stood.

"Dogs eat its young!" Gane snarled, unmindful of the blood reddening his hair and ear and shoulder. "That poxy bird ruined my helmet!"

And Jilain Kerosyris, in the armor of the Lady of the Snowmist, drew a black sword of the Iron Lords and hewed in half a god-bird on behalf of Kirrensark-wark.

It was then the foremost of the returning dark men reached the ship on which the child Snowmist had set her. Dropping to one knee, Jilain struck that man so that his head fell sideways and hung by a shred of skin and muscle while his body wilted. Others rushed to take her, a woman in the armor of one god who wielded the sword of another.

The defenders above were afforded a superb view of the spectacle of that invincible mortal goddess at her work of defending and attacking. None failed to note her surpassing grace and gymnastic ability that enhanced her warrior's skills. Dancing, leaping, lashing, squatting to lunge and slash, pouncing a yard away to chop the fingers that sought to drag a man onto her keep. Her silver armor flashed white fire back at the sun. Her ebony sword hewed amid sundered armor and flying gore. Men fell back spurting blood. She remained untouched, and six men had fallen. More were ordered in to deal with her, and some high above heard the strangeness of an accent different from both theirs and Jilain's.

Jarik saw the monster coming, then, winging in over the sea.

# Nineteen

*Heroes, notwithstanding the high ideas which, by means of flatterers, they may entertain of themselves, or the world may conceive of them, have certainly more of mortal than divine about them.*

—*Henry Fielding*

The metal hawks of the Iron Lords were large; they were to normal hawks as were they to chickadees. What came flapping now over the sea was to the god-hawks as they to termites or wood-grubs. It flew, and it was half the size of a ship, with wings like sails. They flapped.

Of fulvous yellow it was, Jarik saw, and so did other men who stopped what they did, to stare. It came on the wings of a gigantic vulture, the father and grandfather of vultures. Not vulture-black were those wings, though; they were dusty yellow. Its hindquarters and trailing legs were those of a tawny cat the size of a horse. It came over the sea, seemingly from the sea. Flapping in and in toward Kirrensark-wark, and with each sweep of those wings it soared twenty yards while the water stirred below it. Awed attackers and defenders alike saw the sinisterly open mouth below the hooked beak. Yet the creature made no sound.

It bore a passenger.

On its back, astride, sat a figure all of black. Its shape was that of a man and it gleamed blue in the sunlight.

Jarik saw and said nothing. He twisted from Delath, pounced over and between stones, and went pell-melling down the incline to the sea. He ran as if he had been heavily pushed. He had not. He had seen an Iron Lord, riding to battle on the back of an impossible bird-cat; a gryphon. Everyone said such creatures existed; playthings of the gods. Few would swear to having seen one. Many saw one now. And the god on its back.

Men besieged a blue-painted ship with furled sails of green and yellow and a great hawk's head at its prow, in blue. On its deck a woman defended herself from many, masked below winged helm and above impenetrable armor of silvery mesh. At that ship swooped the enormous gryphon, all in silence.

Jarik rushed down the slope in a way that kept him erect only by momentum and the blurry churning of his legs. A man in his way started to straighten up against him, and was overtaken by timidity or wisdom. Dodging to avoid the unstoppable, he fell and roll-slid down and down. One of his comrades failed to get out of the way in time and was bowled over. They fell rolling, tangled and cursing.

Racing pell-mell, Jarik passed them both. He was bellowing two words all the while.

"Jilain! Above! Jilain! Abovvve!"

She was busy, and her attackers were making plenty of noise to swallow the sound of his voice. Jilain became aware only when a great broad shadow fell over the man whose pointy helm and forehead she was hewing, and over her arm and sword. She danced back from the ship's side, then, with the gryphon rushing down at her. Now she felt the down-draft from mighty wings.

Still the shadow was on her, and she sprang aside. She thumped hard against the ship's rail, and in an instant she went toppling over the side onto the sand. Four or five dark men in spear-top helmets, frozen to stare at the descending monster, roused themselves to pounce on their worst enemy.

She still was. The first saw his lean sword shatter into two pieces against her winged helmet. Then a mailed foot kicked him in the approximate center of his body and he fell puking. The second man ran directly onto the point of her black blade. It bit him deep. The fifth was chopped from behind from right shoulder to left nipple, and him in a coat of scale armor. Jarik was there, amid the scent of brine.

The gryphon plunged low and the Iron Lord dropped onto the deck of the ship Jilain had quitted. Despite its fearsome aspect, the flying eagle-cat made no effort to attack. It swept gustily aloft. Desperately, to distract this god of the Forces of Destruction from Jilain, Jarik shouted.

"Annihilation lies dead, great lord. Are you come to be next?"

The god was not to be distracted. The Iron Lord ignored the shout. His goal was her he had to assume was the Lady of the Snowmist, in her silvery armor and his brother-god's sword in her hand. Nor could he be bothered with consideration for his human allies that were in the way. The black god-sword pointed, not at Jarik—whose violent attempt at a leap was foiled by a black-bearded corpse. He fell with a grunt.

Flame from the Iron Lord's extended blade turned Jilain's third and fourth attackers into little suns and danced over them in coruscating yellow-white brilliance. Yet on her, over her and all around her that awful fire flared blue, as if starved for air. She did not become flame, but she did lose her grip on her own god-sword.

"Call it to you!" Jarik bellowed, stumbling upright. "Call *your* sword to you, Jilain! *Call it to you!*"

If she heard, she could not respond. Jilain was a jerkily dancing puppet to the weak blue flame from the Iron Lord's weapon. Beyond rational thought with his fear for her, Jarik hurled his own sword. He did not know that he bellowed aloud for its return.

The Black Sword struck in a miraculous failure. It did not pierce the god-armor, or even strike fully point-first. Yet it banged loudly off the god's arm with enough force to make him lose his grip on his own weapon. Its flame sputtered out as it dropped from his gauntleted hand.

The Black Sword heeled over without turning, and glided hilt-first back to Jarik. Now he was at the base of the attacker ship's prow. So were more of the foreigners, their dark eyes blazing with menace. Jilain, having got to her feet, bounded past Jarik to slash at those Hawkers who sought to hew at him from behind. The dropped god-sword lifted from the sand, to return to its owner. And Jarik, leaping, clutching at the edge of the ship's planking with his shield-hand, struck at the Iron Lord's advanced right leg.

Jarik's shield banged loudly into the ship and he did not fall backward but was catapulted.

The Black Sword had sliced through god-armor, and skin and muscle and bone, to flash free on the other side in a spattering splash of red. Let anyone doubt now that gods bled, or that their blood was as red as any human's!

*Not used to fighting, these Iron Lords*, he thought, even as Jarik slammed to the sand with a teeth-clashing impact that rattled his armor with the sound of dry old haricot pods. It was not, however, his mailcoat or his grunting groan that he heard. What he heard was a cry of pain and horror that echoed metallically within the helm of god-metal the color of jet.

The Iron Lord toppled, and fell off the ship of his human allies. The footless stump of his left leg squirted blood like a mountain spring gone red. His gauntleted hand came down on the yellow-and-nacarat shield of a slain attacker with the sound of an ax against a shed door. The oval shield cracked from end to end.

The Iron Lord's sword fell to the sparkling sand, over a pace from its owner. Jarik, thrusting himself again to his feet, heard a loud sound from several throats and recognized a cry of consternation. A man froze in the act of attacking him, to stare at the fallen god who had come to the aid of him and his fellows. The foreigner stared at a fallen, writhing god; at spurting blood that darkened the sand which swallowed it. Equally horrified into immobility, two of his compatriots fell to the same stroke of Jilain's sword.

Jarik started to the Iron Lord he had crippled, and saw the sand around him darkened by an enormous shadow. He heard Jilain's scream.

*"Jarik!"*

Covered by that shadow as by a patch of night, Jarik yanked his sword to point above his head. At the same time, he hurled himself aside.

His sword struck nothing. He lost his balance in that desperate lunge to escape. He fell to tumble near the edge of the lapping sea. Twisting over, disoriented, he saw the talons of the gryphon, each bigger than the tusk of an out-

sized wild boar, close on the Iron Lord. Then the great
wings beat, one buffeting Jilain as if she had been a doll.
That same wind buffeted Jarik and he squinted in the dust
raised from the sand. While a groan resounded in the helmet of the Iron Lord, the gigantic creature rose into the air
to carry him far from swords. He might bleed to death, but
he would be safe from Jarik's and Jilain's armor-slicing
blades.

Jarik hated that thought. He could not suffer his enemy
to escape so. He risked wrenching his back in twist-
flopping over. In the doing of that, his blade clanged on the
Iron Lord's dropped sword. Letting go his hilt, Jarik
grasped the other sword just below its guard. At the same
time he was lurching to his feet.

The gryphon sprang aloft. The god dangled beneath,
streaming blood. Already the eagle-cat was swinging out
over the sea.

"Return to your *owner*!" Jarik yelled, and hurled the
god's sword the best way he could, point first as though it
had been a short spear.

The sword did not obey, but it did drive true. *Even I
can't miss every time*, Jarik mused, watching the sword
drive twenty feet. Its hilt was starting to sink with its own
weight, when it plunged into the belly of the gryphon.

*I have used you, sword*, Jarik thought. *Return to me*!

He yelled it aloud, but the sword did not respond. It was
not his. It remained lodged, sunk well in to liberate blood,
real blood. The huge bird-thing canted, flapped madly,
flew farther with great flaps of its wings, canted again. It
slid visibly sidewise and down several feet, with blood running off the sword imbedded in its underside. Big eagle-
ragged pinions stroked hard, pushing it up, up, thirty and
then forty feet above the sea. Jarik could only stand and
stare, not knowing that he was holding his breath while he
raged and silently pleaded with the universe.

The gryphon was sixty or so feet up and twice that distance out to sea, still huge. Then it shuddered, lurched, and
again began sliding sidewise.

In a spasm, its talons opened.

Many eyes watched the dropping of a god. He fell like a
stone, splashed like a boulder, sank like . . . iron.

Diving for him in apparent instinct—or on mental

command?—the wounded gryphon lost control and also slammed into the water. Its wings sprang wide as impact drove the sword deeper up into it, almost to the hilt.

"*Jarik!*"

Jilain's voice, and Jarik whirled. He found a man rushing at him behind a long shield of green painted with the head of a blue bird of prey. An ax swung over his head in a silvery rush.

Jarik did not attempt to put his buckler in the way of that chopping stroke. He stood as if frozen—an instant longer, until the ax and its wielder's arms were committed in a downward rush at him. Only then did Jarik drive himself leftward with all the strength of his legs and lurching body. Simultaneously he jerked his sword viciously across between him and his attacker.

The ax flashed down, encountering only air. Its wielder was pulled past by its momentum. Jarik's sword, having swung all the way left, seemed to recoil so that it blurred in a rushing backswing. That horizontal stroke cut the dark man nearly in two, just above the hip.

He glanced back at the sun-sparkling sea. There was no sign of the Iron Lord. Wings widespread to keep it afloat, the god's steed struggled feebly. The water was darkening around it. The gryphon was dying, as its master had to be dead.

*Learn fear and grow lonely, O you last Lord of Iron in your keep without kith*, Jarik thought, and wondered: was it Dread or Destruction who yet lived?

Then he turned back to look at the hillside and along the strand. A general lull had accompanied the falling of the Iron Lord, and his apparent rescue, and now his obvious slaying. The long incline was strewn with corpses and writhing men wounded by arrows or stones. It was alive, too, with many upright men in helmets surmounted by sharp vertical leaves of iron like spearheads. The beach was an ugly jumble of tumbled stones and boulders and a few fallen men. Hundreds of eyes stared past the black-armored man at water's edge. They stared at the impossible flying thing that floated now, a far from permanent monument to a fallen god.

Then a manic figure pounced atop one of the big base-stones atop the hill. He was mailed in leather jerkin and amber-decorated helm. He raised his sword on high and slashed it through the air so that it caught the sunlight like fire.

"Their god is dead! Half of *them* are dead and they've never gained even the hilltop!" Delath yelled. "Into the seeeeea with them!"

And he plunged off the boulder and six mad plunging downhill strides later clove a man's arm from his body so that the foreigner's ax flew to down one of his own comrades.

Another man, bellowing, followed Delath; it was Stirl Elk-runner and behind him a helmetless man Jarik did not know, and there came Kirrensark too. That half-running half-sliding maniac was a youth called Coon, and his shield smashed away an enemy in his path. And here came more, and more still, of the men of Kirrensark-wark.

*Oceanside, by gods' blood*, Jarik thought. *Oceanside! Tomash-ten is reborn here this day, or I swear the Black Sword will bite Kirrensark!*

In seconds, attackers became pursued. One by one and then in a jumbled rushing mass they broke and fled the paler men rushing downhill at them.

Jarik realized that he and Jilain were very much in the wrong place.

"Jilish! They'll flow over us like a flooding stream! Onto the ship again!"

And there they joined. And no attackers could board against the hissing darkly flashing pair of jet-hued swords of the god-metal.

A great and hardly credible victory was won that day. That day four hundred invaders and a god came on behalf of the Forces of Destruction to destroy Kirrensark-wark and then to attack Snowmist Herself, and all fell to a hundred defenders. All. Surely a hundred of the strange walnut-skinned, big-nosed foreigners with the dark eyes were downed by the woman in silver god-armor and the man in black mail, for everything yielded to their swords. The tides carried red-dyed water for miles. The assailants had never so much as reached the top of the bluff on which the wark rose. Attack became battle, and battle became pursuit and hacking massacre on the beach. And when it was done and the odor of blood thick on the air, the victors collapsed panting, exhausted with the slaying. They had even won two good ships.

Jarik bore more than one wound. None would lay him low, much less cripple. His worst debility was that in exertion and armor-trapped heat he had lost pounds and pounds, and sweat enough to fill a goodly jug. He could hardly breathe for panting. Only when the last foreigner had fallen did Jarik Blacksword realize that his sword had taken on the weight of a log at the end of an arm that must surely belong to a seventy-year-old.

Jilain Kerosyris was unscathed, for iron would not pierce the armor of Snowmist, though she had taken many blows and would be stiff on the morrow with, everyone assumed, a rainbow of touch-sore bruises. She and Jarik sank down side by side, surrounded by corpses. Their only aim was to draw breath and not move their arms.

Beside them appeared the child. On Her was the mask of the Lady of the Snowmist.

"My . . . daughter," Jilain gasped out cleverly. But she was hardly godlike now. Moveless she lay, exhausted, already stiffening in every strained muscle.

"Ah, Jilain," the girl said softly. "Ah, Jarik. Heroes."

The Child of the Snowmist went purposefully onto all three ships. She left them to examine dead men along the beach; piled and limb-entangled on the beach. She went then to Jarik. There too stood Kirrensark and a bloodsplashed youth with strange dark markings in his eye sockets.

"The War has begun in earnest," She told Jarik quietly. "These men came from afar indeed. They are of lands called Taris and Barador, domain of the Lord Cerulean and his puppet lords. This attack, and the hawks and Iron Lord with them, means that Cerulean and the Lords of Iron are in contact, and know of us here."

"*Lord* of Iron," Jarik gasped fleetingly even as exhaustion claimed him. For he knew that *their* own mighty weapons, designed to be superior to those of the Forces of Man, to everything on the earth, had claimed now two Iron Lords.

Not many yards away the sea made a gulping noise and the gryphon disappeared beneath the water. It would come in with the tide, most likely tomorrow night's.

"A battle is won," She said in her voice carefully controlled not to sound childish, "a great battle and heroic. Yet the War only begins. We must—"

But Jarik Blacksword, sprawled with an arm across her most supposed to be their goddess, had never fought so mightily or been so wearied, and he lay asleep on that beach strewn with corpses and those wounded men that Kirrensark's people, not slavers, were now turning into corpses. And the words of the child-god must wait for another day.

"It will be as he said," Kirrensark One-arm muttered to his old battle-companion Delath Berserker. "Hereafter this wark shall bear the name of the one we stole from Jarik: Oceanside."

Delath nodded, and squatted beside Jarik of the Black Sword. He would carry him up the hill to the wark—up to Oceanside—and a proper bed, or cease calling himself a man.


This was
the third
of the chronicles
of
Jarik and Jilain
in
War Among the Gods on the Earth

# Fantasy from Ace
# fanciful and fantastic!

# Stories
## ⤝ of ⤞
# Swords and Sorcery

☐ 06586-4   **THE BLACK FLAME,** Lynn Abbey $2.75

☐ 13874-8   **DAUGHTER OF THE BRIGHT MOON,** Lynn Abbey $2.95

☐ 87379-0   **WATER WITCH,** Cynthia Felice & Connie Willis $2.50

☐ 29525-8   **THE GODS OF BAL-SAGOTH,** Robert E. Howard $1.95

☐ 88969-7   **WILDWRAITH'S LAST BATTLE,** Phyllis Ann Karr $2.95

☐ 70801-3   **RAJAN,** Tim Lukeman $2.25

☐ 44468-7   **KING DRAGON,** Andrew J. Offutt $2.95

☐ 81652-5   **TOMOE GOZEN,** Jessica Amanda Salmonson $2.50

☐ 29752-8   **THE GOLDEN NAGINATA,** Jessica Amanda Salmonson $2.75

☐ 05000-X   **BARD,** Keith Taylor $2.50

*Available wherever paperbacks are sold or use this coupon.*